Conspiracy on the Hudson

A Novel

by

Donald B. Keelan

Robin,
All my best wishes
Don Keelan

DORRANCE PUBLISHING CO., INC.
PITTSBURGH, PENNSYLVANIA 15222

Dedication

To the United States Marines who have served, are serving, or will one day serve at the Marine Barracks Washington

Acknowledgments

I have no doubt this novel never would have been accomplished without help and inspiration from a number of friends. To begin, I wish to thank several readers of *The Secret of Camp David,* for which this novel is the prequel. They had told me there has to be a follow-up novel, and it must be a political thriller based on historical fiction.

A great deal of thanks must go to Lyn Parker and Seline H. Skoug. They had the task of typing the many hand-written pages and doing a Herculean job of interpreting my not-so-legible handwriting.

Special thanks must go to the staff at Reposition Inc. for creating over and over again the graphics that provide the reader with a detailed sense of geography within the story. And my gratitude also goes to David Van de Water for his assistance in developing the book's cover.

My thanks to Dr. James L. FitzGerald, M.D., who read my first draft and gave me the encouragement to create the changes that would make the story even more thrilling and suspenseful.

Had it not been for my editor, Tyler Resch, who had a career as a newspaper editor as well as more than a dozen books to his credit, *Conspiracy on the Hudson* might not have been published. His editing skills and attention to maintaining a high degree of historical accuracy were much appreciated and helpful.

Donald B. Keelan
Arlington, Vermont
July 2010

Cast of Principal Characters

General John Anderson: officer in charge at Camp Greentop

Ludwig Berger: German lieutenant colonel, one of trio of agents in assassination plot

Winston Churchill: Prime Minister of Great Britain

Steve Early: Franklin D. Roosevelt's press secretary

Michael Ferguson: professor who reports long-suppressed assassination plot to U.S. President Smyth

Jim Gannon: U.S. Secret Service agent

Herbert Haupt: Operation Pastorius spy who was executed

Gertrude and Hans Hildebrand: German-born cook and housekeeper at Wilderstein estate

Siegfried Holtz: Kathe Schroeder's father

Mr. Kelly: security guard at chemical plant in Beacon, N.Y.

Albert Krupp: head of German assassination team

Radcliffe Lindbergh III: wealthy uncle of aviation pioneer Charles Lindbergh

Ellen McCarthy: agent Jim Gannon's fiancée

Dr. Ross McIntire: Franklin D. Roosevelt's personal physician

Ferdinand Metz: uncle of Gertrude Hildebrand who lives in Bennington, Vermont

John O'Neill: Secret Service agent

Corporal Parker: General Anderson's administrative clerk

Arthur Prettyman: Franklin D. Roosevelt's personal valet

Thelma and Werner Reischman: German agents who work at Vassar College and on Cape Cod

Mike Reilly: head of White House Secret Service

Otto Reinhardt: German-born deputy chief engineer for the New York City Water Department.

Franklin D. Roosevelt: President of the United States

Hyman Ruckenstein and Hersh Morganstein: owners of Hudson View Tourist Cabins

Lucy Mercer Rutherford: friend and sometime companion to Franklin D. Roosevelt

Sergeant Ryan, Trooper Fanelli: New York state troopers who find Reinhardt

Kathe Schroeder: Vassar graduate and German agent in assassination plot

President Smyth: incumbent U.S. President

Kurt and Erich Steiner: relatives of the Hildebrands in Germany

Margaret "Daisy" Suckley: friend and sometime companion to
    Franklin D. Roosevelt

Grace Tully: personal secretary to Franklin D. Roosevelt

Preface

In August 1943, an incident took place at Wilderstein, near President Roosevelt's home at Hyde Park, New York. Great Britain's Foreign Office, the United States State Department, and the Federal Republic of Germany's Federal Foreign Office recently joined in the release of undisclosed, top-secret documents that describe the events.

> Jonathan W. Sommerset III
> Deputy Secretary
> Historical Section
> United States State Department
> Washington, D.C.

Prologue

In 1942, United States Secret Service agent Jim Gannon was employed by one of the largest bureaucracies, the U.S. Treasury Department. Often he would express to his friends and associates what little patience he had for bureaucrats and bureaucracy. The bespectacled, short, and overweight department official now lecturing him was no exception. Since 1924 Otto Reinhardt had been an engineer with the New York City Water Department, one of the world's most marvelous public water systems. Born in Germany and educated in the United States, Reinhardt was made deputy chief engineer in 1939.

"Why must I cover the same ground over and over again?" said Reinhardt, sitting behind the most cluttered desk Gannon had ever seen.

"Because I've never heard it. Three months ago, we were attacked, if you haven't heard," said Gannon impatiently.

Reinhardt fired back, "The FBI and countless other agencies have been here asking the same questions. Do you people ever talk to each other?"

Gannon, an eight-year veteran of the Secret Service, was beginning to see that his quest to know more about how the city protects its vital water supply was not going well. "We do talk to other agencies. But we want the information first-hand, and for that reason I am here, and our meeting was cleared by your supervisor and the commission."

Reinhardt felt the sooner he answered Gannon's questions, the sooner he would leave. "So what is it that you want to know?"

"What security plans do you have in place to protect the water supply?" Gannon asked.

Pride flushed over Reinhardt's face now that he had an audience to hear him explain his water systems—as if he had built, financed, and owned the system that daily served more than seven million New Yorkers. He pushed himself away from his desk, placed a hand behind his head, and started to explain. With his other hand he fidgeted with his multi-colored bow tie. "We only recently, at the start of the war, placed armed guards at the reservoirs: the Ashokan in upstate; in the Catskills, the Croton; the Kensico in Valhalla near White Plains and in Central Park. The rest of the system is underground in huge tunnels. Those aqueducts are so big you could drive a truck through them."

Gannon asked, "How do you get into the tunnels, and are they guarded?"

"No, why should they be? And only a fool would try to go into them," Reinhardt intoned with an air of importance.

"Why is that?" Gannon asked, wondering why a German national would have such a sensitive position now that the United States was at war with Germany.

Reinhardt picked up his pencil and pointed to a map on the wall behind his desk: "If you went into the tunnels, let's say right here, at Cold Spring, you'd be crushed by the volume of water and wouldn't be able to get out until your drowned and crushed body got to Croton, here."

"How does the water get across the Hudson River?" Gannon inquired, waiting for the next Reinhardt lecture.

"Just where I pointed. Cold Spring. About two miles north of West Point. The river is hundreds of feet deep there, and the crossing is very narrow."

Gannon knew the area described by Reinhardt. "There's a steep rugged hill there. How is it that the water can get over it?"

"It's not called Breakneck Ridge for nothing. We pump it. Up on top of the ridge are a series of pumphouses, each containing two ten-thousand-gallon-per-minute pumps that draw the water into eight-foot pipes," Reinhardt explained.

It was still a gray and damp day when Gannon finally emerged from the cavernous water department building in lower Manhattan. It had taken Reinhardt another hour to describe the security and engineering that took place in his water system from the Cold Spring crossing to Central Park. Gannon was still not sure why his boss, Mike Reilly, chief of the White House Secret Service detail, wanted the information. Gannon had felt Otto Reinhardt was partially right in asking why the inquiry from another agency, especially from one that guards the president and searches out counterfeiters.

There also was something about Reinhardt that bothered him. Waiting for the uptown subway at the Foley Square station, Gannon could not shake him from his thoughts. As the Lexington Avenue train pulled into the station and screeched to a halt, he concluded he was being paranoid over Reinhardt's accent and name. It was just a sign of the times, he felt, and along with the shoving crowd of passengers, he boarded the uptown express and headed back to the U.S. Secret Service Office.

Albany 57 Miles

Bennington 100 Miles

North

35 Miles

KINGSTON

Rhinebeck

WILDERSTEIN

9

9G

9W

HUDSON RIVER

HYDE PARK

VALKILL

SPRINGWOOD

CLINTON
CORNERS

44

POUGHKEEPSIE

9W

9

WAPPINGERS
FALLS

9D

FERRY

HUDSON RIVER

NEWBURGH

BEACON

STEWART
FIELD

9

BREAKNECK
RIDGE

301

WATER
TUNNEL

STORM KING

COLD SPRING

9W

U.S Military
Academy

New York 60 Miles

Chapter One

The Present
Washington, D.C.

"Come in and make yourself comfortable, professor," the president said, welcoming Professor Michael Ferguson into the Oval Office.

"Thank you, sir," replied Ferguson as he moved toward the president while transferring an armful of papers to his left hand.

Thanking the secretary who had escorted Ferguson over to the beige twin sofas, President Smyth reached out and gave his guest a hearty handshake. "Let's sit here, and you can tell me all about your visit to Camp David."

The Marist College professor soon realized he shouldn't have brought to the meeting the stack of papers he was now desperately trying to hold onto as he grasped the president's hand.

"Well, sir," Ferguson started to say. The president interrupted and asked, "First, how about some Danish and coffee, professor?"

Finally, setting his papers on the cherry coffee table and feeling relieved that the papers did not end up on the floor, Ferguson replied, "That would be fine, sir."

"Joe Hard, my chief of staff, told me you wanted to see me, and it was quite urgent," the president said as he poured coffee.

"That is correct, Mr. President. It is very serious, and there is a sense of urgency, but you can decide that," Ferguson replied, his lips tightening.

"Well, before you tell me what's on your mind, let me say that I read your report with great interest, and when it is released, surely it will have a significant impact," the president said as he thumbed through the pages of the blue-covered, three-inch report Ferguson had sent to him only three weeks ago.

For Ferguson on this beautiful spring morning in May, it was not his first visit to the Oval Office. The president had called him in February to ask him to take on the assignment of researching the facts surrounding the attempted assassination of the former Soviet Union's Nikita Khrushchev at Camp David in September 1959—an assignment Ferguson had been deeply reluctant to accept.

"Professor, you can't imagine how grateful I am for the thoroughness and completeness that's contained in this document. I was well aware I had asked you to take on the job, and you were hesitant to do so. Am I correct in stating that?"

Ferguson quickly replied, "I just did not want to relive those events, Mr. President. It was that simple."

Setting his cup back on the coffee table, the president responded, "Mike—may I call you..."

"Yes, Mr. President," replied Ferguson.

"The world now has the facts. In 1959 four Hungarian refugees living in Vermont took it upon themselves to attempt to assassinate the leader of the Soviet Union at the Presidential Retreat. The story has never been told, and it needs to be, and you will have played the major role in making that so."

"As a professor of history and a historian, Mr. President, I can't help but say that the story and the events of those days, in September of 1959, needed to be recorded and published. I just didn't want to be the storyteller, and I hope you might understand that, sir."

"Indeed, I knew from having read your report why the initial reluctance. And yesterday I received an e-mail from an old friend who was once an adversary of mine, Mikhail Kaganovich, former First Chief Directorate of the KGB," the president said.

"What was it that he wrote, if I may ask, Mr. President?"

"He wrote…Let me read it to you. Here it is:

Thank you for allowing me to read Professor Michael Ferguson's report. We had knowledge of the attempt on Chairman's Khrushchev's life as well. And like you, we too kept it secret. I should tell you that when we purged Joseph Stalin's files from World War II, we came across material I will send to you. It deals with a similar incident in 1943—of which we were aware, but about which your country and the Brits kept quiet."

"That is hard to believe, Mr. President."

"Well, he goes on, but it's on other stuff, not relevant."

Ferguson watched an aide come into the room and replace the Colonial Williamsburg pewter coffee pot with an identical one. The aide quietly and quickly exited through a side door.

"Mike, why the sudden urgency to meet? What's it about?" the president asked, his tone taking on a serious note.

Ferguson placing his cup back on the saucer, looked up at the president, and said, "Sir, when you sent me to Camp David, it was with instructions to the staff at the retreat that I was to have complete access to all records in the camp's archives, regardless of whether the files were classified as secret, or top secret, for that matter."

"That's what I said, and I hope there were no obstacles placed in your way. Were there?" the president asked.

"Not at all," Ferguson responded.

"Then I don't understand, Mike. Was there a problem?"

"Not a problem, Mr. President. My research discovered there had been an attempt on the life of the president and his guest. And this attempt, similar to the one in 1959, had never been disclosed to the American people. I believe that Mr. Kaganovich was alluding to it in his e-mail, sir."

Now standing and moving to the fireplace mantle, the president said, "This can't be, Mike. Are you certain? When I read Kaganovich's message, I just thought he was pumping up his old agency a bit."

"Yes, it's true all right." replied Ferguson, noting the sudden change in the president's demeanor.

"Another attempt on a president's life. Was it at Camp David?" the president asked.

"No, sir. It occurred sixteen years earlier, in 1943, in Rhinebeck, New York, near Hyde Park. The attempt was made to kill both President Roosevelt and Prime Minister Winston Churchill," Ferguson recalled, now standing and looking directly at the bewildered president.

"I can't believe I am hearing this," the president said.

"It happened, Mr. President, and as far as I know, it has never been told."

"I can't imagine why it hasn't," the president said, hands clasped behind his head.

Pacing the large oval carpet that contained the Great Seal of the United States, the young, handsome, and mild-mannered chief executive said, "Mike, give me the details, and let's just sit down and have another cup of coffee. By the way, are you free for lunch?"

Ferguson politely turned down the offer of more coffee, but in accepting the invitation for lunch, he said, "Certainly, sir, the attempted assault had its beginnings in August of 1943, when two Nazi commandos had entered the United States…"

Chapter Two

August 1943

Jim Gannon of the U.S. Secret Service was growing impatient. He had been sitting in his government-issued 1938 Chevy coupe with his left arm out the window, attempting to make a left turn off U.S. Route 9 onto the private road that would take him to Springwood, President Roosevelt's Hyde Park home.

Southbound traffic was unusually heavy on this Sunday morning. Agent Gannon had come to realize that the worshippers, who only minutes before had been praising the Lord at St. James Episcopal Church just up the road, were now racing home to enjoy the rest of their day. The Lord's work was done for them, but not for agent Gannon. He mumbled out loud that the Episcopalians are doing brisk business this Sunday morning, just like the Catholics down the road at St. Peter's church.

Six foot two, blue-eyed, with jet-black hair, this first-generation Irish Catholic had to skip Mass on this warm and muggy August morning. His boss, Mike Reilly, wanted to see him. Gannon knew well that when the Secret Service agent-in-charge of the White House detail summoned you, all else came to an immediate halt, and you responded.

A break in the southbound lane was all Gannon needed to turn into the president's estate. It would be another quarter mile on a dusty road before he would arrive at what he and his fellow agents called "the big house."

Gannon, peering out his rearview mirror, saw he was creating a cloud of dust as he barreled down the narrow dirt drive, passing eighty-foot elms that stood on either side, erect for generations, like sentries, every thirty feet.

"Christ, Gannon, why do you have to drive so goddamned fast and create a dust storm?" Sergeant Joseph DeVito said as Gannon's coupe came to a stop. He was unable to proceed because the road was blocked by a huge log hung from wires. It was operated inside the gatehouse by the U.S. Army's military police.

"Sorry, Joe," Gannon replied half-heartedly, knowing the dust he raised was now settling on the uniforms and rifles of DeVito and his men. Gannon had a lot of respect for the burly staff sergeant. He was well aware of the sergeant's exploits in North Africa, where the towering soldier had received the Silver Star for rescuing his squad from a German army ambush.

"You know, Gannon, my men's weapons won't be worth a shit with all this dust. And they are going to have to spend hours cleaning them," Sergeant DeVito said, looking at Gannon's identification.

"I'll see if I can get some calcium chloride put on this road. It will keep the dust down," Gannon said, placing his ID back into his suit jacket.

"Yeah, I bet you will. Just slow down, will you?" DeVito replied. He walked back to his guardhouse and ordered the corporal to raise the gate.

Agent Gannon put his car in gear and proceeded. He routinely would have driven to the front of the house and parked near the front porch steps. But today he was not with the First Family, so he steered the car to the drive that would take him to the side of the house where deliveries were made.

He stopped next to the loading dock that led directly into the mansion's kitchen. There he saw Mike Reilly standing at the edge of the dock with his constant cigarette in one hand and a bunch of papers in the other.

"Morning, boss," Gannon said as he pushed the door open.

"Sorry to have pulled you in on your day off, Jim," Reilly said as he moved closer to the steps that led to the loading platform.

"Well, I've only got you to blame for missing Mass, and when Father Paul asks why, I'll tell him," Gannon said with a broad smile that revealed a mouthful of white teeth.

"Father Paul will be presiding at your funeral if you keep pissing Sergeant DeVito off," Reilly responded.

"How'd you know that?" Gannon asked with a smirk.

"Jesus, Jim, I could see the dust storm from here. Try and take it easy. We need those MPs, and DeVito is a good man, okay?" Reilly did not exactly see the humor Gannon felt.

"Yeah, you're right, boss, as always. Those army guys don't have it easy by no means, and I'll be more careful," Gannon said contritely.

Sergeant DeVito was just one of a hundred and twenty soldiers who were assigned to guard the president's home. There were similar numbers at the White House and at Shangri-La, the presidential retreat in northern Maryland. The only difference was that at the retreat, they were Marines. Agent Reilly knew well that he and his agents did not have the manpower to provide for the president's security at any of these locations if it not had been for additional protection provided by the military. And for that he had been much appreciative, and he did not want his understudy, agent Gannon, to make things any more difficult than they were.

Pulling back the screen door to the kitchen, Reilly inquired, "Have you had breakfast yet?"

"No, just a coffee. I came right over from the tourist cabins," Gannon replied.

"Let me see if the chief can rustle us up some eggs, and we can then go over things in the galley. For a change, the place is as quiet as a church," Reilly said.

"Where is the boss?" Gannon asked.

"He's gone to church and will spend a few hours at Wilderstein, due back at three," Reilly said, looking at his watch.

"Mr. Reilly, can I make you something? And how about you, Mr. Gannon?" Chief Orlando asked. The chief petty officer had been in the naval service since 1925 and was assigned to the White House mess in 1933.

"Eggs, toast, and some coffee would be great, Chief," Reilly responded.

"The usual way, yes, over lightly for you, and Mr. Gannon, scrambled, yes?" Orlando inquired.

"That's fine, Chief," Gannon replied to the five-foot-five sailor. Gannon always had wondered how someone so small could have made it into the navy.

"Chief, coming from Manila, you must love this humidity," Reilly suggested.

"I like it a lot, Mr. Reilly. Much nicer than being here in winter and the cold and snow. Any news, Mr. Reilly, on General MacArthur going back to my homeland? I've gotten no word from my family since the Japs invaded Luzon," the chief said as he handed coffee to the agents. "Eggs will be brought to you on the porch in short time."

Reilly and Gannon took their coffee and went out to the porch. Reilly turned and said, "Chief, if I knew anything at all about an invasion by us to retake the Philippines, you know I couldn't say a word. Just have faith, we are going back."

"God, what a view to the river! And that was nice what you told him, boss. Can't imagine what he must be going through, wondering what's happened to his family," Gannon said, gazing at the manicured lawn that swept westward to the shore of the Hudson River.

"Yeah, it's something, isn't it? And a real nightmare to protect. There's just too much property here to cover," Reilly said as he sat at the rattan table and began sipping his coffee. "Not much I can tell him. But I do know we are going to retake the Philippines, if not this year, for sure next year."

"By the way, Mike, who is with the boss?" Gannon asked. He hoped Orlando would not be too long bringing breakfast. Gannon, a devout Catholic, had been fasting since the night before in anticipation that he would get to Mass and Holy Communion.

"He went with Pa Watson and Grace Tully. I can't ever remember the president's aide and closest friend along with his secretary not accompanying him to Hyde Park."

"And Mrs. R.—where is she these days? Did she go back to Washington?" Gannon asked.

"She was going to but wanted to spend a few more days at Val-Kill with some girlfriends from some newspapers, I think," Reilly said. He placed his stack of papers on the table.

Reilly and Gannon had known for some time that it would be a rare event for the president and Mrs. Roosevelt to spend any time together. For years they had their own interest and friends; it was a constant consternation for Reilly, who was in charge of guarding both of them as well as their five children, all adults and leading their own lives.

"Chief Orlando makes the best eggs, but he is as stingy as ever with the ham and bacon," Gannon said, wiping his face with his napkin. "There's a war on, Jim, and the boss wants us to be no better fed than the rest of the country. Orlando has to live with that," Reilly said, scolding his young protégé.

"Mike, you seem a bit on edge this morning. What's up? I feel that something is."

"Very perceptive, Jim. Before he went to church, the boss called me in to tell me his plans for the next few weeks," Reilly said, looking at his notes.

"We've known already that he's going to Canada in a few days to meet with Churchill. Has there been a change?"

"You bet," Reilly quickly responded.

"In what way?"

Reilly looked up at his eager assistant and said, "After their Montreal meeting, the boss is bringing Churchill here for seven days. They want to continue planning for the Second Front. And according to the boss, there is no better place he'd rather be than here."

"Can you blame him? This place is quiet and so beautiful and peaceful. What better place?"

Interrupting, Reilly snapped. "Jim, think for a minute. This place is so vulnerable. And with two world leaders here for a week, it will be a nightmare…if not a disaster."

"I see your point, Mike."

"I'm not sure you're seeing the total picture," Reilly said.

"What have I missed?" Gannon asked, now standing and leaning on the porch railing.

"When you asked a while ago about the boss's whereabouts, I said he was at church and Wilderstein."

"Yeah, you did."

"Do you have any idea what he plans to be doing when he and Churchill are not planning the invasion? He'll be at Wilderstein with Miss Suckley."

"I'm beginning to see the picture, boss," Gannon said.

"Jim, Wilderstein is not a secure place—not from the outside nor the inside."

Gannon interrupted. "Mike, it's only a few miles up the road, in Rhinebeck. We've been there countless times. Why a problem now?"

"For one, all of his visits were random. Being here for the week, they won't be random any more. And second, Miss Suckley's cook and chauffeur, what are their names…?"

"Gertrude and Hans Hildebrand."

"Yeah, that's them, and we still haven't received any word from the Bureau on their clearances," Reilly said, pacing back and forth along the porch.

"Well, we have a week before the boss returns from his trip to Canada. I'll push them on it," Gannon said with an air of authority.

"Maybe we can do that, but the problem is the Hildebrands' parents lived in Germany, Gertrude is pro-German, and the boss once told me she dislikes Churchill. How's that for starters?"

"Holy shit," exclaimed Gannon.

"What I know is that they came to the states in 1928 through a friend and got a job at Wilderstein."

"Why the dislike for Churchill?" Gannon asked.

"All I can presume is what the prime minister had done to her country after the first World War."

"What's their feeling toward the boss?" Gannon asked.

"Good question, but I don't know. But for damn sure we are going to find out, and soon. And another problem is that with the war on, it is a monumental task trying to obtain clearances. Our New York office said they have a three-month backlog."

"You would think we'd have top priority, especially since the cook here will be preparing the president's and prime minister's meals."

"That's going to change," Reilly said as he waived to Gannon to follow him to their nearby office.

* * *

"Daisy, I've never once asked you: How did your home ever get to be referred to as Wilderstein?" President Roosevelt asked his hostess as he sat in his wheelchair on the home's covered, screened porch, sipping his lemonade.

"My goodness, Mr. President, after all these years as my neighbor, you've never wondered about the origin of Wilderstein?" the petite fifty-three-year-old Margaret Suckley replied, touching her lips with her silk handkerchief.

"Well, I can't say I've never wondered about its origin, coming here all these years. It's just that it would slip my mind to ask," President Roosevelt said. He moved his wheelchair closer to the porch's screen opening to admire the estate's magnificent cedars and evergreens.

"Well, with the Depression and now the war to deal with, I can understand, Franklin, that you certainly have enough on your mind," Daisy responded as she joined the president and pulled a chair next to him to admire the view and her guest. Margaret Suckley was one of the few who came in contact with the president who would refer to him by his first name.

"Now, I do recall, a long time ago, when we first met and you told me where you lived. When was that?" the president asked, enjoying the ice cubes in the bottom of his glass.

"There is more lemonade, if you want some." Margaret observed her guest as he sucked on the ice cube, a habit Mrs. Roosevelt had told him, on many occasions, to be lacking in social graces.

"Yes, I'll take a refill."

"It was in 1922 at Springwood," Margaret replied, referring to the name FDR's family had given to their Hyde Park home.

"What happened in 1922?" FDR asked.

"You know, your mother had asked me to come and read to you. I was thirty-one then, and you were forty. You were just back from Campobello and recovering from your polio attack. And I was still grieving over the loss of Papa."

"Yes, indeed I do recall. Mother had you come in and read to me."

"And you had asked at that time what *Wilderstein* stood for. And I said grandfather named it after the Indian settlers. And it means 'wild man's stone.' Now do you remember, you silly man?"

"Now, Daisy, are you getting sassy with the president?" FDR asked his friend as they grinned at each other.

For Daisy it was a welcome sight to see a smile on her dear friend's face, if only for a fleeting moment. She was well aware that the war news was taking a heavy toll on him. From previous sessions with him she had been told that the weekly war casualties were in the thousands. She also knew how much it weighed upon him to have had to inform Joseph Stalin and Charles de Gaulle that the Second Front was not going to take place this year, that it was at least ten or eleven months away.

Earlier in the afternoon, he had told her about Winston Churchill's visit, and that he would be at Springwood for several days. He also surprised her by asking if he and the Churchill entourage could have dinner at Wilderstein on the Saturday night of their visit, with her as the hostess.

"Franklin, how dear of you to choose my home for such a special affair. I am honored, and I will not disappoint you or Mr. Churchill. It will be lovely, and it is a splendid time of year. We should have a delightful evening," Miss Suckley said, wondering how she would ever live up to what she was saying to the president.

Once Miss Suckley had heard of the pending secret meeting between the two allies, she knew that she was one of only a handful who would have been made aware of the visit. If Michael Reilly had known that she had been told, he would have done everything in his power to have the visit cancelled.

"1922, that can't be when we first met, is it?" FDR asked, as he purused his second glass of lemonade.

"You do have a lot of things on your mind. It was at Papa's law firm in New York City. Mr. Roosevelt and Papa were working on some legal matter, and your father was invited up to Crumwold, Mr. Rogers's house."

"When exactly was that, now?" FDR asked.

"It was when I was eighteen, and you were a dashing twenty-eight or something and married, I recall."

"Well, I'm afraid, Daisy, that I can't do a great deal of dashing any more, I'm sorry to say."

"Forgive me, Franklin, for such a poor choice of words, will you, dear?" Daisy pleaded. She rose from her chair, moved to FDR, and placed her arms on his shoulders, her face inches away from his. He placed his glass on the table and put his arm around his hostess's narrow waist. No words were spoken as they focused their eyes on one another.

Chapter Three

As he had done many times before, ever since 1924, when he became a draftsman with the New York City Water Department, Otto Reinhardt was at his drafting table poring over a set of blueprints. His stubby, tobacco-stained fingers were searching for the edge of the blueprint, ready to turn it. On this muggy August morning, Reinhardt, now the deputy chief engineer, was having a great deal of difficulty focusing on the pipes and valves that stared back at him from the thick pile of blueprints. It was seventhirty, and he was expecting a call at nine; a call he was not comfortable in wanting to accept, especially at his office.

In 1919, when Otto Reinhardt was eighteen years old, his parents brought him to the United States. They were part of the German relocation plan that President Wilson had initiated. His Brooklyn-based relatives had persuaded his parents to have him enrolled at Pratt Institute to study engineering. His father always had bragged that Otto was a genius in mathematics. In 1924 Reinhardt graduated, became a licensed engineer, and immediately went to work for the City of New York. The water department wanted minds like Reinhardt's.

Nineteen years later, the now balding and bespectacled engineer felt he was in a deep rut. He was only forty-three years old, but his disheveled appearance gave the impression he was in his mid-fifties. His bachelor's quarters in a fourth-floor walkup apartment in the Inwood section of Upper Manhattan was in the same chaotic state as his office.

On numerous occasions, Reinhardt had told his young secretary and the department's cleaning staff never to touch any of his blueprints, papers, or reports. They were to leave his office a mess. The physical state of his office was always the focal point of gossip for other members of his department. Everyone attributed it to Reinhardt's obsession over his work. No one had known that the "off-limits" rule was due to a more sinister reason that only Reinhardt knew. He wanted it kept that way.

"Mr. Reinhardt, your guests are here for their seven-forty-five appointment," his secretary said. She sought a clear spot on his cluttered drafting board to place his cup of coffee.

"Miss Swanson, show them in, but make sure you come and get me at quarter to nine. I've an important telephone call to take," Reinhardt said as he stood up, placing his Keuffel & Esser miniature slide-rule back in his vest pocket, shaking eraser droppings from his jacket.

"Fine, sir," Miss Swanson replied.

"Miss Swanson."

"Yes?"

"Where are these people from again, and how many of them this time?"

"St. Louis and four, sir. The commissioner wants you to give them a brief history of the water system and how it is being maintained. You know, sir, your usual spiel," Miss Swanson replied with a grin.

"Miss Swanson, has maintenance done anything about fixing this ceiling fan? Five of us in here on this muggy day, Christ!" Reinhardt growled, looking at the lopsided ceiling fan, wavering as it made each rotation.

"I'll inquire, sir."

For years Reinhardt's superiors had called upon him to give tours and to explain the New York City water system to officials from other municipalities. It was a duty he despised. He felt he was the department's perpetual tour guide and not its deputy chief engineer. On occasion he would bring his displeasure to his supervisor's attention. But ever since the breakout of hostilities between his adopted country and Germany, he made few of his protestations known. He felt it was best to remain unnoticed. His position was critical, not only to his employer, but to others and for other reasons that had nothing to do with the delivery of clean drinking water.

For Reinhardt and his staff, it seemed there had been many more tours in the last three years than at any time before. Water department officials from around the country and among America's allies wanted to see how the most elaborate water collection and distribution system in the world was being operated as well as protected.

"Come in, gentlemen, and let's begin. I am pressed for time today, I'm sorry," Reinhardt said curtly as the four officials tried to find a place to sit. It was to no avail. There was only a stool next to the drafting table. Reinhardt did not want visitors to stay too long. He was not interested in human discourse or providing creature comforts to visitors.

"Gentlemen, by the end of today, my department will have distributed over one billion gallons of the purest drinking water in the world. And tomorrow we will do it all over again," the portly engineer said with a detectable degree of arrogance.

Holding his coffee cup and pushing the stool under the drafting table, Reinhardt moved to a wall map of New York state. From a wall hook, he removed a three-foot wooden pointer with a rubber tip at one end and an eyehook at the other. He had noticed that his guests were beginning to perspire, but he made no attempt to ease their discomfort by suggesting they remove their suit jackets. Nor did he open the large window that certainly would have provided the cramped office with a breeze. That the ceiling fan was in need of repair was not his concern. He felt that if he had to tolerate this tour business, his guests were not going to be relieved of any discomforts.

Reinhardt had the rubber tip of his pointer at a spot halfway up the map: "Here's where it all begins. A hundred miles north, at the Ashokan Reservoir. Please note the nearby mountains, the Catskills, and here, just to the north, the Adirondacks. We collect it here, and the water begins its journey south to this point." The far-sighted engineer had taken off his heavy rimmed eyeglasses to focus on the area he was indicating: Storm King Mountain in Cornwall.

"Gentlemen, at this point, the aqueducts are hundreds of feet below the floor of the Hudson River. They transport the water across the river. We bring the water up this ridge at Cold Spring, here, on the east side of the Hudson, the river's narrowest point, well south of the Catskills and the Adirondacks, of course. And if you can recall your lessons in American history, it was near this point that the Revolutionaries tried to stop the British with their logs and iron chains across the river," Reinhardt said. He removed his Longine from his vest pocket. He still had another half hour of lecturing before his nine o'clock call.

He continued, "Cold Spring is the only place one can safely enter the aqueducts and piping."

"Why?" asked one of his guests, wiping his forehead with a handkerchief.

"Because it is where we have a series of pumphouses that pull the water up and then push the water over the ridge," Reinhardt replied, close to being sarcastic.

"Can't that be a breach in your protection if someone can enter at that point?" was a second question.

With a defensive tone, Reinhardt replied, "I'm not at liberty to explain how that area is protected, gentlemen, only that it is where you can first enter the system. So let me continue, if you please." Reinhardt was unwilling to accept that the Cold Spring pumphouses were a serious security matter that had not been addressed by his department.

"From here, gentlemen, the water moves through tunnels and aqueducts twenty miles south-southeast to the Croton Reservoir and is held back by a series of earthen and concrete dams."

"I have to assume these structures are protected around the clock, Mr. Reinhardt?" asked the oldest of his visitors.

"Of course, by a civil defense force made up mostly of veterans from the last war," Reinhardt replied, anticipating the end of his lecture. "From Croton, gentlemen, the flow goes to Valhalla, near White Plains, then on to the Yonkers Hillside Reservoir and finally to Central Park, here in New York City. At all of these stations the water is constantly aerated through a series of one-thousand-gallon-per-minute pumps. Any more questions?" He hoped there would be none.

There was one question. Once again it came from the senior member of the delegation. "Mr. Reinhardt, the system is so exposed, at least it seems to me, and I'm sure to the rest of us. You have hundreds of miles of shoreline around the reservoirs. How do you prevent anyone from poisoning the water? Certainly the guards can't be everywhere."

"You can't," Reinhardt replied.

"So what do you do to maintain purity? To prevent someone from poisoning it?"

Before he could respond, Miss Swanson entered and interrupted her boss. "Mr. Reinhardt, your next appointment is waiting, sir."

"Gentlemen, I can't tell you how we do the specific protection, and that's all the time I have this morning. I wish you all a good day and thank you for visiting with us." Reinhardt did not want his visitors to know there was no adequate protection. The system was too spread out.

The four visitors would like to have asked more questions. Reinhardt's lack of response to the last question did not sit well. Their time was up. Miss Swanson held back the door as they exited.

* * *

It was difficult for the hundred or so men at Camp Greentop to keep their eyes off Kathe Schroeder. In August of 1943 she had been the only female assigned to training at the secret Office of Strategic Services camp, near Thurmont, in Maryland's Catoctin Mountains. Just prior to the attack at Pearl Harbor, President Roosevelt appointed his longtime friend, a New York lawyer and World War I hero, William "Wild Bill" Donovan, to head up a new spy agency. It was to be known by its initials, the OSS. Donovan, who had been a master of organization and a strong believer in the fruits of vigorous training, opened a secret spy-training camp at what was once a recreation area camp for government employees and their families.

Blonde, five foot seven, with a sculptured body, Schroeder was so shapely that one wondered why she was not in modeling rather at a training camp for potential saboteurs and spies. But her intelligence, especially in chemistry, and her fluency in German and French, made her more of a standout. This was evident not only with her colleagues but also with the officers who were training her. It was not difficult for her to translate her knowledge of chemistry into deadly explosive and poison devices.

"Kathe, take off your earmuffs." U.S. Army Lieutenant Greerson was signaling to Schroeder as she placed the last screw into an eight-inch cylindrical canister.

"What is it, Lieutenant? I've got the bomb almost complete," she replied, wishing not to be interrupted.

"The old man wants to see you now, and don't keep him waiting. You know how he gets," Greerson responded.

Schroeder knew all too well how General Anderson reacted to trainees. Despite the fact that she was into her seventh week of training at the camp, from four in the morning until midnight, the one-star army general would never let up with her or her peers. The stress was beginning to show on all the trainees. At times, she thought it was a huge mistake to have allowed her Vassar College organic chemistry professor to talk her into joining the Office of Strategic Services.

"Yes, General, you wanted to see me," Schroeder said as she stood before the camp commander's desk. Schroeder had been in the general's office on many previous occasions, but never with this sense of urgency.

"Colonel Donovan's office at D.C. headquarters relayed a message they received this morning," General Anderson said, motioning to his student to sit in the armless chair in front of his cluttered desk.

"What does that have to do with me, General?" Schroeder asked, choosing not to accept his offer of a chair.

"It seems your mother in Poughkeepsie was brought to the local hospital. St. Francis Hospital, I believe it was—a heart attack. I'm very sorry, Schroeder," Anderson said in his weak attempt at compassion—which was all but ignored by Schroeder.

"How is she? When did this happen?" Schroeder asked, showing only a slight sense of emotion with her hands to her mouth.

"I really can't tell; the message was a bit vague on details. I'm sorry I don't have more information."

Schroeder was silent for a moment and then said, "Sir, I would like very much to request a seventy-two-hour pass. Mother is all that I have as a relative," she pleaded, her voice showing signs of breaking up.

"This all comes at a shitty time, Schroeder. There's nothing more I can say. You and your team are about to leave for Italy in two weeks. I presume you're aware of that."

"Yes, and I'll be back to be with them, but I must get to New York," Schroeder said as she ran her hands through her short blonde hair.

"I figured you'd want to go as quickly as possible. So I've arranged for you to get a ride with a Marine officer from their camp next door, and he'll take you to the train station in Baltimore. That's the best I can do with such short notice. Your request is granted."

"That's most thoughtful of you, sir," Schroeder replied, brushing the wrinkles out of her khaki pants and shirt.

"Just be back here at 0600 on Friday, Schroeder. The allies are in Sicily, and Italy's next, and you're part of it," Anderson said, now on his feet. He gave Schroeder a non-verbal signal that the meeting was over.

As Schroeder left the small wooden cabin and headed back to her Quonset hut to get her travel belongings, she was delighted that her seven weeks at Camp Greentop were finally over. Little did the OSS or General Anderson know that she did not have a mother in Poughkeepsie, let alone one dying from a heart attack. Otto Reinhardt had come through. He had sent the telegram. Within twenty-four hours, she would be able to put on her true uniform and use her own name—Kathe Von Schroeder, captain in Hitler's dreaded and feared SS unit.

As she opened the screen door to the metal hut, for the last time, she asked herself why the Marines were assigned to next door—what was going on there? Strandartenführer Krupp must be made aware. And he will be when she meets him again, in two days' time.

"Corporal Parker, get in here," General Anderson barked to his administrative clerk.

"Yes, sir," Parker said, almost out of breath.

"Send a message to headquarters requesting that I get a copy of Schroeder's complete and full personnel jacket," Anderson said, staring out his window and watching his trainee enter her hut.

"Anything in particular you're looking for, General?" Parker asked.

"Yeah, you might say I am. I want to know more about Schroeder's mother. I wasn't aware that she was here in the states, or for that matter still alive."

"May I ask, what makes you feel that way, sir?" Parker inquired.

"Parker you are the most inquisitive son of a bitch I've ever met. What the hell you are doing up at this remote place, I don't know. You should have been assigned to some intelligence unit where that mind of yours can be better utilized."

"Yes, sir, I tried, but here I am, sir, with you."

"Yeah, I know. There's a bad feeling in my gut about Schroeder that has always bugged me, and I just can't put my finger on it, but it is there," Anderson said.

* * *

"Mr. Reinhardt, there's a long-distance person-to-person call for you. Is this the call you wanted?" Miss Swanson asked her boss as she held the lever on the inter-office calling device.

Looking at the device on her desk, Miss Swanson heard, "Yes, send it in here, and please, Miss Swanson, no interruptions."

"Mrs. Hildebrand, is that you?" Reinhardt asked. He grasped his coffee cup with one hand and talked into the phone stand while placing the hearing apparatus by his left ear.

"*Ja, ich bin's. Haben Sie uns den Fisch schon geschickt?*" Gertrude Hildebrand asked.

"Sprechen Sie niemals Deutsch, wenn Sie mich anrufen. Spechen Sie immer auf Englisch," Reinhardt snapped back.

"Aber ich fuehle mich wohler in unserer Muttersprache und Sie sich doch sicher auch," Mrs. Hildebrand said.

"Das ist scheissegal…hast du mich verstanden/haben Sie mich verstanden?"

Not hesitating, Mrs. Hildebrand said, *"Jawohl!"*

"It is on the train. It left Baltimore at seven this morning," Reinhardt answered, looking at his office door—annoyed that a simple cook would dare to answer him back.

"How many pieces?" was the next question to him.

"There's one now, and it's on its way to Poughkeepsie. It'll be there around one this afternoon, and I'll be sending you two more very soon. I must go." Reinhardt placed the earpiece onto the phone's cradle. Once again he looked at his partially opened door, hoping Miss Swanson did not overhear him telling Mrs. Hildebrand to speak only in English.

Reinhardt's hands were clasped together on top of the desk blotter. He did all he could to keep them from shaking. A mission that was going to have terrible consequences had begun, and he was a part of it.

Chapter Four

"Gertrude, who were you talking to?" asked Hans Hildebrand, standing on the top step that led from the cellar into Wilderstein's kitchen.

He did not receive an answer. He watched his wife remove a strudel from the oven and continued, "And why in German? You know the madam wants us to speak only English."

"Hans, don't you start. I've already been scolded at by that lazy slob of a bureaucrat. I don't need more," Gertrude said, visibly shaken from her conversation with Otto Reinhardt.

"I don't mean to upset you, my dear, but you know we need this position. People aren't hiring these days, and much less are they hiring Germans," Hans said, shaking the dust off his apron.

"Not on my kitchen floor, husband. Outside with that dust. You keep bringing the root cellar into my kitchen. And would you place those potatoes on the counter, there?" Gertrude ordered. She slid the hot pan of strudel onto the oak worktable.

"Was it Otto, Mr. Reinhardt?" Hans asked.

"Yes, you know he wanted me to call him precisely at nine."

"What did he say?"

"It's begun, that's what he said," Gertrude said, her eyes on her husband, who was now sitting at the worktable.

"Tell me all that he said," Hans asked, patiently waiting for her to bring his morning cup of coffee, and when it was ready, a slice of her strudel.

Ever since 1928, when Gertrude and Hans arrived at Wilderstein and were hired by Margaret Suckley as housekeeper, cook, chauffeur, and gardener, they seldom veered from their daily routines.

Each morning it was Hans's duty to go to the root cellar, one level below the house cellar, and bring to the kitchen the vegetables and smoked meat supplies for that day's dinner. At seven-fifteen on this hazy August morning, it was no different. What was out of place, Hans observed, was his wife's noticeable anxiety. It was something he rarely witnessed, and it worried him.

"Hans, we can talk, but only for a moment. Miss Suckley is still sleeping."

"What is going to happen?" Hans asked.

"Mr. Reinhardt told me that Hauptsturmführer Schroeder will be in Poughkeepsie this afternoon. She will take the bus from the train station to her old house on Church Street. He wanted you to pick her up, and I said you couldn't," Gertrude explained, now joining Hans at the table.

The Hildebrands were no strangers to German agent Schroeder. While they never had met her in person, they had been provided with her background at several secret meetings in New York City by Otto Reinhardt during the early months of 1943. It was back in February that the Hildebrands journeyed by train to New York City and then by subway to lower Manhattan and met Reinhardt at a Horn & Hardart cafeteria. It was at those clandestine meetings that Hans and Gertrude were given their instructions and background on Kathe Schroeder, a Vassar graduate and former Poughkeepsie resident. The Hildebrands had nothing but contempt for Reinhardt. They loathed his appearance and the manner in which he presented himself. They resented that he was willing to betray his adopted homeland. But it was the last message at each meeting that garnered hatred in the hearts of Hans and Gertrude. Reinhardt always had been consistent: If he had any indication that the Hildebrands were not cooperating with him, he would inform his superiors in Berlin. It was this message that put fear into the Hildebrands, and Reinhardt knew it all too well.

Otto Reinhardt, as far as the Hildebrands were concerned, was a fifth columnist. He had enjoyed the blessings of his adopted country, but his allegiance was to Germany and its cause. Reinhardt was clever. He did not display any such feelings and thereby escaped the scrutiny that other fifth columnists came under—and who met their fate by being deported.

"I could meet her, Gert. You mustn't get Mr. Reinhardt upset. You know he has deep connections in the old country; he could have Mama and Papa hurt. He can cause trouble for us. You know that as well as I do," Hans said anxiously.

"Can you see now why I wanted you to bring your parents here? Had we done that six years ago, they couldn't be doing to us what they are doing. They are using us to bring in soldiers, and we are part of their awful plans," Gertrude said, her voice breaking, tears beginning to flow.

Hans rose from his chair. He used his wrinkled handkerchief to dry his wife's tears. He knew she was right. He had the chance in 1937 to have his parents immigrate to America and live with them in Rhinebeck. He knew they were now pawns in a military mission for which he and Gertrude had no use. In 1937 Otto Reinhardt had told the German Embassy that the Hildebrands were in a position to some day benefit the Third Reich. Gertrude and Hans loathed him.

"I should have insisted they come to be with us. They said they were too old, they wanted to live out their lives in the village where they were born," Hans said, looking into his coffee.

"You mustn't blame yourself. There was really not much we could do with that swine Reinhardt. I'll never forgive him. And who thought it would come to this?" Gertrude said, wiping her face with her apron.

"Gert, are you going to be all right?" Hans asked.

"I'm fine, Hans. Is the root cellar ready?"

"I've made room for two, but Mr. Reinhardt said there will be more. I don't know how. He wants me to make room for a mixing table and laboratory—for what purpose, Gert?"

"That reminds me, Hans. Mr. Reinhardt still wants you to meet Captain Schroeder at four this afternoon. She wants to go to Beacon and see the Hudson Valley Chemical Company."

"Why?" Hans asked.

"I don't know why, but let's just do it."

"This could be real bad, Gert..."

The annunciator bell interrupted Hans. The arrow on the kitchen wall device, to the right of the kitchen door, was pointing to Miss Suckley's bedroom.

"She's awake. I must get her breakfast. We can talk later," Gertrude said, now on her feet. She put a slice of strudel on a plate that sat on the sterling silver tray. "And Hans, get the cellar ready. Reinhardt's people will be here in two or three days."

"Gert, you didn't answer me. I said I don't like what's happening. Why do they want a mixing table set up in the cellar? And what's the purpose for visiting a chemical factory in Beacon? What are they planning, and are we to be involved? This is not good, I'm telling you." Hans rose from the table.

"Hans, please, not now. You see that I must go to Miss Suckley."

* * *

Jim Gannon was at the wheel of his 1938 Chevy coupe. His passenger was his boss, Mike Reilly. They had just gone by the last sentry post at the president's home. They were on their way to Val-Kill Cottage.

"Boss, I keep meaning to ask you, why does Mrs. Roosevelt live at Val-Kill and not here?" Gannon inquired as he turned south on U.S. Route 9.

"Where the hell have you been?" Reilly responded.

"I've heard certain rumors about the old man's marriage but never placed too much stock in them," Gannon said.

"For your sake, let it just stay as rumors. But so you know once and for all, the boss had an affair back in 1918 or so, before his polio came on. And Mrs. Roosevelt, it seems, never wanted to let the affair pass. From what I have heard over the years, Mrs. R. found a bunch of letters, love letters, that the boss and his former secretary, Lucy Mercer—you know her as Mrs. Rutherford—had sent to each other while he was in Europe during the first war. When he recovered from pneumonia, Mrs. R. confronted the boss with them."

"Don't leave me hanging. Then what happened?" Gannon asked while trying to negotiate through other automobiles on Route 9.

"Well, to tell you the truth, Mrs. R. came to an agreement with the boss. There was to be no more contact with Lucy Mercer, who later got married, but is now a widow."

"So that's why the separate homes and separate bedrooms at the White House?" Gannon interrupted.

"You can say that. And for appearances and for her mother-in-law's health purposes, Mrs. R. stayed at the big house, but in the late 1920s, the boss had the cottage at Val-Kill built. She lives there, and he lives at Springwood. Got that?" Reilly asked sarcastically.

"So why here and not at Top Cottage? It's right near the estate and a hell of a lot easier to protect," Gannon responded, waiting to turn onto Route 9D.

"All I know is the boss wanted a place to go and get away from the big house. He also wanted to be by himself and not living all the time in the same house with his mother. And was she ever pissed when he had the cottage built."

"Well she's gone now, so why does he still use it?" Gannon inquired.

"I can only guess that he wants to be by himself, in a cozier place, isolated like Shangri-La, you know. But in all the years I've been here, the boss never spent an overnight at the cottage."

"Now that you mentioned Shangri-La, his cabin there does remind me of Top Cottage. I know it's wood and not stone."

"If the boss had his way, he would live in a cabin in the woods all of the time. But as events begin to develop, I see things will become even more complicated."

"How so?" Gannon asked.

"Dorothy Schiff is actually going to move next to Top Cottage," Reilly said as he lit his cigarette.

"She's that good-looking dame that owns the New York Post, married three or four times, I've heard," Gannon said.

"Her good looks are only part of what I see as a problem. She's also forty years old, rich, very rich. Her old man was the top guy at the Kuhn Loeb Wall Street firm, and she loves to flirt and party with influential and powerful older men."

"You're not saying she plans to try and make it with the boss—are you?" Gannon asked innocently.

"It's not out of the question. Look, Jim, and keep this to yourself. Ever since he and Mrs. R. had their informal and un-published separation, the boss loves to be around younger women. That's how Miss Suckley came into the picture. And then, up until her stroke two years ago, Missy LeHand. She was not only attractive and efficient, but also half his age."

"Mike, can you blame him? Look what he has had to go through, and now the war. Jesus, I can see him aging almost daily, and I know you can, too."

"Jim, I know that all too well. He's nowhere near the robust fellow I met when I came to the assignment—God, almost eight years now. My only concern is that it complicates things, that's all. Let's drop it." Reilly tossed his butt out the car's window.

Gannon pulled the car up to the Army Military Police's post at Val-Kill and gave the boyish private his identification badge. Reilly leaned over and did the same.

Gannon asked, "Why are we coming here, anyway?"

"Because the boss's secretary told me the president wants to have a picnic here next Wednesday with Mr. Churchill, his family, and some friends. And if Miss Tully hadn't told me, we'd only find out about it Wednesday morning."

"Boss, it's going to be a nightmare to protect this place!" Gannon exclaimed.

"Don't you think I know that? And they all want to go swimming, I'm told, so bring your swim trunks. It will be your job to be in the pond with the boss," Reilly responded, looking over a small map of Val-Kill.

"We're going to need more help," Gannon said.

"Out of the question. By the way, were you able to find out any more on the Hildebrands?"

"I'm working on it, boss, just haven't had the time. But I'll get to it."

"Don't drop it, and keep me up to date," Reilly said.

* * *

"Herr Hildebrand, I was told you were to meet me at the train station. Instead I had to lug all of my stuff on the bus," Kathe Schroeder scolded Hans Hildebrand as he guided the 1938 Packard south on Route 9D to Beacon.

"This car belongs to the madam of the house, Herr Haupsturmführer, and the petrol is being rationed. It's only because Miss Suckley is a friend of Mr. Roosevelt that we can get more ration cards. This sticker here on the windshield allows me to drive on the even day."

"I know all about the goddamn rationing, and don't call me Hauptsturmführer. It's Miss Mayer, and I am a professor at Vassar College. Do you understand?"

"Yes, madam. Beacon is coming up. Where am I to take you?" Hans asked meekly.

The city of Beacon is twenty miles south of Hyde Park. It is an old Hudson River factory town sandwiched between the Hudson Highlands on its east, capped by Mt. Beacon and the Hudson River on the west. The Texas Oil Company research labs had made Beacon its home, as did the popular cookie maker, the National Biscuit Company.

The city's long frontage along the Hudson River, as well as its deep harbors, made Beacon an attractive site for sail and other boat owners. But due to the war effort and gasoline rationing, Beacon's boat flotillas were beached and docked, not only in the half-dozen boat basins, but also on high ground. This observation was registered by Kathe Schroeder as Hans drove her past the entrances to the boatyards.

Captain Schroeder was very familiar with Beacon, not so much because of its history or geography, but because it was home to a half-dozen chemical companies. During her four years at Vassar, she and her fellow chemistry students would spend a considerable amount of time visiting the Beacon plants. Her chemistry professor was keen on his students gaining practical knowledge as well as theoretical. Today, Captain Schroeder wasn't interested in either. The only knowledge she wanted was how she was going to get inside the Hudson Valley Chemical Company. The plant had what she wanted.

"Turn left at the next comer, Herr Hildebrand, and pull up slowly near the building with the smokestack."

"For what reason are we here?" Hans asked.

"Herr Hildebrand, for your own good, don't ask questions, and just do as I order. Is that understood?"

"Yes," Hans murmured. He navigated the large car into an open space on the street, a hundred feet from the smokestack.

Schroeder's response to his question—and the fact that they were parked next to a chemical factory that produced war material—heightened Hans's fears: fears that only a few hours ago he tried to share with Gert.

* * *

"General, there's a Captain Trimble outside. He says it's important he speaks with you," Corporal Parker said, gazing down on General Anderson's desk at Camp Greentop.

"Who the hell is Captain Trimble?" Anderson barked to his orderly.

"He's a Marine, sir, from Shangri-La, sir."

"So?"

"He's the officer who yesterday took Kathe Schroeder to Baltimore," Parker responded.

"And?" The general looked up at Parker.

"You have to hear this, sir, and you're not going to like it," Parker said.

"Show him in, Corporal, and get me Schroeder's file."

"Yes, sir."

"By the way, didn't I request something on her from headquarters?" Anderson asked his orderly as the corporal was about to leave.

"Yes, you did, sir, and it came in about an hour ago from D.C. Do you want that as well?"

"Now what do you think, son? Of course I want it," Anderson said.

* * *

Chapter Five

The late afternoon rush hour was beginning to take shape at New York City's Grand Central Station, and SS Strandartenfuhrer Ludwig Berger was beginning to grow impatient. For the past thirty minutes, he had been waiting at the upper level information center as hundreds of commuters, scurrying in all directions, made him uneasy. Otto Reinhardt was late, and the SS lieutenant colonel had little tolerance for people who were not on time. For that matter, he agreed with his uncle, Heinrich Himmler, the Third Reich's minister of the interior, who had told him, "Do not tolerate incompetence and tardiness. They are signs of weakness." Berger would surely make Reinhardt aware of his shortcomings.

Six-foot-two, with deep-set blue eyes and blond hair, Berger appeared restless and tired. He had been traveling since five in the morning. He had been put ashore at Southhampton, on Long Island's eastern shore, just before dawn, in a rubber dingy paddled by two German sailors from the submarine U-271. Berger's drop-off point was not far from the ill-planned German mission of fourteen months ago. He was well aware why that mission did not meet with success. Berger was determined that a similar fate would not befall his new assignment. He was too cunning, mean, and resourceful to allow it. Furthermore, if he were to be captured, as had been the case with the eight Germans in the prior year's mission, he was prepared.

His suit jacket was lined with a half-dozen potassium cyanide tablets. The ninety-mile journey on the Long Island Railroad was stressful, but he had encountered no problems. He had arrived at New York City's Penn Station two hours earlier and since then made his way across town to New York's other massive train terminal. *So where is Reinhardt?* he wondered, looking at the huge clock on the station's far wall.

"I think I see him, Herr Oberst," Otto Reinhardt said as he and Oberst Albert Krupp descended the marble steps at Grand Central's west entrance.

"Mr. Reinhardt, just 'Krupp,' if you will," the Wehrmacht colonel instructed.

"What do you know about Berger?" Otto asked.

"You don't want to know," Krupp responded.

"Why not?" Otto insisted. They continued down the steps, weaving in and out of the throng of commuters who were making their way out of the station to 42nd Street and Vanderbilt Plaza.

"You'll want to stay clear of him as much as you can. He is ruthless to his core. He also led the raid that rescued Benito Mussolini, and because of that, he is close to the Fuhrer," Krupp said almost at a whisper.

"Good God!" Otto exclaimed.

"And he hates me almost as much as he hates Roosevelt," Krupp added.

"Why?" Reinhardt asked, trying to keep pace with the Wehrmacht colonel.

Attempting to stay focused in locating Berger within the mass of humanity now engulfing the terminal, Krupp replied, "Reinhardt, did you not listen when I told you that Berger's uncle is Himmler, the head of the German Interior Office. He has but one goal in this war: the killing of Jews. The war to him is a means to an end. He's not one bit interested in how it is being played out as long, as he can massacre the Jews in the territories the Wehrmacht captures. Berger is exactly the same, and because I've been put in charge of the mission, he is so angry."

"But you outrank him. You are a full colonel, and he is—"

"You don't understand, Reinhardt. He knows I failed my mission in 1940, in Lisbon, to abduct the Duke and Duchess of Windsor, and he feels he must constantly remind me. Just be careful, that's all," Krupp said. He finally made eye contact with Berger.

"I thought you were captured, detained, or something worse, Oberst," Berger said as he was approached by Krupp and Reinhardt.

"Just 'Krupp,' Berger. And we mustn't stay here. We're too conspicuous. Otto, what have you planned for transportation?" Krupp asked, immediately taking charge.

If Berger appeared tired and restless after his long journey, he was not going to receive any sympathy from Albert Krupp. The colonel had been traveling since midnight, when he came ashore near Annapolis, Maryland. That was also where he was to locate his transportation to Washington, D.C.

The Third Reich needed support from within the United States. It was able to gain such support from selected diplomatic consulates of other countries. From these consulates, the Nazis' entry onto U.S. soil was often provided.

Many of Argentina's diplomatic staff in Washington were either German agents or sympathetic to the German cause. The cultural affairs attaché of the Argentine Embassy had arranged for a car to be left at a fishing pier not far from the U.S. Naval Academy. It was believed that no one would be so reckless as to come that close to the well-guarded naval training college.

Jose Padelia was a naval attaché in Washington at his South American country's embassy. In 1940 he had been stationed in Madrid with most of his time spent cozying up to his counterparts at the Third Reich's embassy in neighboring Portugal. It was during his tenure in Spain that he got to know Colonel Albert Krupp. And it was Padelia who gave the German agents the itinerary of the Duke and Duchess of Windsor's stay in Portugal. Three years later, reassigned to America, Padelia was given instructions to locate an automobile near the U.S. Naval Academy. He felt that once again he was to be part of a plot, even though he was not privy to all its details.

Krupp was familiar with the route he would need to take to get to Washington's Union Station. As German youths, he and his brother frequently had accompanied their father, the vice president of Sandoz Drug Company, on trips to America in the late 1920s and 1930s. Their father had believed it was important for his sons to become indoctrinated in the ways of Americans, particularly their language. Adolph Hitler's rise to power brought an end to the Krupps' sojourns to the United States—until last night.

The forty-five-mile journey from Annapolis on U.S. Route 50 West brought the Wehrmacht colonel to downtown Washington. At five in the morning, he abandoned the car on Third and H Street in the Southeast section of the capital and walked the dozen blocks to the cavernous Union Station. At six-ten he boarded the Pennsylvania Railroad train to New York City. He had been fifteen minutes ahead of schedule. Otto Reinhardt, whom he had met many years ago on one of his trips to New York, was to meet him at Penn Station.

"I have tickets for the 5 of 4 train to Croton. It will be on track 112 on the Lower Level," Otto responded.

"Let's hope we are not sitting all together," Berger interjected, sarcastically.

"I thought of that, Berger. You'll be seated in the second car from the front. Krupp and I will be in the car behind you," Reinhardt responded.

Mumbling, Berger went ahead and walked briskly down the ramp to the awaiting Hudson Line train.

The trio were fortunate to have found seats in the dusty and smoke-filled train. Commuters heading home to Westchester County were occupying nearly every available seat. Young soldiers who effortlessly carried their duffle bags rose from their seats and turned them over to the women commuters, who had for the past eight hours plied their shorthand, typing, and filing skills at offices in New York City.

Krupp and Berger were not comfortable being on a train with so many military personnel, especially their enemy's military personnel. It was not the privates and corporals who gave them concern, it was the dozen or so lieutenants, captains, and two majors they would need to avoid. The two German infiltrators had been warned to be extremely careful and above all not to make eye contact. Krupp felt that he could follow that advice, but was not so sure if Berger would accept it. The one-hour trip along the Hudson was going to feel much longer.

"One Hundred Twenty Fifth Street, Yonkers, Ossining, and Croton-on-Hudson, have your tickets ready," shouted the bespectacled and overweight conductor.

"I hope Berger stays awake to get off at Croton," Krupp said.

"You don't like him. I can see that," Reinhardt responded as they took their seats in the smoke-filled passenger car.

"I guess I am tired, Otto. It's been a long day, and then still more traveling to do. I just want to get to Schroeder's place as soon as possible."

As the car's lights flickered, the train began to roll forward, gradually increasing its pace as it left the station and continued into the dark tunnel under Park Avenue.

Leaning over to whisper, Reinhardt said, "Herr Krupp, this mission will not be another Pastorious, I can assure you of that."

"How can you be so sure, Reinhardt? And drop that 'Herr.'"

Fourteen months earlier, in June of 1942, eight German saboteurs had entered the United States. Four came ashore at Jacksonville, Florida, and four at Amagansett, on eastern Long Island. Their mission was to disrupt America's railroads, factories, and other establishments.

"Because they were not professionals, they never should have come here in the first place. What was the Abwehr thinking to have sent such incompetents?" Otto gloated.

"I know all about it. Berger and I spent the last four months at Brandenburg, at the Quenz Farm, where those poor, unfortunate bastards trained as well for their mission. It was a disaster from the beginning, and we have learned from their mistakes."

"Good Christ, Krupp, it was all over the newspapers here. They were captured within one week by government agents, the FBI," Otto said anxiously.

"The FBI made sure it got the credit; we saw that at our camp. But they didn't discover the group."

"What are you saying? They did."

"No, I'm telling you. Dasch, the leader of the mission, sur-rendered to the government agents. He told the agents where the others could be located. George Dasch went to Washington and exposed the other seven. That's why they were apprehended. That, plus Dasch's group had been initially spotted by the coast sentry when they came ashore on Long Island."

"Are you saying Dasch was a traitor?"

"Yes, he and Ernest Burger. Why do you think that they were not executed last August like the others?" Krupp asked.

"So, can that happen now, this mission?" Reinhardt asked nervously.

"There is a weakness in this plan," Krupp said as he watched the train leave tunnel at Harlem.

"One Hundred Twenty Fifth Street, next stop," the conductor shouted from the front of the car.

"Where, where is the weakness, Krupp? I want to know," Reinhardt asked.

"I'll tell you, but first let the passengers get off."

* * *

Steve Early was as close an advisor to the president as anyone, now that Missy LeHand was no longer at the White House or Hyde Park. He was also a confidant of Mrs. Roosevelt's. To have gained the confidence of both was rare indeed. Early was also the president's press secretary. Mike Reilly always had thought well of Early. Both of them had a great deal of respect and understanding of the difficulty in working for the president.

"Mike, I'm glad you were able to break loose and come over. The boss is in rare form," Early said as Reilly and Gannon make their way up the steps leading to the veranda at Springwood.

"What's up, Steve? Miss Tully said it was important for me and Jim to get over here."

"He wants to see us as soon as he finishes lunch with the big guns," Early responded.

"Who's he with?" Gannon asked.

"Stimson, Knox, and Morgenthau. They've been there for over an hour and half, but I think they'll break soon," Early said.

"Why is he meeting with the secretaries of War, Navy, and Treasury on a Sunday? I thought he came to Hyde Park to relax," Gannon inquired.

"He is relaxing. It's his way. Right, Mike?" Early responded.

"You're right, but just listen. He's pissed at something," Reilly said. He approached the door to the room in which the president was meeting.

"I tell you, gentlemen, there are times I think Lindbergh works for the goddamn Nazis. Christ, a couple of years ago he got Hermann Goering to award him the Service Cross of the Order of the Golden Eagle, and what do you think of that? America's hero aviator, bullshit," the president was overheard saying.

President Roosevelt saw his press secretary with the two Secret Service agents and said, "Come in Steve, you too Mike, and bring that handsome lad with you."

"We can wait outside, Mr. President," Early said.

"No, we're done. Good afternoon, gentlemen, and thanks for your counsel and patience in letting this old fool rant on," the president said to his guests, who now rose from their chairs and prepared to shake his hand.

For many years, President Roosevelt had to endure criticism from Charles Lindbergh as well as from his former ambassador to Great Britain, Joseph Kennedy. It was their belief that the president brought the country into war with Germany and Japan. Mr. Roosevelt's anti-isolationist stance was what caused Germany, Italy, and Japan to be at war with America. Reilly was keenly aware of his boss's antagonists. He had them closely monitored by his department as well as by the FBI. He knew Lindbergh's and Kennedy's animosity weighed heavily on the president, as did the daily news about the war. On this Sunday, they were anxiously awaiting news about the invasion of Sicily.

"Mike, Jim, come in and take a load off your feet. A glass of lemonade will do you all a world of good." The president motioned to the Filipino waiter to get them some drinks.

It never ceased to amaze Reilly how the president could change his demeanor so quickly. Suddenly it was FDR's attitude that Reilly thoroughly enjoyed seeing him, so different from the previous discussion with his cabinet members.

"By the way, Jim, have I mentioned to you what a close resemblance you have to Basil O'Connor? You know Basil, my law partner—or should I say, partner of intrigue?"

Blushing from the president's remark, Gannon responded, "Mr. President, you have never said anything that Mr. Reilly here and Miss Tully haven't heard a bunch of times."

"Well, fellows, as you certainly are aware, Basil is quite dear to me. He's a fellow I have absolute trust in, more so than anyone else. And during these days, that is something that is most precious: trust," the president said, motioning to his guests to sit.

It was Reilly who first had introduced Basil O'Connor to Gannon and gave him a history of the president's relationship. In 1943, the president continued to be a law partner in the Wall Street firm of Roosevelt & O'Connor. It was a partnership that had begun in the mid-1920s, when Franklin Roosevelt was beginning to go out in the public and get back to work. Three years of intensive recuperation from his polio attack enabled him to do so. He desperately wanted to be with people, and to be productive.

Basil O'Connor was at the time only a few years out of law school. He was the strapping, red-headed son of an Irish immigrant from Taunton, Massachusetts who came to Roosevelt's aid when the crippled man fell in the lobby of the office building at 120 Broadway on his first day back to work.

Days later, Roosevelt would recruit this son of a New England mill worker to be his law partner. Roosevelt was to be the producer of clients, and O'Connor did the necessary legal work, and where and when required, attended and participated in legal negotiations.

Fifteen years later, O'Connor's partner, now president and leader of the free world, would frequently call upon O'Connor's skills at negotiating. It was a position that was kept so quiet that only Reilly, Gannon, Early, and Miss Tully knew about it. And that was the way the president wanted it.

"Mike, I had asked Steve to have you come over because I've heard you continue to worry about the prime minister and I having dinner and spending time at Miss Daisy's home. Is that a fair statement?"

"That's correct, Mr. President," Reilly responded.

"Well, I don't want you worrying, and if it means that you need more agents, let's see if Secretary Morgenthau can help," Roosevelt said.

"It's not more agents, sir. It's just that—"

Interrupting, the president said, "It is important, Mike, that from time to time, Mr. Churchill and I get away from here. The matters we will be discussing are profound, and God only knows that Wilderstein is as good a place as any. Last week in Montreal when I saw the PM, he agreed, so let's not fret. All will be fine."

Fifteen minutes later, when Early, Gannon, and Reilly were back outside, Gannon said, "He is convincing, I would say. He speaks his mind, and what else can you do?"

"He's all that and more. For starters, Jim, let's get that material on the Hildebrands and get me the blueprints of the house and grounds," Reilly said.

"You know, Mike, the prime minister will be here next Sunday," Early said as the three men walked around to the front of the house.

"That's the problem, Steve. I know it all too well. Jim, I want you here on the grounds for the next week when the PM and the boss are together."

"That should not be a problem, Mike, but there goes what little I had of a social life," Gannon said.

"Jim, I want a priority put in place for those files on the Hildebrands," Reilly ordered.

Chapter Six

Ever since May of 1942 United States Marines, all one hundred thirty-five of them, together with a dozen German shepherd guard dogs, were stationed at the top of Mt. Catoctin in Maryland's Cumberland Mountains. They were there for one purpose. They were to provide security at the fence that surrounded the secret hideaway of their cornmander-in-chief. For many of the Marines, it was a much less vigorous assignment and less dangerous than what they had been through the previous eighteen months. Shangri-La was the name the president had chosen for his hideaway when he first visited the retreat in April of 1942, and for the battle-tested Marines it was a world apart from Guadalcanal or Midway. They found it as restful and relaxing as did the president and his invited guests. The forested one hundred forty acres was in many respects like the mythical place for which it was named in James Hilton's novel *Lost Horizon*. Yet this was not to be the case for Captain Trimble, the Marine detachment's executive officer, himself a recovering casualty of Guadalcanal. Trimble had been on the island of Guadalcanal for three months. For twenty-one days and nights, he and his rifle company had held the Japanese Marines from overrunning the island's key airstrip, Henderson Field. It was during that slugfest and for his valor that he had been awarded the Navy Cross.

The twenty-five-year-old captain appeared to be much older, more like thirty-five. The horrors of the Pacific campaign were etched in his face. He welcomed his present duty assignment but longed to be back with the Fleet Marine Force. He did not like the fact that next to Shangri-La was Camp Greentop—a training base for saboteurs. He was not bashful in sharing his feelings with his commanding officer or with Secret Service Agent Michael Reilly, who had shared the captain's concerns. Today he was prepared to share those opinions with General Anderson.

"Captain, I heard you wanted to see me. What can I do for you and the Marines?" Anderson said. He took another drag on his three-inch cigar and noticed the navy-blue ribbon with a white strip down the center as well as the purple one on the left side of Trimble's shirt. Their significance was not lost on the general. He was aware that a wounded Marine officer was now in his presence—and a hero as well, one who was awarded his country's second highest medal for valor, the Navy Cross.

"Thanks for seeing me, General. How well did you know that gal that I brought to the station in Baltimore?" Trimble responded.

"Have a seat, Captain. We're not too formal here, got both civilians and military types going through training, you know," Anderson said.

"I'll stand, if it is okay with the general."

"As you wish. Now what is the basis for your question, Captain? Sure, I know Schroeder," Anderson said, not pleased that a Marine captain was questioning him about one of his charges.

"General, I was in the car with her for over an hour and a half, from here to Baltimore."

"So, what about it?"

"I'm coming to that, sir. During that time, I felt there was something fishy, suspicious, something wasn't right," Trimble said.

"Good God, Captain, you'd feel that way about the whole goddamn bunch here," Anderson said in a loud, impatient voice.

Anderson got up and puffed his cigar. He had his back to his guest and was now looking out the cabin window. "They're not Marines, Captain. They're here to train as spies. They're going overseas to do a bunch of dirty tricks to both the Japs and Nazis.

It doesn't surprise me one bit that you feel the way you do—that's good. Schroeder—she's going to Italy to blow up a bunch of bridges, dikes, and railroads. What's important is that she fits in over there."

The officer speaking to Trimble might have outranked him, but Trimble was not going to let the general intimidate him. When you have been given your country's second-highest decoration for valor and still carry the shrapnel from Japanese grenades, one-star generals are not something you fear. And Trimble didn't.

"Look, General, I know you got a bunch of strange people here doing all kinds of weird shit. Me and my Marines can hear your explosions around the clock. But this woman was more than that. Can you tell me what she had in her suitcase that she held onto for dear life?"

"Her clothes, I guess. She's going home to see her dying mother. Why do you ask, Captain?"

"Because there was an odor, and I don't mean from smelly clothes, either," Trimble responded.

"What do you mean, an odor? What kind of odor?"

"The same noxious smell that comes from cordite, gunpowder, TNT, sir, that kind of odor. And if I'm right in assuming that's what it was, what the hell is she doing transporting explosives and bomb-making material?"

"Captain, I don't know what in Christ's name Schroeder might have had in her suitcase. But I'm going to make it my business to find out," Anderson said, looking directly at the Marine. "Furthermore, no one leaves this camp for leave carrying weapons, maps, code books, or for that matter, goddamn explosives!"

"Didn't mean to get you all upset, sir, but..." Trimble replied. He was interrupted by a very distraught general and camp commander.

"Captain, in one hour I'll know whether you're right. And may I ask that for now you keep this conversation between us?"

* * *

"Mr. Kelly, do you remember me, Kathe? Kathe from Vassar College, Professor Freeman's student," Kathe Schroeder said sweetly to the rotund uniformed guard who was sitting on a metal folding chair inside the Hudson Valley Chemical Company's employee entrance.

"Indeed I do, my dear. My, you haven't changed one bit. But I haven't seen you in what, a year or two?" the short and bespectacled Mr. Kelly responded, now rising from his chair.

"I see you're still reading those cowboy stories. What, another Zane Grey?"

"They're Westerns my dear, not cowboy stories."

"Oh yes, you told me that when I first met you."

"So what is the difference between cowboys or Westerns? I'm afraid it's all the same to me, Mr. Kelly."

"My dear Kathe, a cowboy is about one person, one type of job. But a Western, well here's the difference," Mr. Kelly explained while he tried to place his arm around Schroeder's waist.

The last thing Schroeder wanted to hear was the distinction between cowboys and Westerns. It would take Kelly, a Zane Grey fanatic, another five minutes to provide Schroeder with the distinction, and then he asked, "So where have you been, lass?"

"I spent two years in South America, Argentina, and now I'm back completing my master's. Looks like things have changed here," Schroeder said. She leaned beyond the open second door and peered into the vast workroom jammed with factory-floor workers at dozens of work stations.

The Hudson Valley Chemical Company was a sprawling, pre-Civil War brick complex. Since its inception in 1854, its owners over the years had added more and more buildings until they were stopped by the shore of the Hudson River. Then they went vertical.

Three months after the present war had begun, the company no longer manufactured just chlorine. Its total production capacity was committed to the manufacture of explosives, principally nitroglycerin, arsenic, and other highly toxic chemicals and poisons. Its orders came from Wilmington, Delaware. It was now wholly owned by E.I. du Pont de Nemours and Company, and had been since the founder's grandchildren lost the factory in

1934. Their family's business was another casualty of the Great Depression.

"I'm sorry, dear, you can't go in as you did before. The war, you know. Clearances and all that." Kelly maneuvered his short frame next to Schroeder.

"I just can't go in and see my old lab station, Mr. Kelly?"

"I'm afraid not, my dear. But I'll tell you what. In a few minutes or so I'll be on my break, and if you behave, I'll take you around. How's that?"

"That will be just fine, Mr. Kelly."

"It will be like old times to see you pretty girls here once again. It's been mighty dull, I can tell you." Kelly began to remove his black leather security-station belt and clock and placed them on the wooden desk.

"Do they still bring coal in by the old trap door, Mr. Kelly?"

"I'm not supposed to tell you that, but they do, my dear, and a lot more. They operate the factory now seven days a week and around the clock—three shifts, mind you. Not like the old days, and not the same faces, either. If you had gone inside to the manufacturing floor without an escort, you would've been picked up so fast, your eyes would pop," Kelly responded.

"That much security in the old plant?" Schroeder inquired.

"And a lot more. There are guards now going up and down the line. I don't because I'm too old. The stuff they're making, I can tell you it is real secret," Kelly confided, heading toward the factory floor double-swing doors.

"You were wonderful to us girls. You never told Professor Freeman that we went to the coal chute to smoke cigarettes."

"And do you remember why, Kathe?"

"I do. We brought you your favorite cookies, right?"

Schroeder became anxious to get Mr. Kelly to give her the tour. She wanted to see if there were any obstacles placed in the pathway from the coal chute to the finished-goods storeroom. She loathed Mr. Kelly and all of the Mr. Kellys of America. She was thinking in a few days she'd bring him his last batch of cookies.

* * *

The Wehrmacht colonel, Albert Krupp, had been fast asleep ever since the train left the 125th Street station. The train was now slowly pulling out of the Ossining station. He was beginning to wake up. Looking out the window, he could see, up on the rocky hill, the walls of Sing Sing, the infamous penitentiary. He was well aware that behind the prison's twenty-five-foot concrete walls were some of his countrymen. They were fifth columnists, picked up and detained by the American authorities.

His thoughts did not linger with them. He was still reliving his early-morning exploits when he was placed on board the *Biber* midget submarine from its mother boat, U-262. The U-boat was one of eight German navy wolfpack submarines that were on continuous patrol at the entrance to Hampton Roads in Virginia. The *Biber* was manned by one sailor and Krupp. It could only travel at six-and-one-half knots per hour in calm seas, and from where he was put on the *Biber*, he had to travel some twenty miles to reach Annapolis, Krupp's land destination.

For the six-foot career soldier, the three-hour ordeal was debilitating. It was his first encounter with the hardships endured by his fellow warriors who were in the undersea service. The midget submarine had no difficulty getting past numerous mines and channel netting. The *Biber's* operator made it look easy. But Krupp felt the thirty-foot boat was going to be his coffin. He did not have the young enlisted man's confidence in the midget sub's ability.

Krupp was convinced his journey was going to end with a huge explosion when they would ram one of the hundreds of mines or get tangled in the wire-rope nets and be starved for oxygen. The young sailor masterfully guided the sub out of the huge bay area and into the mouth of the Potomac River. Annapolis was not far, but getting there was still going to feel like an eternity to Krupp.

Waking to the jarring of the train as it began to pick up momentum, Krupp wondered if the midget sub pilot ever made it back to U-262. He had been told that the sub's range was only one hundred thirty miles. Its twin twenty-one-inch torpedo tubes were not armed and were instead crammed with additional batteries.

"Albert, we get off at the next station. I'll go forward to make sure Berger is awake. You must be exhausted," Otto Reinhardt said as he maneuvered out of the seat.

"How long have I been asleep, Otto?" Krupp asked.

"Since New York City, about an hour. That's all. Albert, you were about to tell me your concern that there could be someone who could betray us."

"Please sit down. How long have you known the Hildebrands?" Krupp asked as Otto rejoined him.

"About six years. I introduced them to our people in 1937 or '38. I felt that because of their positions they might one day prove useful. Her parents, Gertrude's mother and father, live in Stuttgart. They wouldn't do anything to the Reich that would jeopardize her parents, I'm sure of that."

"I see," Krupp said.

"I'll go and see Berger." Once again Otto got up to move forward into the next car.

"Wait!" Krupp said.

"What is it, sir?"

"You don't know? Fraulein Hildebrand's parents were killed in a night air raid in Stuttgart six weeks ago," Krupp disclosed as he gripped Reinhardt's arm.

"They don't know, I'm certain," Otto said with a worried expression. "And they mustn't know. Because if they did, we most certainly would lose control over them. They would turn on us and the mission. Just as George Dasch did last year—that traitor bastard!"

* * *

Jim Gannon closed the door of his Chevy coupe. He was standing next to a sign that read *Val-Kill Industries*. He had returned to the home of Mrs. Roosevelt to personally go over security arrangements that were going to be needed. He felt his boss was too busy to do it himself, and he would have appreciated Gannon's initiative.

Earlier in the day, Gannon had pushed his boss to tell him more about the unorthodox arrangement the president had with his wife. Reluctantly, Reilly had taken him aside and told him that in 1918 the boss came back from an inspection trip of the Navy and the troops in Europe. He was greeted at the dock in New York City by a doctor and an ambulance. He had influenza and pneumonia. Later Eleanor Roosevelt went through his belongings and found love letters from Lucy Mercer. After five children and twenty-five years of marriage, theirs was effectively over.

Reilly had said that during his recovery from polio, in 1924, he acquired Val-Kill, originally as part of the family's one-thousand-acre estate. Eleanor Roosevelt wanted her own place to do her own thing along with her two dear companions, Marion Dickerman and Nancy Cook. The three women would eventually become so bonded that all the linens, from the bed and bathrooms, were monogrammed *EMN*.

Gannon had already known a great deal about the first lady's friends, but he did not wish to let on to Reilly that he did. Months before, Steve Early had told him about the relationship among the three women and how it came to an end in 1939 after a lengthy legal battle. Reilly had now confirmed it.

According to Early, the break-up was inevitable. When the relationship first began, Cook, the political organizer, and her fellow Syracuse University classmate, Dickerman, brought Eleanor Roosevelt into their world of social causes, peace movements, and women's suffrage—in addition to teaching and furniture-making.

Early had told Gannon that when their boss took office in 1933, the Eleanor, Nancy, and Marion relationship began to unravel, especially when Eleanor met a new friend, the aggressive newswoman Lorena Hickok. That intimate relationship provided no room for Dickerman or Cook. Hickok had made that very clear to the occupants of Stone Cottage.

To the youthful and deeply Roman Catholic Gannon, it was bizarre. He had told his boss that what he was saying was weird and unorthodox. Reilly had warned him to never repeat what he was hearing, that it was none of their business.

Gannon moved away from his car and walked toward the furniture company's dock. He also had to move his mind away from what Reilly and Early had told him. He needed to focus on what protection was going to be required at Val-Kill for the president's picnic next Sunday with Winston Churchill. What he soon had to contend with was far more important than speculating on Mrs. Roosevelt's women friends and their relationships.

Chapter Seven

"Hans, Miss Suckley wants you to take Heather to the veterinarian. She feels the dog might have ringworm or something," Gertrude Hildebrand instructed her husband as she pushed the carpet sweeper back and forth on the Persian rug in the parlor, while her husband followed.

Hans was not pleased with his assignment as he stared down at the aging Scottish terrier resting on the parlor floor just beyond the carpet. Heather knew from observing on countless other afternoons that Gertrude would not come near her spot with the sweeper.

"Imagine wasting petrol for such a stupid thing. When the madam gave Mr. Roosevelt his dog, Fala, she should have given him this one," Hans replied.

"Hans, just do as she wishes. It's not our job to question. You wanted to tell me how your afternoon went with Captain Schroeder. So tell me."

"It's Miss Mayer, Gert, and don't call her 'captain'. Where is the madam?"

"She's at Springwood for the evening. She should be back after ten. What about Miss Mayer?"

"I keep telling you, Gert, the whole thing is not good. She had me drive her to Beacon. And when we got to a chemical factory she went inside. She was gone for a long time. Why would she want to visit a factory in Beacon, and an old chemical factory?"

"What did she tell you when you took her home?" Gertrude asked, no longer cleaning the carpet but leaning on the sweeper's handle.

"She told me nothing. I asked her why we went to the factory, and she said it would be better if I didn't know." Hans placed a leash on Heather's leather collar.

"I haven't met her, Hans, but I know she's up to no good. I'm certain of that. And since she's a captain in the SS, are we in for a lot of trouble from her? What do you think?"

"Gert, with Mr. Reinhardt bringing those other people here, I don't know what their plans are. Why would you visit a chemical factory? Are they going to blow it up?"

"Why would you even suggest that, Hans?"

"Because I know something about Schroeder, Miss Mayer, that's what," Hans said angrily.

"What? What do you know about her?"

"Do you remember a few years ago, before the war, we took the train to New York City and visited the Empire State Building?"

"Yes, but what does that have to do with this, with Schroeder?"

"I'll tell you what. Remember, we also went on the boat to see the Statue of Liberty. When we were there, the guide told us about the other island, Liberty State Park, and what had happened there in the last war."

"I don't remember, Hans. It was too long ago." Gertrude moved out of the parlor.

Following his wife and pulling Heather with him, Hans said, "I still remember. In 1916 there was a big explosion. The island was called Black Tom, and millions of pounds of explosives blew up. People were killed. The explosives were at the dock, getting ready to go to England. This country was not in the war."

"Hans, you've got to get the dog to the doctor's. Why are you telling me all of this?" Gertrude insisted.

"Just wait and listen, will you? That explosion, and the fire at the Roebling Steel Foundry in Trenton, were caused by the same person."

"How do you know all this?" Gertrude asked.

"Because four years ago the German-American Claims Commission said so. They said Siegfried Holtz did it. He was able to escape and died a few years later back in Germany."

"Now, who is Holtz?" Gertrude asked.

"Gertrude, Siegfried Holtz was Kathe Schroeder's father."

* * *

Despite the arduous journey that had begun almost twenty hours ago, when he was put ashore on Long Island, Ludwig Berger never closed his eyes on the train. For the last hour he had stared out the dirty upper window while he kept the lower half open to capture the breeze from the moving train. The Hudson River and its adjacent mountains reminded him all too well of his home in Halle, in Prussian Saxony.

The fact that Albert Krupp, his leader on this mission, came from his village only added to his animus. He was not in charge. Krupp was, and Berger wanted to know why. During their training at the Quenz Farm, near Brandenburg, he questioned his superior's judgment. Berger was adamant that Admiral Wilhelm Canaris, the head of the German Intelligence, was dead wrong in assigning Krupp to lead the mission. Why him? Berger's rescue of Mussolini was legendary, and so was his relationship with Heinrich Himmler, his uncle, the Minister of the Interior.

His trainers at Quenz were well aware of Berger's explosive nature. They also knew he would frequently act irrationally, purely out of hate. His motivation, it was felt, went beyond that which was going to be needed in America.

Nevertheless, the fact that he despised Roosevelt and even more so, Churchill, was sufficient to have him on the mission. Berger's superiors felt it was going to be up to Krupp and Schroeder to work with him, to control him.

Berger did all he could to remain patient as the train began to slow and approach the Croton-on-Hudson station. Ludwig Berger was the most highly decorated officer in the SS. He was also the most feared. He had zero tolerance for any imperfection or incompetence. It did not matter to Berger whether such characteristics were displayed by his subordinates or by his superiors. Berger, when he witnessed such flaws, would lash out. His rage was his signature and the reason why so few in the SS or Wehrmacht wanted to serve with him. On the raid to rescue Benito Mussolini, he summarily executed his second-in-command for having failed to get Berger's team to the top of the mountain on schedule. His calculated viciousness and the resulting murder of a fellow officer were overlooked by the German High Command—because Berger had pulled off a near-impossible rescue and gave Germany a great propaganda victory.

Reinhardt raised his ample frame from the seat he had been sharing with Krupp and began to make his way into the forward car. He was extremely unsteady as he lunged for the brass handgrip fastened to the top of each seat. He believed, though, that the jostling train was not solely the cause of his unsteadiness. Krupp's detailed narrative of Berger's ruthlessness had made his legs cold and wobbly. His forehead displayed large beads of sweat, and his hands slipped off each rail he tried to grip.

Reinhardt was re-thinking, as he entered the next car, the situation in which he was now involved. He did not expect to have been assigned to such a vicious and cunning individual, as Krupp had described Berger. To get away from it all was unthinkable—and too late. Going to the FBI to reveal what was happening would be certain death—if not from the government, then from other fifth columnists. He was now committed, whether he liked it or not. He came upon Berger's seat and whispered to the scowling Nazi, "We get off at this station, Berger. You will need to move back to our car and get off there."

* * *

The Willard Hotel in Washington, D.C., was located both across the street and around the corner from the United States Treasury building. The hotel's history went back more than a century. President Grant was a frequent visitor, especially when he was in office. He had made it a point to meet those seeking favors from his administration who waited in the hotel lobby for him. Thus the press coined the term "lobbyist".

Seventy years later, on a balmy, late Friday afternoon, Ellen McCarthy was also waiting to see someone special. She was delighted that she was able to escape the brutal heat and humidity of earlier in the day and wait for her fiancé in the hotel's vaulted lobby reception area with its many chairs and tables. She was not there alone. There were dozens of hotel guests conversing in the huge and ornately appointed room. The ladies, not unlike her, were wearing summer sundresses with wide-brimmed hats and white gloves. Their male companions were dressed in suits and Panama hats, smoking cigars and cigarettes. The military officers present were dressed in their summer whites and tans.

Lines of would-be hotel guests were patiently waiting behind velvet ropes and brass stanchions to check into one of the capital's most prestigious hotels. Ellen McCarthy's eyes were focused on the activity coming and going through the hotel's revolving front doors. Uniformed, white-haired, and gloved Negro porters were doing all they could to keep up with the steady flow of trunks, suitcases, and military sea bags entering or departing the hotel.

Her focus on the front door hustle was interrupted. "You've been waiting long, dear?" Jim Gannon asked his fiancée.

The twenty-five-year old, a graduate of Marymount College, responded, "Only for a few minutes, James."

Ellen McCarthy, along with Jim Gannon's mother and his fifth-grade teacher at St. Mary's Grade School, Sister Josephine, were the only people who would call him James. Ever since 1941, when he first met Ellen, he could not persuade her to call him Jim. He detested being called James, more so when his boss, Mike Reilly, referred to it. In Reilly's case, Gannon would know instantly that the boss was upset.

The tall and athletic Gannon bent over and placed a kiss on Ellen's cheek. "Let's go in and have dinner, Muffin," Gannon whispered in her ear, using his favorite nickname.

"Where have you been? Are you in a rush?" Ellen asked as she walked toward the corridor that led to the Willard's formal dining room.

Holding on to Ellen's gloved hand, Gannon escorted his smiling fiancée down the hall, ever-observant of the glances they received from the guests. He then said, "I can't tell you where I've been, but yes, I'm in a rush—to see you."

Gannon's courtship of Ellen had begun a little more than two years ago. She was the valedictorian at her graduation. President Roosevelt was also at the graduation ceremony. He was being given an honorary Doctor of Laws degree. Gannon was alongside him. But his eyes were transfixed on the speaker. He could not help falling head-over-heels for the striking Irish American brunette with the most gorgeous green eyes he had ever seen. He personally ran the security check on her, and Ellen was shocked to have heard on their first date how much he knew about her.

For six months after her graduation, Gannon would be able to go out on weekly dates with her. Their getting together became even more frequent when she took a position in government next door to the White House. But for the past twenty months, their visits had been greatly curtailed. The attack at Pearl Harbor had changed their lives as well as their daily routine and responsibilities.

"James, can you honestly afford this place? And on your measly salary?" Ellen asked as the maitre de escorted them to a corner table that overlooked Pennsylvania Avenue and 15th Street.

"For my bride-to-be, why not?" Gannon responded.

"Don't give me that malarkey you're so well known for. There's something up, isn't there?"

"Let's just enjoy this place and, yes, I can afford it, now that you've asked."

"You drop into town and never tell me you're coming. I have no idea where you've been. You're the most mysterious man I have ever known." Ellen glanced over the leather-bound and oversized menu folder.

"Ellen, now look, you work over at Treasury. You know the rules. I can't share with you where I've been, or where I am, or for that matter where I'm going!" Gannon explained as he reached across the white linen tablecloth and clasped her soft hand.

As the assistant to the deputy undersecretary of treasury, Ellen did have some knowledge of what Gannon was saying. What was frustrating to her was his unwillingness to share any of what he was doing with the president.

Gannon had almost finished his dinner of chicken breast, mashed potatoes, and string beans. He was not the sophisticated menu selector that Ellen was. Daintily, she was carving the last piece of her swordfish, something she thought was a rare delicacy during wartime and a rarity at most restaurants. But the fish, along with the creamed scalloped potatoes, was a treat, and unlike her companion, she did not want to rush consuming it—or her glass of Chardonnay. When she glanced up, she saw that Gannon was halfway through his second gin and tonic and said, "James, in three months we are going to be married. I've placed a deposit for one month's rent on a small house in Georgetown. You need to see it. It is so cute, and it is only eighty dollars a month! Do you think we can go in the morning? I'll make an appointment. The landlord, Mr. Marks, lives upstairs with his wife."

"I don't think I can."

"Why not? Do you have any idea how hard it was to find something with the war on? We're lucky we don't have to live in a tent," she said, obviously upset over Gannon's reluctance.

"Dear, I'm flying back tonight, out of Bolling Army Air Force Base to Stewart Field, in Newburgh."

"I have plans, James, for us. Why do you have to go back so soon?" Ellen asked, her face beginning to flush.

"Ellen, you know I can't say. I'll be gone for three weeks. I only came to town to check at immigration on a couple of names," Gannon said. He squeezed her hands and could feel her disappointment.

"What do you have to do at immigration?" she asked, her head down and her eyes staring at the last piece of swordfish.

"I shouldn't be telling you this, but Mike wanted me to personally run down the backgrounds on a couple of German immigrants he is suspicious of, that's all," Gannon said, reluctantly.

"So can you go back later?" she asked him.

"I'm afraid I can't. I'm on a special flight tonight. I've heard that Marshall will be on the plane also."

"General George Marshall?" she asked.

"That's right, and please don't repeat that," he replied.

"James, I know your work is important and sensitive, but I want you to know we have so much to do and not a lot of time to get it all accomplished. I can see that something big might be up. Is that why you'll be away?"

"Can't tell you that, my dear. But I can tell you that when I get the information to Mike on the two people he wanted checked out, I'll give him the information on a character I've always had a bad feeling about."

"Who was that, James?" she asked. Her natural color began to return to her face, and she looked directly at her love.

"You wouldn't know or shouldn't even care. In any event, he's a bureaucrat with the water department in New York City. I met him a few years ago. Christ, was he ever German, and did he l et me know it."

"Have an open mind now, James. It's not in your nature to be prejudiced, especially just because someone's background is German."

"Normally I wouldn't. But this character has a key job, and for years he's been a member of the German-American Bund," Gannon said, hesitating, not wanting to share with Ellen all he had found out about Otto Reinhardt.

As much as Gannon wanted to continue the evening with his beautiful fiancée, he had to get to Bolling. He raised his arm to signal the waiter. It was time to leave. He had to get the information on the Hildebrands to Mike Reilly and also that which he possessed on Otto Reinhardt. Gannon was eager to find out if there could be a connection between the Hildebrands and this fellow Reinhardt. Gannon did agree with Ellen that he was not prejudiced. But his eight years with the Secret Service had developed in him an instinctive suspicion. And in this case, the Hildebrands and Reinhardt prompted that suspicion to come alive. He thought Ellen could easily see that her soon-to-be-husband's mind was not on her, the apartment, or their future. He was deep in thought. It was time for her to see him off. He felt badly for her, but there was not much he could do. She was getting a lousy deal by associating with him. Nevertheless, the feelings they had toward each other were stronger than anything they were working on—or at least for the moment, he thought that was the case.

Chapter Eight

President Roosevelt had just made the difficult and painful transfer from his wheelchair to the soft, cushioned armchair next to his desk. Moments before, he and Margaret Suckley had finished dinner in the dining room at Springwood. She helped him navigate through the long corridor that led from the dining room into his library.

"So Daisy, what do you think of this contraption?" Roosevelt asked his dear friend as she brought him close to the eight-legged mahogany desk.

"I keep meaning to ask you: Whose idea was it, anyway, to take an oak kitchen chair and set it upon two wheels, Franklin? Why the devil don't you get a more comfortable one?"

"Simply because this kitchen chair, as you refer to it, is less conspicuous. People think I'm sitting in a chair. There is no need for me to tell them or show them that I have a great difficulty standing or walking, now is there?" Roosevelt said, clenching the right side of his face as he secured his ivory cigarette holder in his mouth. Shortly before, he had inserted into the holder his favorite brand, a Camel, knowing full well that Daisy loathed his constant smoking almost as much as his excessive drinking.

Several years earlier, before he had contracted congestive heart failure, Roosevelt had been quick with his response to his dear friend's concerns. He told her matter-of-factly that in his physical condition and with all of the geo-political problems with which he had to contend, his several cigarettes and his few drinks were minor and the few of life's pleasures he was able to enjoy. Ever since, Daisy, along with others of the president's closest friends, just let him enjoy what little pleasure he obtained from personal vices, but they were well aware that these habits were major contributors to his failing health.

"Frankly, I think most Americans know of your affliction and don't care what kind of chair you have. You're the one who is so mysterious and self-conscious about it. Now isn't that the God's honest truth, Franklin?"

"Daisy, you're always to the point. Never beating around the bushes. Would you mind terribly if I were to work on my stamps? Ike sent me a bunch he had been accumulating in England."

"Not at all, my dear. I'll just sit here and read my newest acquisition. It's James Hilton's *Lost Horizon.*"

"It's a wonderful book," Roosevelt said. "It's also been made into a motion picture now with Ronald Coleman, I believe, as the leading actor. You know, it was that book that gave me the idea to name the retreat in Maryland 'Shangri-La.'" FDR leaned over his desk and peered through the magnifying glass, examining the details of a stamp from Persia.

"I believe you may have mentioned it to me in May when we went there," Miss Suckley said.

"Daisy, I often have wondered if the reason I was thought of as a loner at Groton and Harvard is because of my insatiable compulsion to work on my stamps and coins. What do you think?"

Recalling what the president's mother, Sarah, once told her, Miss Suckley said, "I know that Grandmeir felt that was part of it. Good gracious, she lived next to you at Cambridge. But no, I don't feel you could ever have been labeled a loner. Just look at you: the most personable and outgoing man I have ever met."

"You are so kind, Daisy. What would I do if I didn't have your companionship?" Roosevelt said, looking directly into Daisy's eyes. She did not immediately respond. Instead she thought about the true sincerity of her friend's remark. She was very keen of the fact that ever since 1941, when Roosevelt lost his other dear companion, Missy LeHand, to a stroke—she was now confined to a nursing home in Georgetown—Daisy was to play an ever more significant role in his life. And it was going to be a role she would have to share with Lucy Mercer Rutherford. Daisy collected her thoughts and wanted to change the subject.

"Franklin, we need to talk about the prime minister's visit."

"What about it, my dear?"

"I'm aware that you and Mr. Churchill will be spending time at Wilderstein. I don't think that is a good idea," Miss Suckley said. She watched him use a tweezers to place the Persian stamp into a small cellophane envelope.

"And may I ask why not?"

"Because at times I feel uncomfortable that you spend so much of your time away from Mrs. Roosevelt. It is one thing when you are in Washington or away on a trip. But here at Springwood?"

"Daisy, you know all too well, and more than most others, that she doesn't care one bit. She is very content to be at Val-Kill with her girlfriends and working on her pet projects. Goodness, it's been that way for twenty years," Roosevelt said matter-of-factly.

"If you say so. It is just uncomfortable at times."

"Also, she knows that I look to you for companionship. And the same holds true for Lucy. Although in Lucy's case, I must ask Anna to show a little more discretion. With Lucy, Eleanor does have a difficult time of it, and that daughter of ours, God bless her soul, needs to realize it."

"To change the subject, Franklin, Mr. Reilly and his boys were all over my house last week."

"Well, I hope they were gentle with your furnishings?"

"Yes, they were. Strangely, Mr. Reilly asked a lot of questions about my staff."

"That's not unusual, just routine," Roosevelt responded.

"Well, it seemed he had a great many questions for me. He's done this before, but never to this length. He asked how long I've known the Hildebrands, where they heard about the positions, and what I knew about their previous employment. Most intriguing, he wanted to know if I had information concerning their relatives who were still in Germany."

"Like I said, my dear, simply routine."

"I thought so too, until he asked to see my telephone exchange billings. He wanted to know if the Hildebrands had my approval to make long-distance calls."

* * *

Otto Reinhardt intentionally avoided the Bear Mountain bypass road that would have taken him, along with Albert Krupp and Ludwig Berger, to Cold Spring, twenty miles north of the Croton-on-Hudson railroad station.

Reinhardt had made the trip up the mountain bypass on many occasions, almost always by himself. When he did, it would take him next to the northern end of the Bear Mountain Bridge. He was well aware of the security that covered this major Hudson River crossing, and also the bridge's importance to the nearby U.S. Military Academy at West Point. Today he elected to go north on U.S. Route 9 to Cold Spring. It was out of his way, but his two passengers made him uneasy, and there were no checkpoints to go through. Even though his 1936 Ford sedan, with its seal of the City of New York on both front doors, would not necessarily prevent him from being stopped and searched, he did not want to risk exposing Berger's mean temperament.

Five minutes north of the Croton railroad station, Reinhardt became fully aware that his passenger, Berger, was anti-social at best, possibly a psychopath. Otto was thankful that Krupp took the seat in front and relegated Berger to the back seat. The ever-cautious engineer guided his car and passengers up the two-lane highway. Why they wanted to stop in Cold Spring was still a mystery to him. His repeated questions to Krupp got the same answer: "Not now." Reinhardt, fifteen minutes earlier, had turned off Route 9 and headed west on New York Route 301. Several miles later he turned north on Route 9D.

"Here we are, Herr Krupp. This is Cold Spring," Reinhardt said as the three men got out of the car alongside a pull-off at the northern end of the Route 9D road and railroad tunnel.

"Tell me, Herr Reinhardt, just where does the aqueduct cross the river here?" Krupp asked. He looked across the Hudson at the majestic peak of Storm King Mountain and its seventy-degree incline down to the river.

"Why do you ask?" Otto inquired.

"Just answer the question," Krupp snapped.

"It is opposite the middle of the road tunnel, there. It's the narrowest crossing," Reinhardt pointed.

"And how is the water brought up and across this mountain, Reinhardt?" Krupp asked, looking up the steep slope of Breakneck Ridge on the river's east side.

"Why are you asking these questions? I don't understand," Reinhardt said, increasingly uneasy.

"Answer the Strandartenfuhrer's question, Herr Reinhardt," Ludwig Berger growled, his eyes shooting a piercing glance at the sheepish engineer.

"Berger, when you see what was built here twenty-five years ago, you might not be so boastful about how we Germans know everything," Reinhardt replied, looking scornful.

"I'm interested, Reinhardt. Tell me what is so significant concerning this area?" Krupp said, wishing to deflect the agitation overcoming Berger and the engineer.

Reinhardt puffed up. He pulled down the bottom of his suit jacket and adjusted his tie and eyeglasses. He was always in his element when asked to describe "his" water collection and distribution system. Despite the present circumstances, Reinhardt welcomed the opportunity. "When I came to the water department, nearly twenty years ago, this water crossing had just been completed, and that was after there had been ten years of planning and construction. The tunnel is over a thousand feet below the level of the river over there."

Krupp followed where Reinhardt's finger was pointing—the center of the Hudson River with Storm King Mountain in the backdrop. Berger was observing, clearly not impressed.

"Why didn't you come over the river with a bridge, an aqueduct bridge?" Krupp asked.

"Herr Colonel, what you can't see is that there are very strong currents in the river coming from the north and, most unusual, from the south. There is much salt water out there that is being pulled up from the Atlantic Ocean."

"Reinhardt, you seem to be so proud of the enemy's engineering accomplishments. It's obvious you haven't been back to the Fatherland," Berger said sarcastically.

Reinhardt had hoped not to have to engage the surly Berger, as had Krupp. But Reinhardt was adamant to not let Berger get his way. "Berger, you and your superiors make a terrible mistake in underestimating what this country can do, especially since it was attacked two years ago. The tunnel that is hundreds of feet below the river's bedrock is over fourteen feet in diameter."

The information about the river's current was intriguing to Krupp. He stored it for the present and asked, "Where and how much water is going through the aqueduct?"

"Daily, about seven hundred million gallons. The water is coming from a reservoir, the Ashokan, about fifty miles away in the Catskills."

"Can we get on with our mission, Herr Krupp? And is the tour over?" Berger asked with a menacing look.

"Berger's correct, Herr Reinhardt. *Danka*, the information is helpful to our mission," Krupp added.

"What's your mission?" asked Reinhardt. He did not receive a response.

"At the top of the hill there is a series of pumphouses that draw the water up and over the hill. But why do you care about any of this, Herr Krupp?" Reinhardt almost pleaded.

"Not now, Herr Reinhardt. In due time. How far north is Hyde Park and Rhinebeck?" Krupp asked, focusing now up the river and noticing two ferries meeting halfway as they traversed the river between Beacon and Newburgh.

"I'm not certain. I'll need to see my maps. I think about thirty miles," was the response.

"And how do we get up to the pumphouses, Herr Reinhardt?" Berger asked.

"Across the road over there, there's a footpath—it takes about twenty minutes," said Reinhardt, now completely baffled by the German agent's questions.

"When you check the pumps, is that the way you go?" Krupp asked.

"Yes, but I never go up there in August. Too difficult, too much heat."

"Let's do it," Krüpp said as he started to walk across the highway to the footpath.

* * *

If there is any one thing that is top priority for the military, it is the protection and safe-keeping of equipment, ammunition, ordinances, explosives, and weapons. It makes no difference if it is a revolver or a thirty-ton tank, bullets or bombs. There is a perpetual inventory taken almost on a daily basis to determine if the numbers on hand are what they should be. People responsible could be court-martialed if there were any unaccountable exceptions. At Camp Greentop, this long-standing military policy had not been carried out. As far as General Anderson and his training subordinates were concerned, it was a policy they didn't have to abide—until this day.

"Come in," General Anderson snapped, somewhat annoyed at the interruption. "What is it, Parker?" he asked.

His orderly, Corporal Parker responded, "It's bad, sir. I'm afraid the Marine captain, Captain Trimble, was right when he said something wasn't kosher with Schroeder."

"What the hell are you trying to tell me, Corporal?" Anderson snarled, now on his feet, still munching the stub of his unlit White Owl cigar.

"The last time Lieutenant Greerson was with Schroeder was the day you called her in to tell her about her sick mother," Parker said. He fumbled with a bunch of papers he was attempting to lay out on the general's desk.

"Yeah, yeah, I remember. We got a wire or a call from Washington. So what about it? And would you please stop shuffling those goddamn papers?"

"Well, it turns out that Schroeder and Lieutenant Greerson were working on some bomb-making stuff. Precisely, ten one-pound packages of C-4, some fuses, and a dozen or so detonators," Parker said, still trying to organize his papers.

"Are you going to tell me that something is missing, Corporal?" Anderson asked.

"More than something, sir. Lieutenant Greerson can only find one package of C-4 and none of the detonators, fuses, and a ten-pound bag of cordite."

"Jesus Christ! I can't believe this shit. Maybe Greerson misplaced it. Where is he now?" Anderson asked, his eyes expressing deep anger at possibly being taken by one of his trainees. Anderson always had known—and so did his boss at OSS, Bill Donovan—that the people they had enlisted to do espionage work were not necessarily the most loyal American citizens. Many of his trainees were not American citizens at all, but were from Eastern Europe, Asia, and South America. They were generally bilingual, intelligent, and fearless. Kathe Schroeder was no exception.

"Lieutenant Greerson went over the inventory three times. He checked out Schroeder's hut, footlocker, and bunk. Nothing. And he'll be right here, sir. He wanted to do one more search."

"How the Christ could this have happened?" Anderson asked, pacing the back of his desk.

"It was pretty clever, sir," Lieutenant Greerson said as he stood at the door to the general's office. "She knew she was going to be escorted off the camp by an officer, in his car, so guess what? No search of her bags by the main gate sentry."

"Are you telling me that this whole goddamn thing had been planned? And there are others involved?" Anderson snapped at his training officer.

"It appears that way. Schroeder is not who we thought she was. Her file that you had requested came up from D.C. an hour ago. Parker, tell the general what you've found," Greerson ordered.

Parker picked up the papers he had placed on Anderson's desk and responded, "Sir, Miss Schroeder does not have a mother in Poughkeepsie or in New York. Her mother's been dead for years."

"Do any of you know what's happening here?" Anderson asked. "A spy has infiltrated the OSS. A German counter-intelligence agent who now knows the agents we are training to send to Europe. She knows our methods, codes, and safe houses. Shit, she has to be stopped—not soon, but now!"

"General, do you want to alert the FBI? It's been several days since she left now," Parker asked meekly, only partially realizing the danger Schroeder posed.

Lieutenant Greerson knew full well the havoc that the material taken from the camp could create. One package of C-4, properly placed, along with other flammables, could easily take out a square city block of buildings or a fair-sized factory. He said, "Sir, I agree with Parker here. We have to get the FBI involved."

"No, not now," Anderson said, relighting his cigar and staring out the cabin's window. "This is what we'll do: We will suspend training this group; Schroeder knows them. Then I want all the codes changed, and relocate the safe houses. Parker, get me a line to Colonel Donovan and make sure the line is secure. How the Christ did his people let Schroeder get up here in the first place? What kind of background checks are they performing?"

Lieutenant Greerson, West Point-educated and multilingual, never had a problem with his commander—or, for that matter, making suggestions to him. "General, do you have any idea what her mission might be? By now she must know we have found out about the missing explosives and that her photograph is going to be plastered on every post office wall around the country."

"I don't want her picture posted anywhere. It could cause panic, as well as make us and the program look like a bunch of fools for letting her get in here in the first place. As far as her mission goes, we've haven't heard of any sabotage so far. But what if it ain't blowing up buildings or bridges? What if her mission is to go after our military or political leadership? And who in God's name is helping her—because she can't be doing it by herself?"

Chapter Nine

The Hudson Highlands are among New York State's most scenic places. The views from atop the highlands of the majestic Hudson are breathtaking. The area is also steeped in history. The mountainous strategic location played a key factor in the colonists' goal to hold back British forces from coming up the river from New York City to capture West Point. They knew all too well the importance of the area. General Benedict Arnold and Major John André, spies and traitors, also knew the importance of the area. The leadership of the British army had its own set of goals along with help from Arnold and André. They were determined to capture the territory around West Point and drive a wedge into General Washington's forces. One hundred sixty-five years later, Wehrmacht Colonel Albert Krupp had his own ideas of mischief here.

Krupp, Berger, and their unofficial guide, Otto Reinhardt, finally made it to the top of Breakneck Ridge. Along the way they had to stop several times. Reinhardt had in his rucksack dried knockwurst, bread, and a thermos of water. His two companions were famished, having had little or nothing to eat since they left their submarines twelve hours earlier.

Colonel Krupp appreciated the food, even though it was dry and not very tasty. Berger was more vocal and critical. He felt Reinhardt should have made better plans for their meal. Nor did his criticism stop at the quality of what Reinhardt had served; he was repeatedly berating the man's physical condition, which became most evident on their way up the mountain.

Resting at a small clearing at the summit and wiping his face with his coat sleeve, Berger said sarcastically, "Herr Reinhardt, you said it would take only twenty minutes. It's taken us nearly one hour."

"It's the heat. I needed to rest, and anyway, I've never come here at this time of year. It's too exhausting," Reinhardt responded, bent over and looking down at the ground.

"You're a disgrace to the Third Reich. Just look at you. What kind of soldier are you, anyway?" Berger demanded, as Krupp explored the views at the southern side of the clearing. Krupp had overheard Berger's berating of the engineer but made no attempt to interfere, thinking it was typical Berger. The out-of-condition engineer would just have to get used to Berger, even though Krupp partially agreed: Otto was terribly out of shape.

"Look Berger, I'm not a soldier. I'm not a member of the Third Reich. I'm only here to provide assistance to your mission, which I don't know much about," Reinhardt shouted at Berger, who was taken aback by the still perspiring and out-of-breath engineer. "Furthermore, if what we have heard here in America is true, the cause for Germany is lost, and the repercussions to the Fatherland and its people will be many times worse than what happened after the last war."

Krupp no longer stood on the sidelines, taking in the view of West Point and the surrounding mountain directly across the river. He was keenly aware that Reinhart's comment would provoke Berger. And it did.

"You piece of shit. I should kill you right here for your remarks about the cause." Berger moved threateningly toward the smaller Reinhardt.

Reinhardt wouldn't let up. "We hear rumors that the Wehrmacht is killing Jews all over Europe, by the thousands, in Hungary, Poland, Germany, Greece. Men, women, and children. Is this what the war is all about? You're a sick bastard, because if that is true, it's not my war."

Berger had become incensed. He reached into his suit jacket pocket and pulled out a pistol, a Luger, and with his left hand cocked the slide. Krupp immediately lunged between the two and shouted, "Enough. I've heard enough!"

Krupp pushed Berger back. He faced the enraged Nazi and held down Berger's right hand, which held the cocked Luger. Berger would not relent. Standing two inches taller than his leader, he leaned his head around Krupp's and shouted, "You filthy swine. How dare you question the Fatherland's eradication of the lousy Jews? Yes, we are eliminating them, but like cockroaches, they keep coming. There's no end to them, but we will destroy them in every country we conquer. You understand this, you Jew-loving bastard?"

Staring at the enraged SS lieutenant colonel, Reinhardt shook his head in disgust. He was thankful Krupp leaped in and blocked Berger. But again, he wished he never had become involved. The situation was now beyond his control. He was in the company of an animal, a crazed animal.

Krupp whispered into Berger's ear, "Put your weapon away, and get control of your emotions. You're a German officer on a critically important mission. Harming Reinhardt is not a part of our mission, do you understand?"

Berger nodded reluctantly.

Walking over to a clearing and motioning Reinhardt to come with him, Krupp asked, "What is this rumbling noise I'm hearing? And what is the purpose of those brick buildings up ahead?"

Nervously, Reinhardt, still looking back at Berger, who had placed his automatic pistol back into his jacket, explained, "That's the water coming up from the aqueduct, and those buildings are the pumphouses."

"I want to go into those buildings. Can you let us in?" Krupp asked.

"Yes."

As they walked over to the one-story building's steel door, Krupp leaned over and whispered to Reinhardt, "Herr Reinhardt, the Wehrmacht has had nothing to do with what you said. It is true, but it's the Gestapo and Berger's SS who are behind the roundup of Jews and others. And Herr Reinhardt, don't provoke

Berger. He's half insane with hate. If I had my way he would not be on this mission."

"Albert, when are you going to tell me about the mission?" Reinhardt asked, having regained his composure and beginning to feel more comfortable with the Wehrmacht colonel.

"Tonight in Poughkeepsie, when we get together with Schroeder."

* * *

Poughkeepsie was not unlike many other tired old Hudson River cities. It was the seat of Dutchess County, and its geographic location, halfway between New York City and Albany, made it a major trading stop for Hudson River commerce. In the 1850s, it had become a significant stop for whaling and coal ships. Later it was the key stop for trains from New England before they went west to Chicago and beyond.

In August 1943, Poughkeepsie was in the business of producing goods for the war effort. The sprawling International Business Machine plant no longer made calculators, but guns. Even Poughkeepsie's two hospitals, Vassar Brothers and St. Francis, were well into the war effort. They provided post-operative care to the hundreds of area servicemen now home and recovering from wounds inflicted upon them in places halfway around the world. Poughkeepsie also was known for its many churches, of all faiths. So many had been established there that one street was named Church Street. Three houses from the Baptist Church was an 1870s, two-story wood-frame house with a spacious wrap-around porch: 128 Church Street. On the side of the house was a pea-stone driveway leading to a barn-like structure that had been converted into a three-car garage.

From the street, Kathe Schroeder could not be seen as she paced back from the kitchen through the ornate dining room and into the parlor that had two Pullman car fabric-covered sofas. Her eyes were fixed on the electric clock above the 1928 high-top General Electric refrigerator. The hour was approaching six o'clock in the evening. Where were Reinhardt, Krupp, and

Berger? Could they have been detained? Did they ever make it to New York City? Why hadn't Reinhardt called?

Neatly laid out on the Formica kitchen table was a straight-line floor plan. It was the final draft of what she visualized as the layout of the Hudson Valley Chemical Company's first floor. A dozen crumpled draft copies had been strewn on the tile floor.

Suddenly she stopped pacing. She could hear the crunching of the driveway gravel and the barking of a dog. She went to the parlor's side door that led to the porch and saw Hans Hildebrand maneuver the huge Packard sedan into the rear of the driveway. He previously had informed her that he would be in the city to take Heather, Miss Suckley's dog, to the veterinarian. She hoped he had not forgotten that he also was to bring her the dimensions and room layouts of his mistress's house.

Looking around to see he was not being followed, and concerned that a Packard would draw unwanted attention, she held the screen door open for Hans and said, "Have you heard from Reinhardt?"

"Yes. He called from a telephone booth in Beacon. They were delayed, stopped by a state policeman. Reinhardt was not paying attention and went through a stop sign and nearly collided with the police car."

"What incompetence," Schroeder exclaimed. "And Krupp and Berger in the car only draws attention."

"They should be right here. That was almost an hour ago," Hildebrand said. He removed his hat and followed Schroeder into the kitchen.

"Did you bring me what I wanted, Herr Hildebrand?"

"Yes, but why do you need these dimensions?" he asked, glancing at the plan on the kitchen table.

"Herr Hildebrand, in a few moments you will be meeting two very dangerous people. I suggest you do what you are told and don't ask questions. We will ask the questions. Do you understand?"

"Yes," Hans said meekly.

"Have you placed the wooden crates in the root cellar as I instructed?"

"Yes," he said. Suddenly he heard a car enter the driveway. "Here they are."

"Herr Hildebrand, you must go now. We will stay here, and in three days, we will come to Wilderstein. Make sure all is ready."

"Miss Schroeder, you have told me nothing about what's going on. My wife and I are scared and worried. Every time I ask, you tell me nothing. Why are you coming to Wilderstein? For what purpose? At least you can tell me that, can't you now?" Hans asked as he placed his hat on and followed Schroeder to the side door porch.

"Herr Hildebrand, the more you and your wife know, the more danger you'll be in. Also, by knowing our mission, you very well could compromise it. For now just don't ask questions, and above all, don't ask when you meet those two out there," Schroeder ordered Hans as she led him onto the porch.

* * *

From the outside, the converted barn looked like a typical four-bay garage, with an apartment on the second floor. At Springwood the old, converted structure was now an office as well as sleeping and eating quarters for dozens of Secret Service agents who made up the president's detail. Reilly and Gannon were housed at a nearby motel. Another thirty agents were housed in the basement of the nearby Vanderbilt estate. At Springwood's barn, the second-floor layout had a appearance similar to that of a big-city firehouse. There was a large table in the kitchen for meals, flanked by eight wooden chairs; a lounge area with two old, stuffed sofas centered around a floor-model Philco radio; and a room off the kitchen that contained a dozen military-style bunk beds with adjoining metal lockers and foot lockers.

Off to one corner of the living room was a series of short-wave radio receivers and transmitters, along with six telephones. Manning the electronic array was a U.S. Army warrant officer and a corporal. They were part of the White House Army Signal Corps, whose mission was to keep the president in communication with other government leaders at all times, and in particular with his military commanders. In essence, this was the heart of the president's communication center at his Hyde Park estate.

The early-morning rain shower drove Jim Gannon and Mike Reilly to come in and have a cup of coffee in the center's kitchen. Any of the off-duty agents were either sleeping or listening to the commercial radio. Jack Benny and "Amos and Andy" were by far their favorite shows. This morning's radio broadcast was the replay of the previous day's Brooklyn Dodgers-Boston Braves baseball game.

Mike Reilly sipped his coffee, looked over his cup at Gannon, and said, "I'm sorry that your and Ellen's wedding plans are going to have to be put on hold."

"Boss, I've been with the service eight years. When will I ever have the time to get married?" Gannon responded to the bad news—which Reilly did not want to have to convey.

"All I can tell you, Jim, is that while you are on this detail, it is best for you and for Ellen to do just what you've been doing and hold off on your wedding until you get reassigned to investigative work. Then you can settle down. Our work is a marriage breaker. It's too demanding, and after the last two years, you should know that."

Reilly was well aware of his young assistant's dilemma. He too was enduring the hardships that the assignment to District 16, the White House detail, placed on them and others. Reilly last saw his wife of eight years, Roby Priddy Reilly, of Anaconda, Montana, in October of 1942. And then it was only for four hours, while the president made his tour of America's Western defense plants.

Ever since December 7, 1941, when Reilly was given command of District 16, he often wondered if he should have completed law school training at George Washington University and joined the investigative team at the Farm Credit Agency. The thirty-five-year-old agent appeared closer to forty-five. Not unlike his boss, the job was aging him daily. Less than two years ago, he worked along with twelve other agents in providing protection for the president. Reilly was now responsible for a revamped District 16. He had seventy agents in his care.

"Will it get any better?" Gannon asked. He got up to refill his coffee cup, trying to avoid the hanging, typewritten papers known among the fellow agents as Tully's laundry, which covered a small section of the kitchen.

Grace Tully was never bashful about coming up to the Secret Service Command Center. Moments before, she had left to return to her office in the main house and was seen hanging typed sheets of paper on a clothesline in the agent's kitchen. They were papers with the president's signature, which, on correspondence or bills, could never be blotted. The signed sheets needed to be hung and dried. The service's kitchen was ideal and was devoid of curiosity seekers.

"Not until this goddamn war is over," Reilly said, staring into his near-empty cup and grasping it with two hands. "What did you find out in D.C. about the Hildebrands?"

"I spoke to this guy at Immigration, Sidney Kessler, and he gave me the lowdown on them. They are who they say they are. They do have family back in Germany. They were never members of any German group, especially any political ones. They frequent German beer fests and go to church in Germantown—the Lutheran one, heavily dominated by German immigrants or first-generation German-Americans. That's about it."

"Well, we didn't come up with much either," Reilly said as he began to pace around the kitchen, glaring at the flashing lights on the radio setup in the adjoining room. "We did, however, check their telephone calls, and what sparked my interest were a bunch of calls to the New York City Water Department."

"Why so?" Gannon asked.

"Because they don't use New York City water. They use well water. Matter of fact, we just ran a test of it, and it's okay. So why the calls to New York?"

"I bet I know who they talked to: A guy named Reinhardt. Otto Reinhardt, an engineer or something like that," Gannon said.

"That's right. How do you know him?" Reilly asked, somewhat surprised.

"For two reasons. About two years ago, I checked out his department when I was on temporary assignment in New York City. The service wanted the details on security for the whole water supply. He's a bureaucratic ass, if you ask me."

"That's interesting. What else?" Reilly inquired.

"When I was in D.C., I also ran a check on him. I just never was able to get him out of my head, you can say."

"And?"

"He's been a member of the America First Committee and a member of a bunch of other pro-German causes. Boss, I didn't have time to check out this America First thing, so what is it?"

"It was a fairly large group, organized around 1940. They didn't want the country getting involved with the situation in Europe, and they did have a lot of influential people involved. Lindbergh was the most prominent, I believe. Some felt that the committee was pro-German."

"You said *was*. Where does it stand now?"

"The committee dissolved when the Japs attacked us."

"But I believe Reinhardt might have picked up with the other German groups after that, maybe."

"That's interesting. I want a follow-up on this. Let's also meet with the Hildebrands and find out why the calls to Reinhardt. Also, let's be in touch with Reinhardt's superiors and get more information on him," Reilly ordered. He poured another cup of coffee.

"Do you smell something, boss?" Gannon asked, well aware of Reilly's intuition for perceiving things that are not right.

"Yeah, I do. Especially since earlier today I heard from agent Cheeder at Shangri-La that one of Donovan's OSS agents, at Greentop, was not who she was supposed to be."

"Holy shit!" Gannon now on his feet. "What are you saying?"

"What I'm saying is that the Marine commander at Shangri-La told Cheeder that a Kathe Schroeder, a trainee, blew camp a few days ago, along with a suitcase full of explosives— explosives that the OSS trained her how to use..She has since vanished. Nobody knows where she is."

"Sounds like an FBI problem, not ours," Gannon replied.

"You would think, except for one problem."

"What's that?"

"Schroeder told General Anderson, her boss, and the Marine captain who drove her to the train in Baltimore, that she was going to Poughkeepsie—two miles down the road from where you and I are now having coffee."

Chapter Ten

Hans Hildebrand maneuvered the heavy Packard around to the rear of his mistress's Rhinebeck home. He pulled up on the hand-brake and climbed out. He was still shaking from his experience on Church Street. His anxiety was evident, despite the fifteen-mile drive up U.S. Route 9. He was perspiring, his breathing was short, and his weather-beaten face—gained from years working outdoors—had turned ashen.

"Hans," shouted Gertrude Hildebrand. "You've left Heather in the car. What's wrong with you?" She watched her husband slowly walk up the stone path to the back porch stairs.

"Oh, I'm sorry. I'll get her," Hans said. He turned around and headed back to the car to retrieve the barking terrier.

"Hans, what is the matter? You're shaking. Was there any trouble?" Gertrude asked, drying her hands on her apron.

"Gertie, please, let's go inside. And would you get me a glass of water?"

Running ahead of both of them, Heather sprinted up to the porch and through a hinged pet door at the bottom of the screen door. Gertrude, meanwhile, waited for her husband and reached out and clasped his shaking hand.

"Come in, Hans. You must sit down and tell me what hap-pened. We can talk. Miss Suckley will be back from Val-Kill in an hour. Miss Tully called and told me she went to Val-Kill for a swim with Mr. Roosevelt, and that Mr. Early will bring her home."

Gertrude Hildebrand had never seen her husband in such a state. Her first concern was to get him to calm down. She had no idea how he had managed to drive from Poughkeepsie to Wilderstein and not crash Miss Suckley's car. She just wanted Hans to sit at the table and stabilize. She placed a pewter pitcher of water on the table.

Hans's composure slowly returned, and he gulped down his second glass of water. "Gertie, something terrible is going to happen. I saw awful-looking people come to Fräulein Schroeder's house. I don't think they saw me. I was pulling out of her driveway when they entered it. I stayed on the street and watched two of them run from their car into the house."

"How many were there, Hans, and who are they?"

"There were three. Two of them, very tall. They looked like soldiers: broad shoulders, closely cropped haircuts—and swift. They went up the porch stairs in two steps. The driver was short and fat. He didn't run. He walked slowly. He had huge glasses and was bald. Gertie, he looked like Joseph Goebbels. I'm not sure, but he also looked like Reinhardt," Hans said, his voice still anxious.

"The head of the Nazi propaganda and Adolph Hitler's ally is here in Poughkeepsie? That can't be, Hans. It must be someone else. It has to be Mr. Reinhardt. He's the one making the plans. He told me that on the telephone."

"So I'm wrong, but he looked like him, I'm telling you. There is something wrong here, and we are involved. We must do something, I tell you."

"Hans, my dear husband, please relax. You must take it easy. You'll make yourself sick."

"I'm okay now, Gertie, but in three nights they'll be here. That's what Schroeder said to me. What can we do?" Hans pleaded.

"We'll wait and see, and then we'll do something," Gertrude responded.

"Gertie, they are out to do harm to Mr. Roosevelt and Mr. Churchill. I know it. Otherwise, why else come here?" Hans brushed his hand on Heather's furry back while the dog lapped water from her bowl.

* * *

"Well, do we know anything more, Corporal?" General Anderson barked. He stood next to Corporal Parker's desk in the outside office of the general's cabin at Camp Greentop.

"For starters, sir, we know she did go to Vassar College in Poughkeepsie. She was part of some student-sponsored and college-supported refugee program which began in 1937 and ended just this year," Parker recited, reading from his notebook.

"Parker, I don't give a shit about Vassar's commitment to refugees. Do they know where the hell she went, who she's staying with?"

Ignoring his commander's tirade, Parker continued, "There's more, sir. She was one of about twenty scholars who were brought here. And she never got a master's in chemistry from Vassar. They don't award master's degrees, sir. She was, however, a lab assistant during her four years there."

"Parker, you're not telling me anything that's useful. Do you have anything that is?"

"I'm coming to it, sir."

"Well, please hurry up, if you don't mind," Anderson ordered sarcastically, knowing well that his trusted orderly was irreplaceable and was not swayed by the general's impatience.

"As it turns out, sir, the telegram that was sent to headquarters about Schroeder's mother being sick has been traced to a Western Union office in Lower Manhattan. Chambers Street, I believe."

"Now that is helpful," Anderson replied.

"There's more," Parker said as he flipped several more pages in his notebook. "Schroeder's sponsor at Vassar was Otto Reinhardt, an engineer with the New York City's Water Department."

"You're doing good, Parker," Anderson said.

"And Reinhardt works in Lower Manhattan, sir."

"Parker, get me our New York office. I want this guy Reinhardt, or whatever his goddamn name is, picked up and questioned about his connection to Schroeder."

"I'll get right on it, sir. But before I do, just one thing, sir."

"What's that?"

"Schroeder, sir, Kathe Schroeder, is Kathe von Schroeder, a captain in the SS. And General, we can't be going around picking up people for questioning. We're not authorized to do any work here in the states. We would be violating every rule in the book. We've got to call in the FBI."

"Parker, I know the goddamn rule book. I helped write the thing. But Schroeder is our problem. Christ, we've trained her to be an assassin. I'll tell you what. Let's not call the FBI. Let's call the New York office of the Secret Service. Let's move, Parker. She's got a three-day head start on something that could very well be a potential disaster."

* * *

The Dutch elms, oaks, and maples that lined each side of Church Street in Poughkeepsie were screening the late afternoon sun as it moved across the mountains of the Hudson Highlands. Fräulein Schroeder did not seem pleased. The three men had entered her house from the side porch in front of the garage bay, where earlier Hans Hildebrand had garaged his employer's Packard.

Before anyone presented greetings, she barked an order to Otto Reinhardt. "Herr Reinhardt, quickly move your automobile into the garage. The markings on its side will draw attention. Let's hope no one has already noticed. You should have used a car less traceable."

"Do you know how difficult it is to get petrol, Fräulein Schroeder?" Reinhardt asked with a note of resentment. The bureaucrat was not accustomed to taking orders from a female.

"I'm not interested now. Quickly," she snapped.

The corpulent engineer had exited the parlor and gone to the porch. Berger said, "He's a disgrace, and we must get rid of him."

"Not now," Albert Krupp said. "In due time. We need more information on the water tunnels. We also need his maps and keys."

"If I were in charge, Herr Krupp, he would be gone by now. I don't know why we wait," Berger said.

"Well, you're not in charge, and that's that," Krupp snapped back at his subordinate.

"I see you haven't changed, Herr Berger. Still the same old Berger," Schroeder said bitterly.

Schroeder's level of contempt for Berger was much higher than Krupp's. Her time in America, and the absorption of its culture and freedom, provided a level of distance from that of Berger's homeland, where female agents, out of fear, were beholden to the ruthless and cunning Nazi. Berger's sexual advances toward them had to be acknowledged and reciprocated. Any other approach meant death or retaliation to the female agent's family. Berger had the power and influence. Schroeder was free from it. She was independent and adamant that in due time he would get that message from her. She harbored nothing but contempt for him.

"Herr Krupp, would you please draw the curtains and then come into the kitchen? I have some sandwiches. You must all be hungry," Schroeder said, impatient with the tension Berger was creating.

"We'll wait for that. While Reinhardt is outside, I want to go over the mission," Krupp commanded. "When are we getting into the Wilderstein, and who was that in the automobile that pulled out of your driveway when we were coming in?"

The three Nazis were sitting in the parlor when Schroeder responded: "Wilderstein is ready. That was Hans Hildebrand, Miss Suckley's chauffeur and gardener. He has prepared the cellar for us. His wife, Gertrude, is Miss Suckley's cook and housekeeper. They don't know that we are going to kidnap her guests. President Roosevelt and the prime minister will be taken four nights from now."

"That is no longer the mission, Fräulein Schroeder," Berger responded gleefully.

"What are you saying, Strandartenfuhrer?" Schroeder asked, not at all pleased with what she had just heard.

"He's right, Fräulein," Krupp said. "We are to kill both of them and destroy the water system. That is why we need the chemicals from the Beacon factory and the explosives."

"When did our orders change, and why am I only finding out now?" she asked.

"Late yesterday, High Command sent a message to our submarine commander, and it wants them both dead and the water system that feeds New York City destroyed in such a way that it will take years to repair. The disruption and fear it will create will surely set the Americans back. The three of us will be bringing the war to the heart of America," Krupp added with pride.

Chapter Eleven

Stewart Field Army Air Force base, located on the outskirts of Newburgh, sixty miles north of New York City, was like many other military posts during wartime—a beehive of cargo planes headed to Europe and Africa ferrying much-needed war supplies, medicine, and food.

In between arrivals and departures of the giant B-17s, B-24s, and C-47s, the Army's fighter-plane pilots were practicing their own take-offs and landings. The base was only an hour or so from Hyde Park, assuming one met the ferry at the right time. One would have to cross the Hudson by ferry from Beacon, twin city to Newburgh. The next crossing was many miles to the north. It was because of the ferry ride that Mike Reilly never was able to persuade FDR to fly from Washington, D.C. to Newburgh. The ferry crossing would have placed the president at risk to underwater demolition experts. Instead, the crippled president was willing to endure the ten-hour automobile trip up Route U.S. 1 to New York, crossing the Hudson from New Jersey at the George Washington Bridge. Unless, of course, Roosevelt elected to use the special train that was always at his disposal.

At least Reilly drew some comfort from the fact that not all was lost. The Stewart base and its contingent of fighter planes provided air security to the president's residence at Hyde Park. Inquiring news and magazine photographers were in for the shock of their lives when they chose to enter the restricted air space over Springwood or Val-Kill. A chance photo of the president or his guests was not worth the risk of being shot out of the sky by the trigger-happy Army Air Force's second lieutenants.

Mike Reilly and Jim Gannon were standing on the runway ramp, awaiting the arrival of the camouflaged C-47 as it was being maneuvered over to its parking spot by an army sergeant who was hand-signaling the plane's pilot. On board were General Anderson and his aide, Corporal Parker.

"I can't tell you how much I appreciate you coming, General, and on such short notice," Reilly said to Anderson as they made their way to the airfield's Quonset hut that was the air base's operations center. Gannon and Parker followed their bosses. "This is my aide, Mike, Corporal Parker," Anderson said as he and Reilly shook hands.

The base commanding officer had made the rear office in the operations center available to the four. Reilly asked, "Can I get you gentlemen a drink? Lemonade, iced tea, or something?"

"Iced tea, Mr. Reilly, would be fine. Hell of a lot warmer here than the Maryland mountains," Anderson replied.

"Same for me, sir," was Parker's reply. He knew from his boot camp training that the meeting in a Quonset hut on such a warm day would be most unpleasant. Fans, not air conditioning, were the only comfort the Army provided.

"I don't mean to rush, Mr. Reilly, but our pilot said he's turning the plane back to Baltimore at 1700 hours, which gives us three hours to go over what we have on Schroeder," Anderson said. He took his seat at the makeshift conference table, and Parker occupied a chair next to his boss.

"That's fine, General. Give us what you have," Reilly responded.

"Parker, fill them in," Anderson ordered.

"Sir, before we left Camp Greentop, we got confirmation that the bogus telegram that was sent to our D.C. headquarters had been sent by an Otto Reinhardt from lower Manhattan."

"How'd you find that out?" Reilly asked as he gave each man his iced tea.

"I'm not supposed to tell you, sir, but we have one of our operators at Western Union's New York headquarters," Parker said.

"So much for the OSS operating outside the U.S.," Reilly commented.

"The war, Mike, is nasty business, and we need to monitor international traffic," Anderson replied.

"I suppose you're right. So what is the connection between Reinhardt and Schroeder?" Gannon asked. "And has anyone picked him up?"

"That's just it, Mr. Gannon," Corporal Parker said. "We thought you might have done so."

"Why?" Reilly asked.

"Because, gentlemen, the son of a bitch can't be located," Anderson jumped in. "Tell them, Parker."

"This morning I put another call into Reinhardt's office. I spoke to a Miss Swanson, his secretary. Initially she gave me the runaround, but then when I told her she could be arrested for obstruction of justice, she broke down. Somewhat of a reach on my part, I guess," Parker said.

"I'd say it was, but what did she tell you, Corporal?" Gannon asked.

"She said Mr. Reinhardt hasn't been seen or heard from in three days. That he had gone off to check on the security at the upstate pump stations and reservoirs."

"By himself?" Reilly inquired.

"Yes, and he had picked up a water department vehicle at Croton, which he normally does."

"How did he get from New York to Croton?" Gannon asked.

"According to Swanson, he usually goes by train from Grand Central," Parker responded.

Anderson asked, "Mike, do you see a connection to the president here?"

Reilly paused for a moment and then replied, deliberately, "Yes, very much so, I'm afraid, General. You see, we have evidence that the housekeeper and chauffeur of one of the president's acquaintances made and received frequent calls to and from Reinhardt. Independently, Gannon here had Immigration check on Reinhardt, and we uncovered that he is a Nazi sympathizer."

"Good Christ," Anderson responded.

"Corporal," Gannon said, "I understand that there is a connection between Schroeder and Vassar College. Is that so?"

"There is, sir." Parker said. "Schroeder went there and got a degree in chemistry. When I called the college, I got nowhere. A snotty official told me they don't give out information. All I wanted to know was where she lived off-campus and who she hanged out with while a student."

"Jim, get on the horn and call the president of the college. Tell him that on our way back to Hyde Park, we want a meeting with him. If he gives you any lip, tell him he'll be arrested," Reilly said sternly.

"Mike, do you think there is a possible connection with Schroeder being at Greentop, the missing explosives, and the president's retreat at Shangri-La?" Anderson asked.

"I don't really know, General. There very well might be. Christ, the two places are right next to each other," Reilly said.

For the next two hours, the discussion went from analyzing one possible attack to another. Follow-up lists were developed. Reilly told Corporal Parker that when he completed his tour with the army, he should apply for a job with the Secret Service. General Anderson was not pleased with the recruiting suggestion until he was informed that he and Corporal Parker were going to be temporarily assigned at Hyde Park under orders from their boss, OSS Director Donovan, as well as from Secretary of the Treasury Morgenthau. Reilly had arranged for this only hours before the general's plane had landed.

Mike Reilly was convinced that if he had any chance to uncover a plot to harm President Roosevelt and the prime minister, he would need all the help he could get. Anderson and Parker, as far as he was concerned, knew Schroeder and could identify her. Weeks' worth of detective work were contained in their heads. He needed to pry it out. Colonel Donovan and Secretary Morgenthau had agreed. General Anderson's replacement at Camp Greentop was already at work checking and rechecking the identities and credentials of the remaining spy students. Having one Schroeder was enough. The OSS did not need another.

Chapter Twelve

Of the seventy agents now assigned to the president's detail, Secret Service Agent John O'Neill was by far the biggest and strongest. At six-feet-five and a muscular two-hundred-forty pounds, the former Notre Dame football tackle was FDR's aide when it came to lifting him in and out of his wheelchair. Today FDR was engaged in his favorite sport, swimming. The brownish water in the lilypad pond at Val-Kill was his second favorite swimming place. Nothing, of course, could take the place of the soothing and mineral-laden waters of Warm Springs, Georgia. The president needed those waters now more than ever. Agent O'Neill would frequently pass on to his boss, Mike Reilly, that the president was becoming more frail by the day. The war was indeed taking its toll.

"Franklin, it's time you came out. An hour in those cold waters is long enough," Eleanor called as she stood on the dock, watching her husband dog paddle some ten yards from where she was standing.

"Just a few more minutes. You know how much I enjoy this. And it's not that cold. You should try it, and get Daisy to come in as well."

"We're just fine as we are, Franklin," Eleanor said. She pulled up the hem on her ankle-length white dress.

Meanwhile, Daisy Suckley was sitting in a canvas chair, sipping an iced tea and observing the conversation. She knew FDR would just as soon have been at the pond with her and without Eleanor.

"Franklin, I'm going to have Mr. O'Neill come in and take you out right now. You must get on with the planning for Mr. Churchill's visit. He'll be here in twenty-four hours, and I'm still at a loss as to what your plans for him are. You are aware I'll be leaving in the morning," Eleanor said. She motioned to agent O'Neill to lift her husband out of the pond.

Agent O'Neill was ready physically, but not mentally. He knew all too well how much the president enjoyed the water and how infrequently he had the opportunity to do so. In just a short few weeks, the pond's temperature would dip to sixty-five degrees from today's seventy-five.

O'Neill, clad in blue swimming trunks and an undershirt, stood waist-high a short distance from the president. FDR could see that his bodyguard felt the same way he had: just a few more precious minutes.

Arthur Prettyman, the president's long-time valet, was fixing a blanket in the president's wheelchair as agent O'Neill lifted his precious cargo out of the water and onto the dock. Fala was right behind him, yelping. He too didn't want his master to leave the pond. For him, the cool waters were a welcome relief to the hot and humid August day.

Daisy went over to Fala and dried him off. She was very fond of the Scottish terrier, even more so when she was told by FDR that it was the best gift he had ever received, her gift to him.

As Prettyman was drying the president, FDR knew Eleanor was right. It was time to prepare for the visit of Prime Minister Churchill. It was going to be a difficult visit. FDR was informed earlier in the day that Churchill wanted to know why a Second Front in Europe could not get under way as soon as October, and so did Joseph Stalin. FDR had felt it was too soon. He had his work cut out for him. The brief hour in the pond and its small pleasures were fleeting. It was time to get back to the chaos of the world.

* * *

Captain Schroeder had her guests for two days and two nights. She wanted to get on with the mission. It was becoming too dangerous to just be sitting around the house. Sleeping in the same house with Berger gave her additional stress. She locked her bedroom door. The fully loaded Luger was kept under her pillow. Even with these precautions, she sensed the doorknob to her room was being turned late in the evening; Berger was on the prowl, but to no avail. The neighbors soon would become suspicious; already a close scare came when the postman, having inserted the previous day's mail into the slot in the front door, elected to peer in the parlor window. He was observed doing this by Reinhardt, who, after seeing him from the dining room, went into a panic.

What was more disturbing to Schroeder, as well as to Krupp, was the electric meter reader's entry into the back yard. It was the time of the month when the meter was due to be read. What was not expected was when the overweight, uniformed checker went to the side of the garage and urinated against the garage, just below the window. Four pairs of eyes observed him. Reinhardt had removed the New York City Water Company seals from the garaged car. It was Krupp who had Berger lower his Luger. The meter reader survived, buttoned his pants, and left. Never did he realize how close he had come to being a casualty of war, only because he needed to relieve himself.

Moments later, standing around the dining table, Schroeder's guests were looking at a map of the Hudson Highlands when Krupp said, "Once more, let us review tonight's operations."

"Must we? I know what I have to do," Berger interjected.

"Shut up and listen," Krupp snapped. "If we fail tonight, there is no purpose for our being here," he continued, staring at Berger.

"Schroeder and I will enter the factory. Once we are out, we will make our way along the tracks, south to Cold Spring, here at the boatyard," Krupp said, pointing to the Cold Spring Harbor boatyard on the map.

All along, Reinhardt was wondering why he got involved with this bunch. Once again, he was near a state of anxiety. He was perspiring profusely just standing next to the table. He was well versed in reading maps, but why Cold Spring, and why the visit? Two days ago it was the pumphouse. He kept wondering.

"Meanwhile, Reinhardt, you will provide Berger with the keys to the water tunnel pumphouse. Are you certain, Herr Reinhardt, that the maps are still in the pumphouse?"

"Yes, I'm sure. But must I go? My office must be wondering where I am. I've not checked in for two days. I'm not a secret agent. I'm an engineer, an office worker," Reinhardt pleaded.

"What you are is a disgrace," Berger told the perspiring bureaucrat.

"Berger, what you are is an ungrateful bastard," Reinhardt retorted, "You wouldn't have come this far if it were not for me and my allegiance to the Fatherland. You might threaten people back in Germany, but you're not in Germany. You're here in America, and I don't feel threatened by your looks or words." Reinhardt adjusted his vest and checked his pocket watch while looking directly at the two Nazis.

"Enough of that," Krupp demanded. "Now that the signs are off your car, we will use it to get us to Beacon and you two to Cold Spring."

"We must get rid of it as soon as we can. They'll be looking for it, and for Herr Reinhardt as well," Schroeder added.

"If there are no more questions, let us go now," Krupp ordered, glancing at his audience. "And Berger, it will be your job to get us an automobile in Cold Spring. And have Reinhardt here help you."

Chapter Thirteen

Corporal Parker was having a difficult time suppressing his excitement at having been temporarily assigned to the U.S. Secret Service. The twenty-one-year-old Virginian was into his third year as an army clerk, assigned to the OSS training facility at Camp Greentop. Since his time in boot camp at Fort Belvoir, he had done nothing in his brief army career other than be an office clerk. On this warm August afternoon, he and agent Gannon were driving onto the campus of Vassar College in Gannon's Chevy coupe.

It was to be Corporal Parker's first visit to a college campus. Almost all of his able-bodied friends from Newport News, Virginia either went to work at the local shipyard or into the military. His friend Jim FitzGerald was the only person he had known who went to college. Jim had enrolled at the University of Virginia but dropped out and enlisted in the Marines three days after Pearl Harbor was attacked.

"Mr. Gannon, I don't see one guy in this whole place," Parker said as Gannon brought the coupe to a stop at a Gothic gray stone building.

"And you won't," Gannon replied. "It's an all-girls school. Men are not allowed here. Never had been, and never will be. Last summer, in July, I think, I was here with Mrs. Roosevelt and Princess Julianna, you know, of the Netherlands. There's been no change, I'm sure of that."

Gannon gave his passenger a five-minute version of the history of the college. In preparation for his last visit to the pristine school, he had to immerse himself in the institution's folklore. What Gannon would have told Parker was that he had just entered the 1,200-acre campus one of America's most elite colleges, one of the so called "seven sisters", known for educating children from WASP families since it was opened by a beer-brewing king, Matthew Vassar, in 1861. Gannon's boss, FDR, had been a trustee at the college in the early 1930s, and Gannon felt it was ironic that he and Parker were now in search of one of the college's alumni—who could very well be out to harm one of her college's most famous trustees.

"This would be paradise for a guy, especially someone like me—who, I might add, has been stuck on a mountain in the middle of nowhere these past two years," Parker said as his eyes glanced from one side to the other.

"And do you know what, Parker?"

"What, sir?"

"Classes don't begin until September, and hundreds more will be here then. But, Parker, let me just say that the girls here are not your type. You should know that from Captain Schroeder, right?"

"Sir, Schroeder was a swell-looking gal. Every guy in camp had his eyes on her, if not his hands, especially in the close-order hand-to-hand combat workouts. For a while there, I even thought General Anderson was out to put the make on her. But I was wrong."

"Did you?" Gannon asked.

"That's just it, sir. She didn't socialize with no one, let alone a corporal. A couple of the foreign guys would touch her ass, you know, a pat, and she slapped them in the face in a split second. She got the message out that she was off-limits, and she never reported it. The general was aware but didn't do nothing because Schroeder would never file a complaint. I can see why."

Gannon was about to ask Parker about Schroeder's contacts at Camp Greentop when he was interrupted. "May I help you, gentlemen?" asked a woman of middle age, wearing an ankle-length yellow-and-white summer dress with sleeves covering the length of her arms, her head bedecked with a brownish straw hat.

"If you are with the college, you just might," responded Gannon, convinced by the way she was dressed and spoke that his feelings were accurate—Vassar College was snobbish and stuffy.

"I'm the college provost, and you must be agent Gannon. Mr. Gannon, all male visitors require a female escort when inside the gates of the college. I hope you will not be offended," Provost Olcott said as Gannon and Parker got out of the car.

"This here is Corporal Parker, U.S. Army, ma'am; he has been assigned to me," Gannon said and pointed to Parker, not realizing that Miss Olcott's face grimaced at Gannon's grammar.

"Gentlemen, if you would, please follow me," Miss Olcott said. She turned her back and walked to the stone arch doorway marked with a wooden sign: *President's Office*. Standing on the marble steps leading to the door were three Vassar girls. Each was holding on to an archery bow and a quiver full of arrows. They were clad in white blouses, khaki shorts, and white socks with brown-and-white shoes. Their eyes were fixed on the uniformed soldier and the other man, who was dressed in a blue business suit. "Girls, no need to stare. Just get on with your archery. There is nothing here that concerns you."

Gannon and Parker heard, in unison, "Yes, Miss Olcott."

President Henry Noble MacCracken's large office occupied the southwest corner of the building's second floor. It was awash in sunlight, and so was his secretary's office and adjoining conference room. Gannon and Parker were escorted to it by Miss Olcott. An iced-tea setting was laid out on a mahogany table surrounded by four Windsor armchairs. Gannon and Parker had been expected.

Glass-enclosed bookcases lined two of the room's walls. A large mahogany sideboard took up another wall. On top of the sideboard was an ornate silver tea service and twin glass candleholders. Two framed college degrees hung on the wall behind MacCracken's desk. One was from Yale, the other from Harvard. The lettering on both was in Latin.

While pouring iced tea, MacCracken said, "Let me begin by saying that we do not like to discuss our girls' stay here at the college, Mr. Gannon, especially with government people. This is a private institution and has been for close to eighty-two years."

"Mr. MacCracken—may I call you that?" Gannon asked.

"No, you may refer to me as Dr. MacCracken," the former head of the English department said.

"If the situation were not one of the most important national security matters now before us, I can assure you we would not be wasting your time," Gannon replied, not taken aback by MacCracken's aloofness.

"So you say, Mr. Gannon. But why should we at Vassar believe you? Why should we place your work, your so-called concerns, above those of our girls?" MacCracken responded airily.

Gannon was beginning to realize that he was dealing with a snob. Even MacCracken's middle name offered a hint of royalty. Gannon recalled what his boss, Mike Reilly, had told him: don't take any crap from anyone at the college. He was not about to, and replied, "Well, Doctor or President MacCracken, you can either cooperate with us here privately, or before a federal judge, publicly. Either way we will get the information we need. You and this college, I'm sure, don't need the publicity that will surely come out when the press hears that for four years a Nazi agent attended your college. And who, I might add, is now on the lam and in possession of high explosives, as well as bomb-making material, a skill she developed while a student here."

"I wasn't made aware of this, Mr. Gannon," MacCracken said, almost sheepishly.

"Well now you are—and here are my questions."

As agent Gannon and Corporal Parker were about to clear the stone archway perimeter wall that led them out of the college and onto Route 376, Parker glanced to his right to see oncoming traffic. For a moment he was spellbound. Could the driver of the black Ford sedan with an unusual smudge on the driver's door be Kathe Schroeder? Of course not, he concluded, and returned to his summarizing the substance of the two-hour meeting he and Gannon only moments before had concluded with Dr. MacCracken.

Chapter Fourteen

"Gertie, we must talk. I have news about Kurt and Erich. Carl Steiner wrote us from Madrid," Hans Hildebrand said anxiously to his wife as he stood in the kitchen porch doorway, keeping the screen door partially open.

"Hans, come in, close the screen, and be quiet. Mr. Roosevelt is inside with Miss Suckley."

"I didn't know. I didn't see any automobile come in," Hans said meekly, realizing how foolish he was to blurt out news from his cousin Carl.

"Don't feel bad, Hans," said agent O'Neill, who observed the German caretaker come into the kitchen. "They can't hear you, but I can hear them. The boss is getting an earful from Secretary Morgenthau and his friend."

"It is none of our business, Mr. O'Neill," Gertrude said. She prepared another round of iced tea and lemonade for Miss Suckley's guests.

"What are they saying, Mr. O'Neill, that makes their voices heard all the way into the kitchen?"

"Hans, shame on you, too," Gertrude cautioned.

"It's okay, Mrs. Hildebrand," O'Neill responded. "It happens all the time. It's part of the job, and we pay it no mind."

"It's not right. Listening in on others' conversations," Gertrude muttered. She headed toward the swinging pantry door that led to the dining room.

"Mr. President, I want to thank you for meeting with Mr. Karski and me," Secretary Morgenthau was saying as he watched the housekeeper place her tray of drinks on the coffee table. The cabinet member was not mindful that agent O'Neill and his hostess's groundskeeper had their ears to the butler pantry's door, overhearing all that was being said.

"No need to thank me, Henry. You know better. Just how are you today, Mr. Karski?" FDR asked his guest, Jan Karski, who appeared exhausted—as well he should have. He had been traveling for the last eighteen hours to get to Hyde Park. An Army Air Force plane, en route to Stewart Field in Newburgh, had brought the Polish Christian leader from England, with refueling stops in Iceland and Newfoundland.

"Mr. Karski, please sit down and relax. My friend, here, Margaret, has been gracious enough to make her home available so we can meet without being under the microscope of Walter Winchell or Westbrook Pegler," Roosevelt said.

Secretary Morgenthau was not sure whether his friend knew who Winchell or Pegler were. He was about to tell Karski how the two newspaper and radio correspondents felt about his boss when FDR said, "Henry tells me you have important news about the plight of the Jews. Is that accurate, Mr. Karski?"

"Yes, Mr. President," Karski said, expressing hope that the president could understand his broken English.

"What exactly do you know, Mr. Karski?" FDR asked.

"Operation Reinhard, Mr. President, the Nazi code name for the elimination of the Jews. You may know, sir, it was named after that dreaded Nazi, Reinhard Heydrich, who was killed a year ago last June in Licice, Czechoslovakia. Tens of thousands are being murdered in Lublin, Belzec, Sobibar, Treblinka, sir," Karski said, gazing at the carpet under his shoes. His tears were an embarrassment, and Henry Morgenthau moved over to him and gave him a handkerchief.

"Mr. Karski, please do not feel ashamed about shedding your tears in this room. Your coming here under the most difficult of circumstances makes you a hero in our eyes." FDR said, noticing the agreement from his treasury secretary as well as Miss Tully and Daisy Suckley.

"I'm sorry, sir, but there is worse. It's at Auschwitz, in Poland, sir. There they are systematically killing Jews by the tens of thousands. Last week I met with Mr. Eden in London."

"What did he have to say about all of this, Mr. Karski?" Secretary Morgenthau interrupted.

"He said that when I see you I should urge you, Mr. President, to open the Second Front now and also bomb the rail lines into the camps."

"Well, I would expect that from the foreign minister of England, now wouldn't you, Henry?" FDR asked.

"Indeed, Mr. President," was Morgenthau's response.

"This weekend I'll put the question to Winston. I'll ask him to open up Palestine so Europe's Jews can live there, if they can make it out of Europe in the first place."

"That would help, sir," Karski tentatively agreed.

"Mr. Karski, the best way I can think of to help the Jews is to win the goddamn war," said FDR, who leaned forward from his chair, hands tightly grasping his knees.

For the next thirty minutes, Karski described to FDR how he and his organization had secretly entered the Warsaw ghettos and surrounding countryside and obtained the information he just had presented.

FDR knew he was in a quandary. He wanted to get help to the people Karski was describing but without dictating to Generals Marshall and Eisenhower how to fight the war. Both generals were adamant. The Jews would have to wait to be rescued. The plans for the Second Front could not be changed. Furthermore, the death camps were a long way from the coast of France. FDR also was aware that if he ordered the rail lines bombed, his anti-Semitic political enemies would be criticizing him for playing into the hands of his Jewish friends and sacrificing American lives and equipment for his personal cause. FDR felt he had to bring this issue up with Churchill. He knew that Americans would soon know that a holocaust was under way in Europe. And that he had done nothing to stop it.

As the president's guests moved slowly onto the porch at Wilderstein, agent O'Neill gently placed his charge onto the oak wheelchair and guided him to the porch. O'Neill stayed on the porch as well.

In the kitchen, Hans could hear the movement of the guests on the porch and said, *"Gertie, Onkel Carl hat uns Brief geschickt. Kurt und Erich sind bei Nacht und Nebel vonder Gestapo abgeholt worden und sitzen jetzi in einem Berliner Gefäingis!"*

Gertrude Hildebrand wasted no time and responded, "Hans, *sie still*! You know Miss Suckley never wants to hear German in her house."

"Yes, yes, I know, Gertie. I'm,sorry, but I couldn't wait any longer. Do you know what that means?"

"I'm afraid I do, Hans. They want us to work with them. They want us to be a part of this plan. I won't do it, Hans. I won't do it, I tell you," Gertrude said, holding on to the preparation table.

"Gertie, how can you say that? They have Kurt and Erich and your mother and father. They'll kill them if we don't help them. We're already involved. What's the difference if we just do what they tell us?" Hans whispered.

"Hans, I think Mr. Reilly and Mr. Gannon know something. They've been asking questions."

"What questions? Who'd they ask?"

"Miss Suckley asked me this morning why we made calls to Mr. Reinhardt. She said she was asked by Mr. Reilly to find out why we made calls."

"What did you tell her?" Hans asked, drying his sweating hands with a handkerchief he pulled from his overall pocket.

"I told her that you and Reinhardt were cousins. That you had only recently found out that he was in New York City, and that you were inviting him to visit with us someday."

Agent O'Neill startled Hans and his wife when he opened the kitchen door from the pantry and said, "Don't mean to interrupt this family meeting, but the guests would like some drinks out on the porch."

"Yes, right away, Mr. O'Neill," Gertrude responded. She wiped her hands on her apron and watched O'Neill retrace his steps.

"We can't talk here, Hans. It must be later, someplace quiet. And I'm afraid. I don't think Miss Suckley believed my explanation about Reinhardt."

Gertrude Hildebrand knew, even more than her husband, how bad their situation had become. Her nephews, Hans's sister's children, were now prisoners of the Nazis. Her employer, Miss Suckley, was on to her many calls to Otto Reinhardt. She never had mentioned to Miss Suckley that Hans had relatives in New York City, let alone the water department's deputy chief engineer.

From what she gathered from her husband, the recent arrival in Poughkeepsie of the three Nazis made matters even more untenable. She felt that she had to tell someone, but who?

Agent O'Neill pushed the president's wheelchair toward the waiting car. The president was speaking to his treasury secretary as they made their way down the driveway. Agent Reilly, who only a few minutes before had arrived at Wilderstein, was a few steps behind, walking between Miss Tully and Miss Suckley. Jan Karski had left fifteen minutes earlier. When he did leave, it was obvious to all that he was not pleased.

"Henry, I don't know what else I could have told that chap, Karski. We just can't change our plans. And if we bomb the rail lines leading to those dreadful camps, our bombers could very well kill Jews. It would be political suicide," FDR said, puffing on the Camel in his ivory holder.

The president knew he was on the horns of a dilemma. There was no easy solution, but at the same time, if Karski's report was anywhere near accurate, tens of thousands of innocent people were being made to suffer and die. Could he move up the timetable? FDR would raise the issue once again with General Marshall, even though he knew the general was right in not diverting resources from the focus on the Normandy landing, now nine months away. And in the meantime, throughout the countries the Nazis had conquered, thousands of Jews were being rounded up. Roosevelt was going to have to live with his decision, and it would weigh heavily upon him.

Gertrude Hildebrand watched the party leave. She was on the porch gathering the glasses and placing them onto a tray when her heart almost stopped. She saw Miss Suckley motion to agent Reilly as agent O'Neill lifted the president from his chair and into the open car. Miss Suckley asked Mike Reilly to bend down so she could whisper to him. Gertrude's hands were now on her face. Was it too late? Had they been discovered? She needed to get to Hans, who only a few minutes before had gone to the cellar to finish preparations for their German guests.

Chapter Fifteen

The staff that would accompany the president and his wife to Hyde Park at times exceeded one hundred. It would include aides, press, security personnel, medical, transportation, and radio-communication experts. A short distance north of Springwood was the sprawling Vanderbilt mansion, the wartime home for the president's personnel.

Frederick Vanderbilt, Commodore Cornelius Vanderbilt's grandson, outdid his brothers by building his Dutchess County castle in 1895 three hundred feet above the Hudson River. Vanderbilt had incorporated fifty-four rooms and twenty baths into it. In 1938, Margaret Van Alen obtained the estate from her Aunt Louise, Frederick's wife. In 1939 Louise gifted the estate to the National Park Service, and for two years it was open to the public. It was then closed and became the wartime home and office for scores of civil servants. Agents Mike Reilly and Jim Gannon also kept an office in the mansion.

"I can't believe this house belonged to just one guy," Corporal Parker exclaimed to Jim Gannon as they walked down the crushed-stone driveway of the mansion.

"I can, and this was only one of many. The family had a bigger castle in Newport, Rhode Island, and a huge townhouse in New York City. Vanderbilt built the house but a guy named Edward Hyde originally owned the property two hundred and fifty years ago," Gannon said.

"Who was Hyde?" Parker asked, adjusting his uniform cap.

"Governor of New York, I think, and the Viscount of Cornbury."

"Where's Cornbury?"

Gannon, looking now at Parker and Reilly, said, "It's in England. And by the way, Hyde was a transvestite."

"What the hell is a transvestite, and how do you know all this stuff?" Parker asked.

Gannon did not respond. The history lesson was over. It was time to regain focus on the matter at hand, Schroeder and Reinhardt. Reilly saw the change in Gannon's face and wanted to lighten things up, if just for a minute, and said, "It's not like sleeping in the barracks, I suppose, Parker, but just don't get used to it."

"But I can, sir—sure beats the hut at Camp Greentop."

"Tell me, what did you find out from your visit to Vassar?" Reilly asked.

"Initially, this guy MacCracken was reluctant to tell us anything. But he did," Gannon responded.

"Anything that can help?"

"We'll know better later today. MacCracken thought Schroeder lived off-campus, in Poughkeepsie, and he also thought that she may still have the house. So after a half hour or so search of his student files, he may be able to get an address for us. It was highly unusual for a student to live off-campus and not in the dorms. And as Parker here has told us, she was a loner at Greentop. Pretty much stayed to herself, never mixed."

"Well, let's stay on it, and let's do it today."

"Okay, boss. What did you and the general find out about Reinhardt?" Gannon asked.

"You won't believe this. He's disappeared. Gone. Vanished," Reilly said. "Holy shit, just like that! How can that be?"

"According to his supervisor, who is the chief engineer, he's up and left. They said he was going to check out the security at the upstate reservoirs, took a city car, and that was that."

"Do they know why and when?" Gannon asked.

"Three days ago," Reilly said. He motioned to Gannon and Parker to get into the car. "I've got the state police out looking for him as well as the water department's security people."

"For all we know, he could be lying dead from a heart attack in the woods someplace. You know he wasn't in good shape," Gannon said, getting into the car.

"Could be, but I doubt it. Something is not right here. Yesterday at Wilderstein, Miss Suckley took me aside and told me she was not pleased with the response she had gotten from her questioning of the Hildebrands."

"What questions, sir?" Parker asked as he jumped into the back seat.

"The telephone calls to New York City, to Reinhardt, and that it was because Reinhardt was a long-lost cousin, Gertrude told her," Reilly said.

"Mike, there's some kind of connection between Reinhardt and Schroeder. We know from Anderson that it was Reinhardt who sent the bogus telegram to the OSS on the Schroeder matter. But do you have anything on the connection, what it is that they're up to?"

"I don't really know at this point, Jim, but I want you and Parker here to check out where she lived while she was at Vassar. In the meantime, Anderson and I will go to Wilderstein and have a talk with the Hildebrands."

"And with all of this, the old man is to meet with Churchill in two days," Gannon said.

* * *

Night had fallen over the Hudson Valley when Otto Reinhardt brought his car to a stop along the north entrance to the Hudson Valley Chemical Company. The windshield wipers were erratic in removing the rain. He always had the best intentions to have the water department's maintenance people fix them, but never got to it. The problematic wipers became an irritant to Berger during their twelve-mile ride from Schroeder's home. SS Strandartenfuhrer Ludwig Berger kept reminding Reinhardt of his incompetence ever since the car's occupants left Schroeder's house in Poughkeepsie.

Krupp and Schroeder had given up on getting Berger to back away from his endless criticism of Reinhardt. They felt it would be more productive if they stayed focused on their mission. Upon leaving the Poughkeepsie house, Berger snapped at Krupp and Schroeder when he was chastised for his constant picking on Reinhardt. Berger told them he could stay focused and still pick on the "coward".

Krupp and Schroeder got out of the car and felt a sigh of relief—just to be free of Berger. What truly amazed them was how quickly Berger had turned on Reinhardt. The antagonist had met the engineer for the first time less than seventy-two hours before. It appeared to Krupp and Schroeder that Berger was more motivated in doing away with Reinhardt than their intended targets, the two world leaders. Krupp and Schroeder could be seen walking down Water Street, looking for the drainage culvert that led from the plant's outside storage yard to the sidewalk. It would be this point they would use as their entry into the sprawling factory. Berger and Reinhardt passed them as they drove on, south on Water Street to Route 9D, to Cold Spring.

Darkness had come two hours earlier as Berger and Reinhardt were making their way up Breakneck Mountain for the second time in three days. Reinhardt had had an awful time then, when there was daylight. It was much worse this night, when there was total darkness and rain. An hour ago, when they had dropped off Schroeder and Krupp, it was raining even harder. Reinhardt was panting. His suit was being torn from the trail's brambles and thorns. His hands and face were scratched; he was tired, thirsty, and wanted to stop and rest. He kept slipping on the climb, but Berger kept pushing him to get going. They were now within sight of the New York City Water Department's pumphouses.

Dark as it was, Berger was pleased with what he saw. The outline of the fifteen-foot-high brick buildings was in front of them. He already had completed two parts of the assignment given to him by Krupp. He and Reinhardt had lowered the New York City Water Department's Ford sedan into the Hudson River. It was at

Hastings Landing boat launch, where the deep inlet swallowed the car in twelve feet of water. A few blocks from the abandoned car, he saw the second part of his mission being fulfilled. In front of the Cold Spring Inn was a large, black 1939 Buick with the keys in the ignition. How stupid, Berger thought, of the driver, who most likely was inside the inn. Within seconds, Berger and Reinhardt were in the Buick, driving to Breakneck Ridge, a few minutes north of Cold Spring. This time, unlike their last visit to the mountain, they did not pull off and park on the shoulder of Route 9D. Instead, Reinhardt instructed Berger to pull onto a dirt road just south of the mountain's access, which led to an abandoned mansion. The car's owner and the police would never be looking for the stolen car this close to the Cold Spring Inn.

"The keys, idiot," Berger demanded of Reinhardt, who was resting on the ground outside the pumphouse.

"You're a cruel man," Reinhardt said as he passed the keys. Continuing, he said, "What is with you? What is it I've done to deserve this treatment? You harbor so much hatred, it is a wonder you can function. Even your two comrades despise you. I've overheard their conversations several times. They feel if you were not so highly connected with the leaders of the Reich, you would not be here, if fact you would most likely have been shot. Not by the enemy of the Third Reich, but by your own men!"

"I don't care what you think or say," Berger shot back. "You are the lowest of swines, the poorest excuse for a man—and worse, a German." He searched for the skeleton key that would unlock the large, heavy steel door.

"I still don't know why you need the plans, Berger, and why did we dump the car in the river? What in God's name are you people up to?" Reinhardt asked, resting at the entrance to the pumphouse.

"I'll tell you what we are here for. We are going to kill that Jew-loving president of yours. And while we accomplish that, we will also get rid of Churchill. That's part of our mission, so now you know," Berger finally revealed. He used the key from the exhausted Reinhardt to open the pumphouse.

"No, you're not. I'm not going to allow you to do this. I was never told that this was to be your mission. I would have never have been part of it," Reinhardt said, pushing himself up.

"Sit down, you fool, and stay out of my way. You are part of it. Why do you think we are up here and at the chemical plant? After we kill the president and the prime minister, we will destroy your wonderful water system. And with your help," Berger snarled.

Reinhardt became enraged. He brought his hands up to Berger's coat collar and yanked at it. Berger, equally furious, slammed him to the concrete floor and drew out his dagger.

Chapter Sixteen

On the eve of his close friend's visit, FDR's high spirits were coming back to him. Winston Churchill's arrival was less than twenty-four hours away. He had always looked forward to his visits, and the upcoming one was no exception, even with an agenda of topics that easily could have divided the closest of friends.

The news that Eleanor had decided to move up her planned trip to the South Pacific only made Roosevelt more jubilant. She had an innate way of dampening the environment that surrounded the prime minister and her husband. Churchill knew well that Mrs. Roosevelt was not particularly fond of him. As far as Eleanor Roosevelt was concerned, Churchill was everything she was not. His conservative approach to the social ills of Great Britain and throughout the British Commonwealth was the opposite of everything she stood for. Churchill's harsh treatment of the people of Ireland, India, and the West Indies was, in her opinion, no less severe in 1943 then it was before the war. And what infuriated her was that her husband turned a blank stare when she would bring these issues up. She would be departing in a few hours.

The president also was elated over the news that he heard from Harlem, eighty miles south of where he was at the moment. His long-time political ally, Fiorello LaGuardia, the mayor of New York, only an hour before had telephoned him that the riots in Harlem had ended and normalcy was being restored. FDR had been informed that there was a price. Five Negroes were killed, and fifty policemen were injured. There was also several million dollars in property damage from fires and looters. Roosevelt had asked his friend to confirm for him that the melee was attributed to a policeman wounding a Negro soldier who had come to the aid of a woman being arrested. The mayor confirmed it. The fires were extinguished, but not the underlying resentment of the residents of the large New York City Negro community.

Roosevelt was not one to dwell too long on bad news. Nevertheless, he was keen enough to be aware of any political fallout that would arise from the riots. He quickly dispensed with the New York City issue and began to relish the good news from the war fronts that his Secretary of War, Henry Stimpson, had given him before breakfast. The president would be able to share with Churchill the good news that Sicily was about to fall. The German army was in full retreat back to Italy, and in due time Mussolini's Italy would surrender.

Yet, it was the news that Stimpson had provided, that the Soviet army had defeated the Nazis at Orel and Belgoron, that FDR delighted in even more. Marshall Joseph Stalin's forces had finally won a summer victory. FDR felt that maybe some of the pressure coming from Stalin and Charles de Gaulle to begin an immediate Second Front would now dissipate.

Pushing his breakfast tray back and turning his wheelchair so he could face his secretary, Grace Tully, the president asked:

"Grace, where is the prime minister now?"

"I've been told, Mr. President, that he is en route, and that he decided to take the train from Quebec rather than his motorcade."

"Well, if that's the case, he should be here sooner, I would suspect."

"That's correct, sir. Mr. Reilly said he expects he'll be in Poughkeepsie by five o'clock."

"I would have thought sooner," FDR said, and he turned toward his desk to gather up briefing papers.

"Mr. President, according to Mike, the P.M. is planning a stop in Montreal. There is some sort of rally to be held."

"Good God, is he running for election in Canada now too? His visit was to be top secret."

"You know Mr. Churchill, sir; however, you should also know that Mrs. Churchill will not be with him, she's not feeling well enough at the moment and will be staying behind for a few days. Their daughter Mary will be accompanying him."

"Well, Anna will have a partner then. In the meantime, Miss Tully, I want to send a note off to Winston before he arrives so he can be thinking about what's going on in the Pacific, that other war he sometimes doesn't think we're fighting. God only knows I have been taking a heap of criticism from some quarters that I had known about the Japs' intentions. And what's worse, some are now speculating that Winston's people had broken the Japanese ciphers and were aware in advance of the attack at Pearl Harbor."

"You are planning to ask the prime minister about such speculation, Mr. President?" Miss Tully asked.

"I'll wait and see if the right moment comes up, and then I just might."

"I'm ready, Mr. President," Miss Tully replied as she sat next to the boss with her steno pad and pencil.

"Mr. P.M., I want your opinion on just which route we should be taking to breach the Japs' outer perimeter: Burma, China, Manchuria; or the Philippines, Formosa, Korea. And in the meantime, Nimitz wants to go up through the islands. More when you arrive, Franklin."

"Is that all, sir?"

"Yes, will you get that off as soon as possible?" FDR asked.

"Yes, I will, but may I ask you, Mr. President, why don't we ask Mr. Stalin to help out in fighting the Japs?"

"Miss Tully, I should have you work for Secretary Hull. He's the one to whom your question should be addressed. And I'm sure he'll tell you it's because Uncle Joe feels he's fighting the Huns all by himself."

"Forgive me for being so impertinent, Mr. President." Miss Tully slid her chair out from alongside FDR's desk and stood to go to her office.

"Not at all, my dear. On the other hand, you're not going to be able to ask the secretary of state. He's on a secret mission in Moscow working with the Soviets and China on drafting the proposals for the new United Nations."

* * *

Jim Gannon turned his car onto the tree-shaded driveway of the Vanderbilt estate. As he had done countless times before, he brought the car to a stop at the military policeman's sentry post. Along with the president's estate at Springwood, the Vanderbilt's sprawling estate was patrolled and guarded by members of the Army's military police units. The not-so-young military policeman wearing a white helmet and white pistol belt that held his .45 caliber sidearm approached Gannon's car and said, "It's okay to go on, Mr. Gannon. I guess you can vouch for your passenger?"

"That I can, sergeant, he's one of yours. You can log him in 'Corporal Parker on temporary assignment to the Secret Service.' Or do you need to see anything else?"

"Parker," the sergeant said, "What's your serial number for the log book?"

Parker recited his number, and the men were given approval to move on. "By the way, there's a real knock-out of a lady waiting to see you up at the reception center," the M.P. said.

"You're kidding, Sarge. Who is she?"

"Don't really know, Mr. Gannon. She was logged in about an hour ago by the previous relief, came in with a bunch of people from Treasury," the M.P. said as he moved from Gannon's car and lifted the suspended gate log barrier.

Ellen McCarthy was not waiting in the reception room. She was standing at the mansion's grand marble entry, leaning against a giant Romanesque column. Her green and white summer dress was partly covered by a white cotton cardigan sweater. Her tan hat with a small green flower highlighted her beautiful brown hair and fair complexion. Her white-gloved hands were clasped in front, clutching her handbag. From the look on her face, she immediately knew that the approaching car was being driven by her fiancé, Jim Gannon.

"Holy shit, the M.P. was right. What a babe! She's gorgeous," Parker exclaimed as they pulled up to the mansion's front steps. "I'll need to introduce myself to her, and soon!"

"Not so fast, Corporal—that's my fiancée. And what in God's name is she doing here?" Gannon asked, bringing the car to a stop and attempting to get out at the same time.

"You never told me about—" Parker was saying when he heard: "James, I thought I would not get to see you." Ellen rushed down the marble steps and into the arms of Gannon. Stripping off her gloves, she placed her arms around his neck.

"Ellen, what the devil are you doing here? How did you get here, and do you have any idea what's happening?" Gannon asked as he looked into her face with his arms around her shoulders.

"Is that all you can say, James? You haven't seen me since last week, and now I'm here."

"I'm sorry, muffin, it's just that things are crazy. In a few hours an important world leader will be—"

"I know. Mr. Churchill. That's why I'm here, too." Ellen held tightly to her fiancé's hands.

"You're not supposed to know that. Very few people do," Gannon said, his eyes now glancing around and over Ellen's shoulders to see if she might have been overheard.

"Nonsense, dear, a lot of people know. It's just that his visit is not in the newspapers or on the radio. Censorship or something like that, I guess."

"Ellen, so what brings you here, and at this time?"

"Well, if that's what's important to you now, James, I'll tell you. The undersecretary and my boss are here to brief Mr. Churchill and the president on the government's plan to rebuild Europe after the war and how much the allies will need to spend on the effort," she said matter-of-factly.

"And your role?" Gannon asked.

"James, you make it sound like I'm being questioned—a suspect of sorts. Well, if you feel that finding out what I'm doing here is more important than asking about our apartment in

Georgetown and the wedding plans, I'll tell you," Ellen said as she pulled away from him.

"I'm so sorry, dear, it's just that things are insane. Let's walk over to the bench, there, by the pond. We can talk freely. I love you, you know that? And your dress and hat are just stunning."

"I know you love me, and I love you. But you seem so stressed. You're so hurried, and it appears you don't want to spend time on plans for our wedding or even the apartment."

"It's that water department fellow I had told you about at the Willard, remember? He's into or up to something that is not good. It's why I'm with the army corporal you saw in the car, Corporal Parker. I shouldn't be telling you this, but Parker here and his boss, General Anderson, train our spies. One of them can't be traced, and we think there is a connection with the fellow from the water company—but we're not sure."

Gannon felt he had told Ellen enough. Possibly too much. He also knew that she held a top-secret clearance. Nevertheless, he needed to justify why he was staying away from Washington.

The couple spent that next hour at the pond, getting caught up with all that was happening in their lives. It was during their time at the pond that Gannon told his fiancée that their wedding date was going to have to wait a bit longer. It didn't sit well with Ellen.

* * *

Corporal Parker had begun walking over to the couple. He stopped abruptly and saw Gannon patting Ellen's watery eyes. The corporal reversed himself and headed back to the mansion's front door. The fact that Mike Reilly wanted to see Gannon and let him know there was a break-in at a Beacon chemical factory the night before was going to have to wait—just a few more minutes. Parker was becoming fond of his new friend and enjoyed being with him. He would have done anything just to get off Maryland's Catoctin Mountains and away from Camp Greentop's paperwork and the camp's isolation. He felt now he was working with normal people. Potential spies and saboteurs were strange people. Most of those in training at Greentop were of foreign origin, which made it even more of a spooky matter for Parker. Until he had been assigned to Camp Greentop, the country boy that Parker was had never met someone not born in America.

Chapter Seventeen

Brian Kelly had worked at the Hudson Valley Chemical Company since 1919. He took the job of night watchman thirty days after he left his World War I Army unit, the Fighting 69th. He was proud of his service to the famous New York military unit. Almost every one of the company's employees had heard his stories of his service in France during the Great War. They were also knowledgeable of the fact that Mr. Kelly was an orderly to Colonel William "Wild Bill" Donovan, the regiment's commanding officer and now the director of the OSS, Kathe Schroeder's superior. Everyone loved Mr. Kelly

On this sunny Tuesday morning, Mr. Otis, the plant manager, did what he had done on countless mornings before. At his desk, just outside the processing room, he would look over Mr. Kelly's security-time-clock punch sheets. The holes in the circular sheet of paper would tell him that on the night before, Mr. Kelly had made all of his appointed rounds, and on a timely basis. But on this morning, there were no time clock sheets from Mr. Kelly. It was the first time in twenty-four years that time sheets from Mr. Kelly were not on his desk.

Mr. Otis got up from his desk and was about to leave his office when the intercom on his credenza rang and his secretary announced, "Mr. Otis, Mrs. Kelly is on the telephone. Her husband never came home this morning, and she is asking if he is still at the factory."

Five hours would go by after Mrs. Kelly's call. It was time for Mr. Otis to restart the plant production and have his employees get back to their assignments. He was not mentally prepared to call Mrs. Kelly, but he had to. Her husband was found dead by a New York state trooper. His body was underneath the loading ramp on the westerly side of the building. His throat was slashed. It was determined that he was executed by a professional assassin. But why? The call to Mrs. Kelly had to be made.

Having been provided with the factory's inventory records, the investigators concluded that chemicals and poisons had been removed. Specifically, it was discovered that five gallons of hydrogen ammonia and five quarts of arsenic had been taken. But still no one could figure out why. And why was Mr. Kelly murdered?

* * *

"Be careful with that stuff, you fool," barked Schroeder as Berger lifted the chemical container into the trunk of the car, the same Buick that only an hour ago he had stolen in Cold Spring, near the village dock.

"Where's Reinhardt?" Krupp asked Berger as he carefully placed the arsenic vials into a box in the car's trunk.

"He's dead, and good riddance," Berger snapped as he slammed the trunk closed.

"What do you mean he's dead? How did it happen? You were to watch him, Berger," Schroeder demanded.

"He got me to the pumphouse and gave me the maps and keys. I felt his services were no longer needed. So I killed him. His body is locked up in the pumphouse. No one will find him for weeks."

"And what if they find him tomorrow and begin a search? Our mission will have been compromised," Schroeder snapped. All three got into the Buick, with Schroeder at the wheel, Berger in the back seat. They headed up Route 9D to Poughkeepsie.

"I don't think there will be a problem. He told me he is the only one who goes to the pumphouse, normally for routine inspections," Berger said. "He was useless to us and to the

Fatherland. He was a disgrace. You see, Herr Krupp, I don't hesitate to liquidate anyone who I find not helpful to our cause. You, on the other hand, will tolerate complacency, mediocrity, and incompetence. If you acted like me, the Duke and Duchess of Windsor would now be residing in Berlin. Instead, they are in England."

"Berger," Krupp said disgustedly, "you have put us all in jeopardy. There was absolutely no need to kill Reinhardt. You are exactly what I was told to expect."

"What is that, Herr Oberst?" Berger asked sarcastically.

"Nothing but a blood-thirsty, treacherous killer. No feelings, no sense of morality. Just an outright gangster and a disgrace to the German Army."

"Well, Herr Oberst, you should know I'm not in the German Army. I'm in the SS, and I can kill anyone I damn please."

"Now we have two dead civilians," Krupp mumbled as he stared out the windshield of the stolen car.

"What do you mean, two?" Berger snapped.

"He's referring to my killing the nosey watchman at the factory. He caught Herr Oberst removing the chemicals. And he recognized me. He had to be eliminated," Schroeder said matter-of-factly. She slowly brought the car to a stop at an intersection in the village of Wappingers Falls.

"What do you mean, Schroeder? He recognized you, how?"

"It's not for you to know. He's dead and that's all there is to say," Schroeder responded, her eyes fixed on an oncoming car.

"I want to know, Herr Oberst. How was Schroeder identified by a night watchman?" Berger insisted.

"It was—"

Schroeder was interrupted by Krupp, who responded, "She did her university field and lab assignments at the chemical factory. It was back then that she befriended the watchman. Does that satisfy your curiosity, Berger? Because that's all you're going to get. And the Duke and Duchess are not in England. They're in Bermuda. And it was one of your types who foiled our mission to capture them, just so you know."

Berger broke his five minutes of silence and said, "Well, you see, Herr Oberst, Schroeder here is as much a cold-blooded killer as I am. You're the one that needs to be prepared. Not us," Berger said, knowing he was provoking their leader.

Krupp did not respond. He had, in his career, many encounters with others who held similar mindsets as Berger. They were all in the SS, or worse, the dreaded Gestapo. Their loyalty to the Führer was uncompromising. Krupp had seen many of his fellow officers disappear or be executed for their crossing an SS or Gestapo officer. Later there would be time to deal with Berger. He promised himself that if their mission was accomplished, Berger was not going back to Germany. Germany's cause was lost, and in part because of the Bergers of his country who aided in Germany losing the war—on a daily basis.

The road sign read *Rhinebeck 7 Miles* as the trio passed the entrance to Springwood. Berger broke a silence that had endured for the past twenty minutes, saying, "How stupid Americans are. Just look, we're driving by the entrance to their leader's home. And only a sentry post. Never would this be the case with our Führer's place at Berchtesgaden."

* * *

"Hans, where did you move their car?" Gertrude Hildebrand asked her husband, who entered the kitchen looking worn, tired, and upset.

"I brought their Buick to the Poughkeepsie railroad station. I left the keys and everything just as I found them. I wanted it as far away as I could get it," Hans continued and asked, "Where are they? Are they staying put in the root cellar?"

"Yes, for now. They wanted food, so I brought them coffee and strudel," Gertrude said, though tears began to flow.

"What is it, Gertie?" Hans came toward her.

"Hans, what have we done? They are frightening. You've seen them. They don't care one bit about us or what could happen to us."

Three hours earlier, Schroeder, Berger, and Krupp had entered Wilderstein. While in the village of Hyde Park, Schroeder had telephoned Gertrude Hildebrand and was told that only she and Hans were at the estate. Miss Suckley had gone to Hyde Park.

The Nazis wasted no time in getting onto the estate, along with all of their weapons of destruction.

Each of them had to make two trips to the car to unload their equipment, including the chemicals and poisons. They had them placed carefully in the cellar, but soon they would be moved again.

When Schroeder had turned over the keys to the '39 Buick to Hans, he also gave her the keys to the twenty-eight-foot motor launch in the Wilderstein boathouse.

Earlier, Schroeder and Krupp had agreed that their best escape route would not be Miss Suckley's Packard, but by boat. They would have to move quickly and get back to Cold Spring and Breakneck Ridge.

"Gertie, we have no business here any more. We must leave. You know the madam did not believe us when she questioned us about the telephone calls to New York City. And I agree with you. These people are killers, and they are now here in the house," Hans said, his voice breaking.

"Erich and Kurt, Hans. What happens to them if we don't obey? I don't want to ask."

"Gertie, when I came back on the bus from dropping off their automobile, I realized we can't help Kurt and Erich any more. These people are going to kill the president and Mr. Churchill, and God only knows who else gets in their way."

Almost whispering so not to be overheard by the German agents in their root cellar, Gertrude said, "The dog, Hans. Can you hear her barking? She's in the cellar. She's found them, and—" Gertrude was interrupted by the echoing sound of the Luger's blast. Heather was no longer barking. Her sense of smell and hearing was too much for Berger. Fala's mother had just become another casualty of war.

Chapter Eighteen

For forty-five minutes, Corporal Parker had been sitting alongside his new-found friend, Jim Gannon. They were driving into Poughkeepsie on Route 44. Earlier they had been in the village of Clinton Corners, an hour's drive northeast of the Hudson River city. It was the third of five locations that Vassar College's president, Dr. MacCracken, had reluctantly given them as possible residences for his college's alumna, Kathe Schroeder.

The estate in Clinton Corners was intriguing to Gannon. It was owned by the uncle of world-famous aviator Charles Lindbergh. Both the aviator and his uncle were widely known as no friend of Roosevelt or of his policies toward Germany.

The Lindbergh mansion was deep in the woods, a mile off Route 82. The seven-hundred-acre estate was being maintained in an immaculate condition. One would never know that a war was on. Parker and Gannon could not help but notice the manicured lawns as they drove up the pea-stone graveled, quarter-mile driveway. An almost endless white-board fence bordered each side of the driveway. Where, they asked, does the estate's owner get the paint? The entryway was also lined with mature elms and maples, spaced precisely from each other and well trimmed.

Gannon and Parker had wondered how Lindbergh was able to get sufficient rations to provide fuel to maintain such a place. Parker made no pretense about his feelings. As far as he was concerned, Lindbergh was just like other influential and wealthy people. They got all the ration coupons they needed. It was families like his that had to scrounge for ration books for food and fuel.

After Gannon and Parker arrived at the mansion, they walked up the dozen marble steps to an ornate oak front door. They did not have to announce their arrival. An elderly, white-haired man was leaning on a cane at the opened door. He was dressed in a blue blazer, white shirt, and bow tie. His tan trousers were much too large. His loafers were shined to a gloss. To Gannon and Parker, he was a true blueblood. They knew they were in for a bit of trouble when they would question Mr. Lindbergh. They also did not miss the aging aristocrat's unwelcoming smile. Lindbergh asked them to follow him to his library.

Seated in an ornate, wood-paneled library, Gannon wasted no time in commencing his questioning. Radcliff Lindbergh III had made it clear to agent Gannon and Corporal Parker that he resented their questioning him about the Vassar student who once rented the apartment over his carriage house. His belligerence went on for five minutes. It came to a sudden halt when Gannon produced a pair of handcuffs and told the aristocrat he was going to be placed under arrest. Asked why, Gannon informed him it was for interfering with an official government investigation and possibly harboring a foreign agent.

Lindbergh, who had been known before the outbreak of hostilities to be outspoken over the way in which the U.S. State Department was treating Germany, suddenly went limp. His face became ashen. His hands could hardly hold the top of the cane. And his tone abruptly changed. He disclosed to Gannon and Parker that Schroeder had stayed at his estate during her first and second semesters of her junior year at Vassar, that she had left to be closer to the college, and that she had rented a house in Poughkeepsie.

Lindbergh, in fact, became a font of information about his former tenant. Parker and Gannon were to hear that Schroeder was the niece of a well-known Cologne banker, and that her uncle, Kurt von Schleicher, was the bank owner who had funded the Nazi party in 1930 and in 1933. Furthermore, they learned that Schroeder earlier had been educated in Paris, and that her uncle recruited her for the SS. How Lindbergh came to know all of Schroeder's background, Gannon was willing to postpone learning. For now, he was interested in the current whereabouts of Schroeder and of the rented house in Poughkeepsie.

* * *

Gannon's eyes were transfixed on the slow-moving traffic as he and Parker approached the downtown section of Poughkeepsie. His mind was not on the cars ahead of him, but on the last meeting with his fiancée.

He had left Ellen at the Vanderbilt estate seven hours ago. He knew it was going to be weeks before he could see her or talk to her. Once again, he thought of resigning from the Secret Service. He felt the Service was stealing his life. Constantly, it was interfering with his relationship with the only girl he had ever loved. Earlier in the day, he had to tell Ellen their wedding plans must be postponed. When Ellen had asked him until when, he had no response. He wasn't going to lie to her. His suggestion of eloping, by going to Elkton, Maryland, just brought on more tears. She wanted a church wedding, a Catholic church, with all of their families witnessing their vows. She had discounted the travel and accommodations limitations brought on by the war effort. She told him she felt she was not up to trying to get around his schedule. In turn, he did not want to lose her. His only choice was to resign. He would talk to his mentor, Mike Reilly, but not now. Mike had too much going on, and he needed to be there for him—even more so than for Ellen.

The silence in the car was broken when Parker asked, "What are you thinking about?" The car's two-way radio interrupted. It was agent Reilly calling.

"Where are you, Jim? Over."

"About three blocks from Poughkeepsie's city hall. We're on our way back from Clinton Corners. We've got some pretty good intel from someone who knew Schroeder and her background, especially her background in Germany. Now we want to run down two leads on places she may have rented in Poughkeepsie."

Moments before, Gannon had asked Parker to pull out from the glove box the map of Poughkeepsie. Parker located Church Street, then told Gannon to make the next two left turns. Church Street was at the end of the second left.

"Well, the running around might just be done. Over."

"What do you mean? Over." Gannon glanced over at Parker.

"What do you have as your next locations? Over."

"One is on 128 Church Street, and the other is 317 Hudson River Drive. Why?"

"Go to the Church Street address. I think that will be the one. But don't go in. We will send backup to you first. Over."

"Jim, why there? Over."

"Because we've been informed that an electric meter reader had called in when he heard that Reinhardt was missing. Said he saw a car, with a NYC Water Department decal on it, at the 128 address."

"So you think that's it?"

"I'm almost one-hundred-percent sure. We've contacted the water department. Still no word on Reinhardt, and no one in their department resides in Poughkeepsie. Over."

"Jim, Parker and me are parked in front of the Baptist church. We're three houses away, no sign of any activity at 128. Over."

"I'm on my way. The old man is here with the package. Don't move until I get there, understood? Over."

"Understood. Over and out."

* * *

Great Britain's motorcade had come to a stop directly in front of the four-columned front porch at Springwood. A U.S. Army Jeep had escorted the three limousines up to the house. The president and his daughter were only a small part of the welcoming group standing behind the three-foot white balustrade. Roosevelt was on the south wing, leaning ever-so-subtly on the arm of his trusted security agent, Michael Reilly; Secretary of the Treasury Morgenthau; the military's Chief of Staff General Marshall; Harry Hopkins, who was only recently released from a hospital; and a dozen lesser officials were all on the north end of the porch, their backs to the sun, waiting for Mr. Churchill to alight from an oversized Packard touring car.

Reilly tried to focus on what was happening directly in front of him when he caught a glimpse of Margaret Suckley. And immediately he reminded himself that he was to go to Wilderstein with General Anderson and interview Miss Suckley's servants, the Hildebrands.

The president continued to place more of his weight on Reilly's right arm. The president's seven-pound leg braces could only do so much, and for the next few minutes, it was up to Reilly to do the rest. *When will Churchill ever get out of the car?* Reilly thought to himself. He knew more than most that standing, if only for ten minutes, brought excruciating pain and discomfort to his boss.

A courteous round of applause broke out as the British prime minister exited his car, cane in one hand, a six-inch cigar in the other, along with his black bowler hat—all trademarks of the legendary leader of the embattled British Empire.

Quickly moving up the four steps, with his daughter Mary trailing behind, as well as a half-dozen other British dignitaries, Churchill extended his arm to the president. Those on the porch patio gave an even more enthusiastic applause. Roosevelt was obviously pleased once again to meet with his dear friend and wartime partner.

"Welcome back to Springwood, Mr. Prime Minister," FDR said as Churchill clung to his hand.

"It is so good to be here, Mr. President. We have much to discuss, and I must say I've never seen you look so well," Churchill responded.

If asked, Mike Reilly would not have agreed with Churchill, whom he had met the year before in Casablanca, as well as at other meetings between the two world leaders. The president's health was failing, and he and only a handful of other close associates knew it only too well. One of them, Dr. Ross McIntire, FDR's personal physician, was standing just to Reilly's left. The doctor had always confided in Reilly about the president's health issues. Earlier in the day, he had asked Reilly not to have the president exert himself.

"Winston, I am so sorry we don't have a band here. I so much love hearing 'God Save the King.'"

"Well, Mr. President, I too will miss hearing 'The Star Spangled Banner,' the most moving national anthem I've ever heard."

"Shall we go in, Winston, and have some tea and cake? You must be half-starved from your arduous journey," FDR said.

"I'm more dying of thirst than from hunger, and I'm certain you cannot help but notice, Mr. President," Churchill responded. They moved through the oversized entrance crowned with a half-moon window.

Once inside the mansion and away from photographers, Reilly, along with Anna Roosevelt and Arthur Prettyman, gently placed their charge in his wheelchair, with the prime minister taking over the duty of pushing the chair to the president's study.

Churchill and Roosevelt were alone. All of their family, friends, and aides had left them to themselves. It had been preplanned. The two political giants wanted to be with each other for an hour and then go for some pre-dinner refreshments.

"Franklin, I just don't know how you do it. Bear up with so much stress surrounding you," Churchill said, accepting his second glass of whiskey.

"Winston, it is so important that I do not show the strain in front of others. They need to know that we will prevail, we must prevail, and we will," Roosevelt responded. He placed another cigarette into his trademark holder.

"Well, the reports this morning from Italy are good, Franklin. Mussolini is through. The Italians certainly will come over to us, is how we now see it."

Looking at his colleague, FDR said, "I'm hoping for just that. And later we will meet with Generals Marshall and Eisenhower and review their plans for the Second Front."

"In Moscow, discussions for a future United Nations will certainly go much smoother for Hull and Eden if they can tell Stalin that we have set a date for the invasion," Churchill said.

"I'm well aware of Stalin's anger at our progress, but that son of a bitch should not have sided with that other son of a bitch,

Hitler, three years ago. He has no idea, nor does he care for the fight that is taking place in the Pacific and the men and material losses we have endured," Roosevelt said, puffing on his Camel.

"I agree with you," Churchill began.

The president interrupted: "And Winston, the pressure this office is under by the Jewish groups is relentless. Even my dear friend Morgen, Secretary Morgenthau, is demanding action to rescue the Jews of Europe. History will not be kind to us, Winston. We now have positive confirmation. Hitler and his gang are massacring them by the thousands. And my dear friend, I am deeply saddened by Great Britain's decision to take over Palestine and have Europe's Jews move there. This will only create future problems with the Arabs for all of us."

Churchill was not happy with what he had just heard. He felt he had not come to Hyde Park to hear about the Jewish problem.

* * *

Bill Travis and his older brother had fished for sturgeon in the Hudson River since just after the last Great War. The contents of the fish's stomach were the closest anyone would come to caviar this side of the Baltic and Caspian Sea.

Their twenty-two-foot boat, painted a deep red, had been a common sight in the Cold Spring section of the dark and deep waters of the river. As on other summer afternoons, they brought their boat close into shore on the river's east bank, a hundred yards north of the Route 9D road and railroad tunnel.

What had never happened to them suddenly occurred. There was a loud screeching sound as their boat's small propeller collided with an underwater obstacle. The Travis brothers couldn't believe they had hit a rock. They knew the waters too well.

"Good God almighty, Ned, we hit a car!" Bill screamed out, and he started to lift the boat's engine out of the water.

"Bill, hold the boat. I'll go in and see if there is anyone in the car," Ned said. He quickly went over the gunnels and into the dark, cold waters of the Hudson.

Chapter Nineteen

Mike Reilly and General Anderson were in a sprint as they raced toward Reilly's car. It had been more than an hour since he had instructed Gannon to just observe the house at 128 Church Street. He was hoping Gannon's lack of patience would not rule the day, but that he would wait before he and Parker entered Schroeder's safehouse.

Reilly had turned over the security of watching the president and his guest to his other trusted and experienced aide, John O'Neill. The burly O'Neill also would have with him Churchill's security protection detail from Scotland Yard, so Reilly felt he could leave.

"Any news from the New York City Water Department yet?" Reilly asked the general, who had been following up on that part of the investigation.

"Nothing on the whereabouts of Reinhardt, but just before we left, there was a police notice we picked up from Cold Spring," Anderson replied. Reilly maneuvered the car south on Route 9 toward Poughkeepsie.

"Anything we can use, General?"

"Don't know yet. It was noted that a car was fished out from the river just north of Cold Spring, near a railroad tunnel. And the car had markings on it; that was all."

"General, take—" interrupted Reilly.

"Mike, please call me John."

"Fine. Take out the map in the glove box there, pinpoint where they found the car. And then locate the water department, where they have their Hudson River crossing. General—John, I mean—how does an agency as secretive as the OSS let a Schroeder type slip by? I mean, you guys go through more of a background check than we do in hiring agents. Unless, of course, they're assigned to the White House detail." Reilly maneuvered the car through traffic just north of the Poughkeepsie city line.

"Mike, I'll admit this is a real screw-up. Schroeder's file is nothing short of impeccable—all the right references, smart, tenacious, and fluent in three or four languages, as if she came right out of France or Germany. I know it's not a good reason, nor am I really answering your question, Mike. I'm giving you the bureaucratic bullshit line."

"Yeah, you are."

"The truthful answer is we are so desperate in our attempt to infiltrate agents into Europe, especially into France and Belgium."

"The Second Front effort?" Reilly said.

"Exactly. And if the invasion is to have any degree of success, we've got to get intelligence on German defenses and also get a better understanding of the strengths and weaknesses of the local resistance."

"So along comes a Schroeder, I guess."

"Right again. She was perfect. We were initially training her to blow up Nazi weapons, factories, oil and ammunition locations in Italy. And if she is what we think she is, all our efforts have been compromised. This is especially so if she has had communications with her Nazi handlers since she left Greentop."

"Good God, what a mess we've got! It's even bigger than just a possible assassination plot now," Reilly said dejectedly.

"There are two things that really worry me. What is she up to, and how many people is she working with? And how many other Schroeders have slipped through?" Anderson wondered as he marked two points on the McNally New York State road map.

"Chief, O'Neill here," the voice on Reilly's two-way radio shouted out. "The boss and the package are going to the furniture company for a swim, not to Daisy's place. Over."

"Okay, John, stay in touch. Over and out," Reilly responded.

"What does he mean by the furniture company?" Anderson asked.

"For about ten years Mrs. Roosevelt, along with two of her close girlfriends, Marion Dickerman and Nancy Cook, built furniture at Mrs. Roosevelt's Val-Kill. It's been closed for some time now. It's a couple of miles from Springwood, sort of her hideaway. Over the radio we use the code phrase 'furniture factory.' Not too subtle, I know."

"You mean the president and Mrs. Roosevelt don't live together?" Anderson asked innocently.

"It's a long and tragic story, but my telling it is going to have to wait. What's on the map?"

"Your intuition is right. The water department's river crossing is about a hundred yards or so from where the car was discovered. And when I overlay it with the map Gannon gave us, the water department's pumphouses are up on the hill, right here," Anderson said, pointing to the brick buildings on the site plan.

"John, get on the radio and have our guys at Springwood call the state police. Have them send a detail up Breakneck Ridge to the pumphouses. I'm sure they're going to find Reinhardt there. Let's hope the son of a bitch is still alive and can tell us what the hell is going on," Reilly barked. He turned their car down Church Street, where he immediately saw Gannon and Palmer sitting in their car, thirty yards from 128 Church Street.

* * *

The root cellar at Wilderstein was not a hospitable place to spend any length of time, especially for three people and for forty-eight hours. It was damp, humid, and cold, even on this August afternoon. The cellar's old fieldstone walls were dripping with sweat.

Located eight feet below the huge cellar at Wilderstein, the root cellar had not been fully used for at least twenty years. There was just not the need for it. The house that Margaret Suckley's father had rebuilt in 1888 no longer enjoyed the parties, celebrations, and family gatherings. Only a fraction of the vegetables and smoked meats were now stored there.

The Hildebrands were what was left of the estate's two-dozen servants. Gone also were Miss Suckley's siblings, all five of them and their offspring. And worse for Margaret Suckley was that most of the family's fortune was either lost in the Great Depression or spent to maintain the estate. A small trust fund was all that was left for her to use to keep up the appearance that she was of wealth. Only her close companion, Franklin, knew her lot. On many occasions, ever since she was hired to read to him in 1922, during his rehabilitation from polio, he secretly gave her money to keep Wilderstein operating for her—indeed, for both of them.

"Strandartenfuhrer Berger, if you touch my legs once more, I'll slit your goddamned throat. Do I make myself clear, you filthy swine?" Schroeder warned, getting quickly to her feet and clutching her dagger.

"You liked every bit of it, and you know it, too. It is so obvious," Berger responded, shifting his body on the wooden crate next to the corner of the root cellar.

"What's obvious is you are scum and Herr Oberst is right saying you are a disgrace to the Third Reich," Schroeder said, her hand still on her dagger, glaring at Albert Krupp.

What was being played out in the dimly lit room did not come as a surprise to Krupp. He had been told in Germany that Berger had nothing but contempt for the opposite sex, that he treated female contemporaries with abject disrespect. The untimely deaths of six or seven Berlin prostitutes were unofficially linked to him, but never officially proven. His uncle, Heinrich Himmler, in a high position of authority, was always there to cover up his nephew's nasty deeds.

But Krupp also knew of another deep-seated reason for Berger's behavior. Like his uncle, Berger deeply resented the fact that his grandmother was not of German descent. She was from Poland and a Jew, so Berger was paranoid about his family's ancestry. It could spell disaster for him as well as his other relatives who were in the top echelons of the Nazi party. Berger, once he had any inkling that someone was suspicious of his background, would secretly have that person dispatched, never to be heard from again. He was unaware that Krupp had any knowledge.

And Krupp, had he been back in Germany, would reveal this. But they were not in Germany; they were in a claustrophobic room.

"Would you two control yourselves? Where is your SS discipline?" Krupp ordered.

"Just keep the swine away, Herr Oberst. Is that too much to ask? And Herr Oberst, can we get rid of the dog's carcass? It is beginning to smell, and it's disgusting to look at, thanks to Berger here," Schroeder replied.

"Look, we have another day and night to spend in this hole. I know it is unbearable. I'll go upstairs and see if it is safe for us to go out for some air. And then we can take the dog out and bury it someplace in the garden, but not until then. Don't leave until I get back. And Berger, act your rank, that's all I ask of you. Do you understand?"

"Heil Hitler, Herr Oberst," Berger said, now on his feet and saluting, heels locked in place.

Krupp did not return the arrogant subordinate's salute. He walked toward the root cellar stairs.

* * *

"They shouldn't have killed the dog, Gertie," Hans Hildebrand said, sipping his coffee in the kitchen. "What do we tell the madam when she wants to know where Heather is?"

"We tell her she broke from the leash when you took her outside. She chased after a Canada goose. Then she ran down to the boathouse, and she'll be back. She's done it before. What else can we say?" Gert proposed, folding recently ironed embroidered napkins.

"Gertie, have you thought of what I said, that we must pack up and..." Hans was saying when they heard the cellar door open and saw Colonel Krupp standing at the door.

"Is there anyone else in the house, Fraulein?" he asked.

"No, Herr Oberst. Just me and Hans."

"That's good. When will your mistress be back? And what have you heard of the plans for tomorrow?" Krupp asked. He made his way into the kitchen, brushing off dust from his pants and shirt. Gert made no comment about his doing so.

Hans said, "She could be back at any time. She drove herself. She didn't tell us. What plan—"

"That's good. I want to bring Schroeder and Berger up here for some fresh air. That cellar is despicable."

"What plans are you referring to, Herr Oberst? We know of no plans, do we, Gertie?"

"Look here, old man, we are not here to play some game," Krupp suddenly confided. "We know from Otto Reinhardt that President Roosevelt and Prime Minister Churchill will be having dinner here tomorrow night. And he was told that by you two. Our mission is quite clear. We are to assassinate them. And if you know what is good for you and your family in Germany, you will assist us. Can I be more clear than that?" Krupp's eyes were cold as steel, staring at the two servants.

"At eight o'clock, Herr Oberst, dinner will take place here. That's what we've been told by Miss Suckley. We expect at least twelve for dinner," Hans said meekly.

Gert Hildebrand's hands were shaking. The napkin she had been folding was on the floor. Here eyes began to swell. *What are they going to do to Miss Suckley?* She asked herself, and then she asked Krupp.

"She is of no concern of ours, Fraulein. Nonetheless, they all must go," Krupp said.

"And Gertie and me, Colonel. What about us? Are we to go as well? Are we part of this horrible plan of yours?"

"Old man, do you have any idea what Churchill and Roosevelt are doing to our homeland? Have you not seen the results of the day and night bombings of our cities? Munich, Dresden, Cologne, and hundreds of others are now in ruins. And you dare say our horrible plan? Are you not loyal to the Fatherland?"

"We were just as loyal as you are, Herr Oberst. But we did not bring this disaster to our country. That horrible leader to whom you salute, Heil Hitler, brought this on us."

"Old man, I'd advise you to keep your mouth shut. If Herr Berger heard what you just said, he would kill you instantly. Do I make myself clear? I'm a soldier, not a Nazi party member or a fanatic. He is, and I've seen his work."

"So, Colonel, what happens to Hans and me?" Gert asked, hoping her husband would stop provoking Krupp.

"If you are in the house when—" Krupp was interrupted by the sound of Miss Suckley's Packard pulling up to the side porch.

* * *

Margaret Suckley, fifty-two-year-old distant cousin of President Roosevelt, was doing what she always had done after a visit to Springwood. She was recording her day's activities in her diary. Ever since 1933, when her relationship was rekindled with her dear friend, Daisy had become a dedicated diarist. No aspect of her encounter with FDR or those she might have met on that day, or on any day, went unrecorded.

For Miss Suckley there were only two joys in her sheltered life: being with Franklin, especially being alone with him, and coming to her study at Wilderstein and making a lasting record of what had transpired on that day or evening.

Today was no exception. She was also aware of the fact that in doing so, she was far removed from the accomplishments of her distant ancestors, Robert Livingston and Henry Beekman, seventeenth-century lords of the Hudson Valley. While chronologically Miss Suckley was one hundred fifty years removed from her ancestors, she would often feel that her life's accomplishments were rather shallow, and at times this wore on her. And so did residing on the huge, inherited estate when so many Americans were living in substandard housing. On many occasions, she would wonder what her dear friend Franklin thought about her surroundings. He never broached the subject with her.

With her two-inch diary opened, her Parker pen in hand, she began to write:

Friday, August 13, the P. met W.C. and his entourage on the patio. Mrs. R. had left for the Pacific soon after the ceremony. Mr. C. has no hair and looks like a huge barrel of a man. P. was happy I hung up painting done by Mr. C. on their Casablanca meeting. Anna and Arthur helped P. into his wheelchair. P. looks tired and needs rest. I'm off to...

"You called for me, madam?" Gert Hildebrand asked, entering the small, semi-dark study.

"Yes, and we will need to set the table for fourteen guests, not twelve, as I had requested," Miss Suckley said, blotting her last entry.

"Will you be giving me the table cards and the names, madam?"

"Of course. Would you read off to me who you have so far?"

Picking out of her apron pocket the typed list of guests for dinner at eight in the evening at Wilderstein, Mrs. Hildebrand read, "Mr. & Mrs. Winston Churchill; his daughter, Mary; Foreign Secretary Anthony Eden and Aide; Lieutenant Colonel Montgomery; Mr. Harry Hopkins; Anna Roosevelt; Mr. Wallace, and of course, the President and you, madam."

"Mrs. Hildebrand, that's only eleven. Whom have you left out?"

"I don't know, madam. I thought I had written down everyone, please forgive me," Mrs. Hildebrand said, not looking up from the paper in her hands.

"Are you all right? Is there anything wrong? Anything you want to tell me?" Miss Suckley asked.

Attempting to hide her emotions, Gertrude said, "No, madam. It's just that Hans and I know how important tomorrow night will be for you, and that you want it to go well."

"And it will, Gertrude. Just be yourself. We've done these dinners on many previous occasions. And would you add Dr. and Mrs. McIntire and Mr. Steve Early? That's all for now," Miss Suckley said, and she returned to her diary.

Gertrude nodded and began to leave when her employer called out, "I haven't seen Heather today, or for that matter, this morning. Would you ask Hans to locate her and bring her here? Oh, by the way, Mr. Reilly will be here tomorrow afternoon to meet with you and Hans. He said he has some questions he would like to ask both of you."

* * *

Franklin Roosevelt, if he had the opportunity to do so, would have liked to spend every waking hour of each day in the water, whether it be the soothing waters at Warm Springs, Georgia, or the pool inside the White House. Today, in early evening, was no exception. But at Val-Kill, the pond's water temperature was seventy degrees, and the president did not mind it at all. It was a different situation for his bathing companion. The short and stocky Churchill, eight years the president's senior, had a difficult time trying to stay warm in the pond—while holding onto his scotch and keeping his cigar from being extinguished.

"Franklin, my enemies in the Labor Party would never ask me to endure the hardship I am now experiencing in this dreadful lake," Churchill said to his friend who was floating nearby or being held up in the giant arms of agent O'Neill.

"Winston, I'm surprised at you. You, the former First Lord of the Admiralty, afraid of a little chill in the water! Initially, I had in mind a swim in the Hudson, but that can be a bit chilly, even in mid-August."

"Indeed, you are a compassionate host, Franklin. Mr. President, you must come to my home at Chartwell. I have finished building a pond there. And I must say, the water is much kinder to one's body. But are we to discuss the planning of the Second Front while my skin and body are near freezing?"

The daughters of the two great world leaders, Anna and Mary, sat on the Adirondack chairs at the pond, watched, and listened.

"I must say, Anna, that your father hides his discomforts so well. I only wish my father could do so," Mary Churchill said to her hostess between sips of her iced tea.

"Mary, what you see is what he wants everyone to see. He does all he can to be smiling, cheerful, and full of enthusiasm in front of all who come in contact with him. But I assure you that when he is by himself or with his companion, Daisy, or even with Mrs. Rutherford—and my mother knows nothing about this—he is a different Franklin. Without them he is melancholy, depressed, and feels very much alone."

"Then there's not too much difference between your father and mine. Papa goes and hides at Chequers as much as he can, and paints. There are times that I feel he is carrying all of Great Britain on his shoulders."

"Mary, I believe I know exactly how you feel. Your father's Chequers is comparable to a new place my father goes to, Shangri-La. But on top of everything our fathers must be concerned with, I've heard rumors that there may be some people, four or five, who could be out to bring harm to them," Anna said. They watched the two world leaders gambol in the pond.

"My God, Anna, I was not aware of this. I don't think Papa is, either," Mary said anxiously.

"Please don't be alarmed. It might very well be a rumor. There are so many reports that my father's Secret Service receive. Please don't repeat what I said. Our fathers have too much already to deal with in these next few days."

Chapter Twenty

On this early evening, Church Street in Poughkeepsie seemed no different than most small urban streets in America. Front lawns no longer had their grass but were blooming with Victory garden vegetables. Cornstalks were hip high. Tomatoes were abundant and beginning to shed their ripe greens for red. Sunflowers were as high as porch railings.

Houses displayed signs in their windows: *We have a son in the military.* A few had the small white flag and Gold Star, meaning the home had lost a son in the war. A half-dozen ten-to-twelve-year-old boys were indifferent to it all. They were engaged in a game of stickball. An old broom handle and a rubber ball were all that was required for hours of fun in the middle of Church Street.

Reilly slowly maneuvered his coupe over third base and pulled up behind Gannon's car. All four men got out and met on the sidewalk a few houses up the street from 128 Church Street.

"Hey mister, what's going on?" the young outfielder shouted to Reilly.

"Not to worry. Just keep playing, and pay no attention to us," Gannon responded.

"Yeah, I bet," the youngster mumbled.

"Mike, the place is deserted. We've seen nothing, in or out, in the last hour," Gannon reported.

"Hey, kid, come over here a minute," Reilly beckoned to the redheaded, freckle-faced player.

"Hey, guys, wait a minute," the boy shouted to his friends.

"Look, I'll give you a quarter if you tell me what you know about that house, the one over there," Reilly said to the youngster, pointing to Schroeder's one-time residence.

What happened next, Reilly did not want to happen. All of the ballplayers came over to see what the three men in suits and the army corporal wanted with their Curley. Reilly now needed a handful of coins to offer them in exchange for information about the house.

Curley was forthcoming: "That house had nobody living there for a long time, and all of a sudden, there's a bunch of cars and people going in and out of there."

"When was that?" Gannon asked.

"Early this week. You should have seen the big car that pulled in there, a Chrysler or Cadillac, I think."

"No, it wasn't a Caddy. It was a Packard, and the guy behind the wheel was in uniform, Georgie," the older of the boys said.

"Georgie's right," Curley said. "And remember, we kept telling him to move it so we could keep playing."

"Was he in an Army or Navy uniform, Curley?" Anderson asked, "Something like this man's uniform?" as he pointed toward Parker.

Georgie responded, "We ain't dumb, you know. We know the uniforms. I collect all of the military patches, you know. It was a gray uniform, and he had a gray hat. You know, like the guy, the Negro driver in the Charlie Chan's pictures."

"Did you see anyone else come in?" Reilly asked.

"Yeah, the other night, remember guys, they kept hitting the horn because we wouldn't move off the street. A short guy in glasses and two mean-looking big guys," Curley recalled.

"And they might've been cops, you know," Frankie, the only Negro among the six boys, said.

"Why do you say that?" Gannon asked.

"I know cops when I see 'em, but these cops may have been detective cops, you know, they didn't have uniforms," Frankie said as he looked at his teammates.

"I don't know if you're right, Frankie. The car did look official and all that. It had these markings on the side," Georgie said, and continued, "Are you guys cops?"

Reilly sent the boys back to their stickball game. He had given each of them a quarter, and they felt rich and totally excited. Reilly was grateful. For a dollar and a half, he had received valuable information.

For only a brief moment, he wondered if he could rely on what Curley had said about three men in the car. Who were the others with Reinhardt? And once more, what are they planning?

"Chief, are you thinking what I am thinking?" Gannon asked. The four made their way across the street and walked toward 128 Church Street.

"The Packard, the gray hat, the gray jacket. You bet I am, Jim," Reilly responded as he walked a pace in front of Anderson and Gannon, with Parker in the rear.

"General, some of the pieces of this puzzle are falling into place, and it's not looking good," Reilly concluded. He and the group made their way toward the front porch of Schroeder's house with his .38 revolver drawn and held next to his right thigh.

Gannon also had his service revolver drawn and said, "Miss Suckley owns a Packard. Her chauffeur wears a gray uniform when he is driving the car. The chauffeur, Hans Hildebrand, and his wife, Gertrude, have made a bunch of calls to Otto Reinhardt in New York City."

"Well, it makes sense what the kid said about the three guys in the car," Parker said, standing behind Gannon.

"What are you saying, Parker?" Reilly asked.

"It came over the radio in Jim's car. He had stepped away at the time. After the car was fished out of the river, a state trooper in Wappingers Falls reported that a car with New York City markings and with three men inside nearly ran into him four days ago."

"So, Corporal, when were you going to tell us about this?" Anderson, in his officer demeanor, asked of his subordinate.

"Sir, I just didn't think anything of it, until the kid mentioned it," Parker retorted sheepishly.

"One other thing to note in the puzzle, Mike," Gannon offered.

"What is it?" Reilly asked.

"The guy me and Parker met up in Clinton Corners, Radcliff Lindbergh. He told us Schroeder worked at the Hudson Valley Chemical Company in Beacon. Not really worked there, but was on some sort of college training deal."

"Isn't that the place that had the break-in, Mike?" Anderson asked.

"Sure was. We're going in, Anderson. Parker, stay behind us and—"

Reilly was interrupted by Gannon. "Boss, we don't have a search warrant. We just can't go in."

"Jim, the hell with a warrant. This is a matter of the utmost national security. For all we know, these people very well could be plotting something drastic against the country, or for that matter, to harm the president," Reilly said. He raised his leg and brought it crashing down on the front door of 128 Church Street.

Frankie, surrounded by his pals, exclaimed, "Holy cow, did you see that? They're cops all right. I told you guys."

* * *

To hike up to the top of Breakneck Ridge, there are three ways to go. From the north, south, and east, long winding paths make for an easy two-hour trek. For more adventurous and experienced climbers, the sheer three-hundred-foot cliff would be the most challenging. For New York State Troopers Sergeant Ryan and his partner, Trooper Fanelli, climbing the path to the top of the road tunnel was the best approach. From there, it would be a climb with hands on rocks and shrubs for support, bent over almost all the way up, but a faster route than taking the worn-down paths. The two Troop K troopers earlier had received orders to climb to the top of Breakneck Ridge and see if anything was out of the ordinary. Trooper Fanelli was a hundred feet ahead and wondered if the climb was too much for his sergeant, who was fifteen years his senior and weighed close to two-hundred-twenty pounds.

"Sarge, should I slow up for a while, let you catch your breath?" Fanelli asked. He looked down at his perspiring partner and at the same time took in the view of the U.S. Military Academy across the Hudson at West Point.

"Fanelli, if you ever want to make corporal in this troop, you'd watch what you say. And keep your eyes sharp. Look here, a handkerchief, and there appears to be blood on it."

"I'll come down, Sarge. Hold on."

"No," replied Ryan, "Let's keep going. We're almost there."

The last two-hundred yards up the mountain for Ryan were the most difficult. If the thorned bushes were not attacking him and his uniform, the footing underneath kept sliding away. He envied Fanelli's youth and energy.

Finally, standing in front of the water department's pump-house, dripping in sweat, Ryan and Fanelli were perplexed to have seen the metal door ajar that led into the pump room. The large Yale brass lock was on the ground. Instinctively they drew their Smith & Wesson .38s and went inside. The noise of the huge pumps was deafening, and so was the sound of tons of water being lifted from the valley and pulled up the mountain. The cast-iron pipes were large enough to drive a fair-sized pickup truck inside them.

Ryan was not pleased that such a crucial facility was not attended, no security. Worse, the door was left open. His bewilderment would be short-lived. Fanelli tapped him on his shoulder, pointed, and shouted, "Sarge, on the floor, by the control panel."

Guns still drawn, the troopers approached the short, bespectacled man in a dirty, brown three-piece suit. There was blood ever-so-slowly oozing from his neck. His eyes were closed, and his legs were drawn up under his body.

"Can this be the guy they're looking for?" Fanelli asked.

"It has to be. Who else can it be but Reinhardt?"

"Sarge, what do you think happened to him? Who the hell would cut his throat?"

"Fanelli, I don't know. But look, his arm, it's moving. The poor son of a bitch is still alive. How the hell can that be?" Ryan exclaimed.

"You're right, and he wants to tell us something," Fanelli said. He got down closer to Reinhardt and placed his ear close to Reinhardt's mouth. He heard faint words: "You've got…"

"I can't hear what he's saying, Sarge. His voice is shot, and there's too much noise in here," Fanelli said.

"Pick him up, and take him outside," Ryan ordered.

Each trooper took an arm and lifted the water department engineer up and away from the blood-stained concrete floor. Within seconds Reinhardt was outside and his body gently placed on the shaded grass, the unabated noise no longer surrounding them.

"Fanelli, get a handkerchief on that wound. Put pressure on it. What in God's name happened here? Who did this?"

"He's still whispering, Sarge. He wants to tell us something."

Reinhardt croaked, "You've got to stop them. They're going to do something bad."

"Who is going to do something?" Fanelli asked, his Stetson hat now off as he knelt next to Reinhardt.

Fanelli got no response as Reinhardt fell into unconsciousness.

"Who's going to do something?"

"Fanelli, you've got to get down to the car, get help up here and tell the barracks what we've found," Ryan ordered. "Also, let them know what we heard. Now move it, and I'll do all I can to keep this poor bastard alive."

Within seconds, Trooper Fanelli had disappeared on the same path he and Sergeant Ryan had used to ascend the ridge.

* * *

Fanelli had been gone at least ten minutes. Ryan kept asking Reinhardt to tell him more. "Who is going to do something?" he kept repeating to the pathetic engineer.

Suddenly he heard, "How can we help? What happened?" the tallest of three climbers asked as Ryan knelt over Reinhardt and applied pressure on the neck wound.

"Where the hell did you guys come from?" Ryan asked, dismissing immediately the notion that they had anything to do with the attack on Reinhardt. The climbers were dressed in military fatigues, helmets, and cartridge belts, and had M-1 carbines slung over their backs. Each climber was rolling up yards of climbing rope and climbing gear.

"West Point, Sergeant. I'm Captain Ritter, and my platoon is working their way up the cliffs," the six-foot-three blond, athletic soldier said to Ryan.

"Captain, I need your help. We've got to get this guy off this mountain and to Highland Hospital in Beacon. It's a matter of national security. Any chance you can lower him with your ropes?" Ryan asked.

"Can do. But first let Lieutenant Smyth here attend to his wound. The lieutenant is a doctor," Ritter said. Smyth quickly moved to the now-unconscious Reinhardt.

Smyth made an instinct evaluation of his patient and said, "Captain, this guy's in bad shape. He's hardly got any pulse, and he's cold. Appears like a lot of blood loss, and sir, he's going into shock. We've got to move him real soon, and even then I don't think he'll make it. God, he's hardly breathing."

As more of his platoon came over the top of the cliff, Captain Ritter immediately took charge of the scene once he had heard the urgency in Ryan's and Dr. Smyth's remarks. Eight hundred feet below, Fanelli was on his car's two-way radio and couldn't believe what he saw happening. A wire basket was being carefully lowered, attached to a half dozen ropes and guided by four soldiers at the bottom of the cliffs. *How did Sergeant Ryan pull this off?* Fanelli asked himself, when he heard the sound of an ambulance coming down Route 9D from Beacon. Captain Ritter had used his platoon's radio to send a critical message to West Point. It was from there that an urgent call for help was radioed to Highland Hospital in Beacon.

"Control, this is Fanelli. The subject is on the ground. Cancel the rescue party," Fanelli said into his radio mike.

Chapter Twenty-one

Agent John O'Neill had taken up his position at the edge of the Val-Kill pond dock. His back was to the water, and he did not wish to have the early-evening shade block his eyes as he watched his charge, FDR, holding court a short ten paces from him. The strapping agent was not at all pleased that the president had so many friends and advisors around him. The heated discussion that was taking place was also unnerving him.

Vice-President Henry Wallace had never been a close friend of Winston Churchill. He certainly never had the deep and warm relationship that his running mate had, nor did he want to. Wallace, as far back as 1939, when America's Neutrality Act was being debated in the Congress, felt there was too much interference by Churchill. And he had always believed that FDR was too involved and too cozy with the pompous British leader.

Wallace, along with the president's naval aide, Admiral Wilson Brown, Chief of Staff General George Marshall, Margaret Suckley, Mary Churchill, and Dr. McIntire, as well as another half dozen Anglo and American military officers, were all listening to the martini-sipping, cigar-smoking prime minister. What came next from the mouth of the stout leader of the British Empire was totally unexpected.

"Franklin, how do you feel about joint British-American citizenship? We are two peoples with such common roots, language, and heritage. With it, we can, once we bring this war to an end, dominate the world with Anglo-American democracy."

It was exactly what Roosevelt did not want to hear. His daily dealings with other Allied leaders, and especially de Gaulle and Stalin, would have been even more difficult than they already were if they had any inkling of what his friend was proposing.

Henry Wallace was on his feet. He was furious. He said, "With all due respect, Mr. Prime Minister, that is exactly the type of thinking that will wreck the alliance the president is trying to achieve."

"Oh now, Henry, don't get your dandruff up. I'm just putting out an idea I believe has great and lasting merit," Churchill responded, taking another puff on his cigar.

Agent O'Neill was wondering if the British leader might have had one too many martinis when General Marshall suggested, "Mr. Prime Minister, General Eisenhower is putting together the coalition for Operation Overlord, and General Graves has thousands of scientists engaged in the Manhattan Project. At this time, I can assure you we can't afford to have any such statement on world dominance."

The mention of General Eisenhower, the supreme allied commander, only provoked Churchill to continue to dominate the discussion. Only a few hours before he had heard from FDR that Field Marshall Bernard Montgomery was not going to be the leader of the invasion of Europe, news that did not sit well with Churchill. As far as he was concerned, Eisenhower had never been in combat. Montgomery had, in all of North Africa and in Sicily. FDR was ready for Churchill's retort and had made it clear to him. The invasion needed someone who could pull together almost two million soldiers and sailors from a half-dozen countries. Montgomery was not the one who could orchestrate this mammoth undertaking. FDR was emphatic about having Eisenhower, not the pompous Montgomery; he had told Churchill his position was not negotiable. Churchill was not in a position to argue once his friend made his case. He knew his cause for Montgomery was a lost one. It was time to move on and plan the invasion.

Henry Morgenthau, drink in hand, and wearing a three-piece suit that appeared not exactly the attire to be wearing on this sultry August evening, had joined the circle and commented: "Mr. Churchill, we must stay focused on what is in front of us. And when we defeat Hitler, we must do everything to get into our hands their atomic bomb research and scientists. They cannot be sent to the Japs or, for that matter, be captured by the Soviets."

"Gentlemen, gentlemen, you are beating up on our guests. There will be plenty of time to discuss these matters. Now let's hear from Daisy. She has a presentation to make," Roosevelt said. He raised his glass and smiled toward his friend, Winston.

Agent O'Neill was now more relaxed as he watched Margaret Suckley present her book, *The True Story of Fala*, to Mary Churchill. Little did she know at the time that the mother of Fala lay dead in the root cellar of her estate.

* * *

"Nothing in the cellar but dirt and dust, Mike," General Anderson said as he came through the door of the cellar at 128 Church Street.

Reilly and Gannon were searching through the furnished house, looking for the slimmest of evidence that this was indeed Schroeder's old hideout, when Gannon shouted out, "This is the place, boss."

"How do you know?" Reilly asked. Anderson stood next to him in the kitchen.

"Look here, near the wall phone, the number on the wall," Gannon said, pointing to the telephone number written on the beige floral wallpaper.

"What about it, Jim?" Reilly asked.

"It's the number for the New York City Water Department, Mulberry 7-6000. I've called it enough times."

Reilly was about to respond when Parker entered through the back kitchen door holding in each hand two large car-door seals. "Look what I found in the garage," Parker said.

"Good work, Corporal," Anderson said as he read the seals: "City of New York Water Department."

"John, did you find out who the owner of the house is?" Reilly asked General Anderson as he took one of the seals from Parker.

"I was about to tell you, Mike, when you were kicking down the front door. Werner and Thelma Reischman, German immigrants. They lease the house out and work as cooks on Cape Cod from June to early September, I'm told."

His mind racing, and only half paying attention to Anderson, Reilly barked an order to Gannon: "Jim, call this in and have the lab boys comb through every bit of this place. And so things are legal and on the up-and-up, get me a search warrant. That judge who the boss likes, Judge Hand, will issue it."

As Gannon exited through the back door, the other three men moved into the living room, which was cluttered with newspapers, crumpled sheets of writing paper, and ash trays full of expired cigarettes. Earlier, they had concluded that nothing of value was obtained when they had rummaged through the three upstairs bedrooms.

"Parker, you and the general here go through every one of those crumpled papers. There's got to be something that can tell us what Schroeder and Reinhardt are up to. And maybe we can find out who the others are," Reilly said as he used a poker to shift through ashes in the parlor's fireplace. The search for information went on for fifteen minutes, when Gannon rushed through the parlor's porch door, out of breath. He shouted, "We can stop looking for Reinhardt."

"What do you mean?" Reilly asked, still on his knees.

His hands rested on the parlor's drop-leaf table as Gannon explained: "When I made the call for the lab boys, I was told Reinhardt is in a hospital over in Beacon. He was found, barely alive, by a couple of troopers on top of Breakneck Ridge—with his throat slashed."

"Is he going to make it?" Parker asked meekly, wondering if he should have said anything.

"Don't know, but from what little I got, he is near death," Gannon said, regaining his composure.

"That changes everything," Reilly said, joining Gannon at the table.

"How? What are you thinking, Mike?" Anderson asked.

"We've got to get Reinhardt to tell us what the hell is going on and who tried to kill him," Reilly said.

"One other thing, chief," Gannon said.

"What is it? And it better be good," Reilly said, staring down at the table, deep in thought.

"The troopers were able to hear Reinhardt say that something bad is about to happen."

"That's it. Jim, I want you to get over to Beacon and find out what you can from Reinhardt. Don't take any bullshit from the docs if they say you can't speak to him. You got that?"

"Yes, sir."

"What I can't figure out is why someone would want to kill Reinhardt. And his throat was slashed—it sounds professional. Who else would have known he was up at the pumphouse?" Reilly mused.

"Could it be that it was one of his own, someone he was helping to get up here?" Anderson said.

"You may not be far off, John. Could be Reinhardt's usefulness was over? I just don't know," Reilly said.

"John, I'm going to drop you off at Springwood. I want you to get all you can on who the Reischmans are. We must know if they are in any way part of whatever it is that Reinhardt is talking about. And Parker, you've got the house. Wait for the lab guys, and while you're waiting, keep searching for evidence."

"Where will you be, boss?" Gannon asked as he made his way out the side door.

"I'm going to Wilderstein. I want to ask the Hildebrands some questions, and they better not try to mislead me, if they know what's good for them."

"Sir," Parker said quietly.

"What is it, Parker?" Anderson snapped.

"How does one get some chow around here?"

"Can't blame you for asking, son. Slip one of those kids a quarter."

"There's a sandwich shop down the street," Reilly said. He went out the front door wondering what was about to happen. Were his president and his guest in imminent danger?

* * *

Even the Oberst Colonel Albert Krupp would have acknowledged that the conditions in the root cellar at Wilderstein were
unbearable. He had never experienced anything like it in his
twelve years in the Wehrmacht. His thirty-six hours hiding in a
horse stable in Portugal while waiting to kidnap the Duke of
Windsor in 1940 were at least bearable compared to the dark,
damp, dingy root cellar. But it was the lack of fresh air that was
the most uncomfortable part of their ordeal, not helped by the
fact that any need to relieve oneself was restricted to a pail in the
corner. He felt that, in some ways, the horrible conditions trig-
gered Berger to go after Schroeder. Berger was an animal, as far
as Krupp was concerned, and the root cellar was his cage. And
not unlike an animal in a zoo's cage, anything or anybody near
him was fair game.

Two hours earlier, after he had heard Miss Suckley was going
back to Val-Kill, he decided to get Schroeder and Berger out of
the wretched hole. Over at the boathouse, Berger had been relentless in his animosity toward Schroeder, and his disdain for
Krupp was not letting up, either. He still resented that Krupp
was chosen to lead the mission over him.

Five minutes after entering the boathouse, they once again
checked their equipment and supplies. Krupp was convinced
Berger's neurotic temperament would somehow, somewhere, interfere with the mission. Yet, at this late hour he had no other
choices; he somehow had to deal with it. He said," We can't be
here for too long. In a few minutes, we must get back to the root
cellar."

"Herr Oberst, the key is in the boat's ignition. Will it be there
tomorrow night?" Schroeder asked, cleaning her Luger.

"I had asked the Hildebrands about that, and they said they
always leave the key in the boat. And that's where I moved it after
Hans gave it to me the other day," Krupp responded. He was
folding up his map of Dutchess County and studying the charts
of the Hudson River he had picked up earlier from Miss Suckley's
boat. He needed to memorize them. There would be no time tomorrow night. And the rock outcroppings in the river as well as

its currents were going to test his skills—not to mention the patrol boats operated by the Coast Guard that guarded the Hudson two miles west, south, and north of FDR's Springwood.

"You trust those two too much, Krupp, and they easily could betray us," Berger said. He assembled the workings of his machine pistol.

Ignoring the treacherous Berger, Krupp asked Schroeder, "Have you covered up where you buried the dog?"

"No one will know where it is, Herr Oberst," Schroeder replied.

"Krupp, don't ignore me. I'm telling you the old couple will somehow betray our mission, and you must do something now."

"Like what, Berger, kill them?" Schroeder snapped.

"Yes, kill them and put them with the dog."

"Berger, you are a sick bastard. Do you know that?" Schroeder said as she snapped the bolt home on her pistol and stood up.

"Look, you bitch, you're just as sick. You slit the throat of the old guard. I'm willing to admit I'm an assassin, why aren't you?"

Schroeder lunged at Berger. She let her Luger fall and yanked her dagger from its scabbard. Her dagger was at his throat. She was about to push it when her arm was yanked back by Krupp. Berger's eyes were white with fear. His smile was his way of showing he had no fear—though he did. It was Krupp's instant reaction that saved his life, and he knew it.

Krupp, still holding onto Schroeder's arm, used his free hand to remove the dagger and place it back in Schroeder's scabbard. "Of all the people the SS could have sent on this mission, I get you two. Do either of you realize what is at stake here? We are about to destroy the two leaders of the Fatherland's greatest enemies. And you want to destroy each other. Why don't I just let you do it?" He stared at Schroeder and Berger.

"Herr Oberst, he is a swine, and I'll kill him if you don't keep him away from me," Schroeder said as she wiped her lips with her sleeve.

"No you won't, Hauptsturmführer Schroeder. You will do your job as you were trained to do. And that is an order. I will deal with the Strandartenführer, do you understand?" Krupp said.

Berger got to his feet, realizing he was seeing Krupp as he had not seen him before.

Krupp wanted peace between his two officers so he could provide Berger with the information that Schroeder had shared with him the night before. It was about how they were going to make their way back to Germany. With the unplanned death of Reinhardt, Krupp's plans for after their mission were completely changed. He had developed a revised exit plan and had shared it with Schroeder, but not with Berger. Calm was slowly taking over the chaotic scene.

"Herr Berger, what was the most difficult aspect of the rescue of Mussolini? And was it the same with the aborted attempt on extracting the Duke and Duchess of Windsor?"

"How to escape. It always is," the sullen Berger responded.

"Exactly," Krupp agreed. "And for good reason. There will be much confusion and chaos tomorrow, and we need to go over the escape from here and from Cold Spring."

Schroeder had her back to the two officers. She was gazing down the river toward the Poughkeepsie railroad bridge that linked the town of Highland with the city of Poughkeepsie.

"Tell Berger about your landlord, Schroeder. Tell him about our comrades, the Reischmans. And do it on the way back to the house," Krupp ordered.

* * *

For Thelma and Werner Reischman, their annual three-month stay on Cape Cod was always eagerly anticipated. The summer of 1943 was no exception. It was their fifth summer working as cooks at the posh Irish-American Travel Lodge in Dennis Port. The thirty-two-year-olds had spent most of their youth in Chicago. Lake Michigan for them was not anything like the Nantucket Sound or the Atlantic Ocean. The gray weather-beaten shingle houses of Hyannisport, with their well-tended gardens, were for them a world away from the teeming tenements of Chicago's south side.

Their jobs on the Cape also allowed them to escape the heat and humidity that always seemed to get trapped in their other residence at 128 Church Street in Poughkeepsie. Their time spent in the kitchens at the travel lodge was also a respite from the steam, noise, and smells of the huge galley at Vassar College, where they toiled from late September to June.

"It will take us eight hours, Thelma, if there is little traffic," Werner responded to his wife's question as he steered the borrowed Ford coupe west on Cape Cod's two-lane Route 6.

"We should have told Mr. O'Malley we were leaving, Thelma. He's been good to us. Not many people would hire Germans, you know."

"I left him a note. I put it on his desk. I wrote him that your Aunt Louise had suddenly passed away in New York City, and that after the funeral we'd be back on Sunday night. He's got the FitzGeralds to do the cooking while we're gone. What else would you want me to do?" Thelma said. She poured coffee from her vacuum bottle into a small metal cup.

"You're right. We have a long journey, and we must get to Cold Spring on time."

"Why do you think Fraulein Schroeder was so impatient in wanting us to meet her in Cold Spring?"

"I don't know. But ever since she moved into the house, I felt something strange about her. You know the girls at the college. She's not like any of them," Werner said.

"Werner, do you know what day this is?"

"Yes, I can't get it out of my mind. It was one year ago when the government of Roosevelt killed Cousin Herbert in the electric chair. How could I forget?"

Chapter Twenty-two

As she had done on many occasions, Gertrude Hildebrand had completed the last of the dinner place settings in the formal dining room at Wilderstein. The sixteen-foot mahogany table was covered with a brilliantly hand-embroidered tablecloth made from the finest cottons of India. It had been a gift from Franklin Roosevelt to his dear friend when she first started to read to him in 1922. He had received it in 1916 from the U.S. Fleet admiral during one of his naval inspections in the Mediterranean. Eleanor was never happy about her husband's generosity to Margaret Suckley, and less so over the gift of the rare tablecloth.

The table's china and crystal, all fourteen sets, had come from Miss Suckley's family home on New York City's Madison Avenue. It was a residence her father had maintained until it was lost along with many of the family's possessions in the financial panic of 1883, and again during the Great Depression. Margaret had wanted the china, silver, and crystal saved. Even when her brother, Robert, was losing the family fortune by being on the wrong side in trading Reichsmarks, she kept the heirlooms from him. She refused to feed his insatiable desire to sell family possessions to offset his losses.

Gertrude Hildebrand was near exhaustion as she glanced over the fully dressed table. She was wondering what she might have overlooked when Hans came in and said, "Gertie, they're back in the cellar. The two young ones went at each other. I saw all of it while I was collecting these flowers."

"Please, Hans. I need to think. Put the flowers in the four vases I set out on the sideboard," Gertrude said. She placed three pairs of large Waterford crystal candleholders strategically on the table.

"Gertie, you are too old to be doing this any more. You look so tired. You and I are doing the work of twenty servants. That's what I overheard Madam Suckley tell Mrs. Rutherford. There were over twenty in help here for a long time. And now there are two: me and you," Hans said. He cut the stems on the roses and gently placed them into the vases.

"Hans, I'm all right. We must get the table set. Miss Tully called, and the staff at Springwood will be preparing the supper. Were you able to start the old roadster? It hasn't been out of the garage in two years, I'd say."

"I only had trouble finding the petrol. I siphoned it from the tractors. I think we have just enough to get us to Bennington, Vermont. And Gertie, as long as we are far enough away from this place, I don't care if we run out."

Gertie placed a finger to her lips. "Hans," she whispered, "You mustn't say anything. They may hear us. Just what were they fighting about?" Gertrude asked. She swept her hand over the tablecloth to smooth out a wrinkle.

Hans whispered, "When does Uncle Ferdinand think we're coming? Was he pleased we're coming to visit him? I told him to expect—"

Hans abruptly stopped, and Gertrude followed his gaze. She was startled to see Berger at the cellar door. He had three containers in his hands, and as always his eyes were full of rage and contempt.

"How long must we wait for some water? Just what are you whispering about? From now on I want one of you to stay in the cellar with the rest of us," Berger said. He pushed the canteens into Hans's chest.

"We can't do that. We must be here. The madam will be suspicious. She already is," Gertrude pleaded.

"You low-life swines will do what you are ordered. Make no mistake. Otherwise, I'll kill you myself. I don't trust either of you, especially now that we don't have the leverage of your mother and father, Fräulein Hildebrand."

"What about mama and papa? Are they safe? We were told that they were," she questioned the arrogant Nazi.

"They're safe all right. They, along with hundreds of other Germans, were killed in an air raid not long ago. Now you see why I don't trust you to keep our mission secret, but if you don't, you'll join them."

Berger, who stood close to six-foot-two, towered over the housekeeper and the gardener. His face was drenched with sweat, and so was his shirt. His clenched fist was the size of a hand-held sledge hammer, and he raised it to bring down on the dining room sideboard. He turned and saw Krupp enter the room.

"Just what the hell is going on here? Berger, what have you said to these people? And why is Fräulein Hildebrand crying?" Krupp demanded.

"I want one of them in the cellar. I just don't trust them," Berger responded with a scowl.

"I'll give the orders here, Strandartenführer. Is that clear?" Krupp barked, glaring at Berger.

* * *

"Mr. Gannon, if you want to get anything from this fellow, you'd better hurry. He doesn't look like he's going to make it," Sergeant Ryan of the New York State Police said, escorting Jim Gannon down the first-floor corridor of Beacon's Highland Hospital.

Gannon was visibly annoyed, having lost precious time changing a flat tire on the way from Poughkeepsie on U.S. Route 9. The normally thirty-minute trip took more than an hour. All the while, Otto Reinhardt was inching toward death in the hospital's emergency room. His body had received four pints of blood, and the transfusion appeared not to have any effect. Two doctors and three nurses were working feverishly over him, preparing another transfusion, when Gannon entered the room and was immediately struck by the smell of ether and iodine.

"Sir, you have no business here. You must leave at once," demanded a slim, white-uniformed, and masked nurse, who was carrying a metal tray of surgical instruments to the operating table.

Gannon recalled Mike Reilly's last instruction: "Don't take any crap from the docs that you can't speak to him." He moved closer to the patient and the team of medical people and announced, "Let me make one thing clear to all of you. We have evidence that this man is part of a large plot to do harm to the country and possibly the president of the United States and the prime minister of Great Britain. I am a United States Secret Service agent, and yes, I do have business here. Is that clear enough?"

"Well, agent, whatever your name is, that is perfectly clear," said the attending doctor, who never took his eyes off the patient. "And if you insist on staying in here, nurse Grinwald will give you a surgical mask, gloves, and a gown. How can we be of any assistance to you?"

"The name is James Gannon, sir. And this here patient is Otto Reinhardt, a fifth columnist and a key suspect in a conspiracy," Gannon said. He allowed the young blonde nurse to dress him in surgical room attire.

"So what exactly has he done that brings the Secret Service into our small hospital, Agent Gannon?" the doctor asked.

"Officially, it is classified. All I can say is he is a key suspect. Is there a chance I can talk to him?"

"Well, if you must, then you better get up here and stand at the head of the table. He's been slipping in and out of consciousness, and when he does say something, it is mostly incoherent," the physician said crankily.

Placing his gloved hands on the side of the operating table, Gannon leaned over and whispered into the dazed patient's ear, "Reinhardt, what did you mean that something bad is going to happen? When is it to happen? Where is it to happen?"

Gannon straightened up and took a step back. His eyes were on Reinhardt's face. He was hoping his lips would move from under the oxygen mask. "Can he hear me, doctor?"

"I believe he can. Just keep asking, and if he moves his lips, we will remove the mask. But you won't have long to listen. He needs the oxygen."

"Otto, who did this to you? Where are they now?" Gannon continued.

Precious minutes went by, and Gannon received no response. The young nurse kept calling out the heart rate and blood pressure: "120 rising, 100 over 60; 130 and 90 over 60, doctor."

"Reinhardt, you're dying. You need to tell me who did this to you. Can you hear me?" desperately Gannon pleaded.

"I think he's trying to speak, Agent Gannon. Go ahead, place you ear by his mouth, and I'll take away the oxygen, but you have less than thirty seconds."

"There's eight of us, it was Ber—they're going to destroy the—and hurt—they're staying in—" Reinhardt gasped.

"Reinhardt, who's Ber? And what are they going to destroy? Who are they going to hurt? Otto, tell me. I need to know. You were trying to tell me where they are staying. I need—" Gannon was almost shouting into Reinhardt's ear when nurse Grinwald interrupted.

"The readings are flat, doctor. We are losing him," she announced.

"You must stand back, Agent Gannon. He's going fast, if he's not gone already," the younger doctor said, and he replaced the oxygen mask.

Gannon took a half-dozen steps back from the table as he watched the doctors use their hands in attempting to revive Reinhardt's heart. For three minutes, and with perspiration flowing from their foreheads, the medical team continued. Suddenly they stopped.

"He's gone, Mr. Gannon. There was only so much we could have done. He had lost over four pints of blood by the time he had come in here," the senior doctor said apologetically.

"You did your best, doc. You all did. Thank you. I have one more thing to ask: that you speak not a word of this to anyone. The Secret Service will come back and take care of the remains. Any questions?"

There were none. Gannon left the room and went immediately to the hospital administrator's office. He wanted the patient's death suppressed and no bureaucratic mixups. He had to telephone Reilly. It was no longer just Reinhardt and Schroeder. There were six more, and who were they? He asked himself as he wrote out orders for the hospital about what to do with Reinhardt's body. And all along he wondered what more he could have learned from Reinhardt if he had not had to stop and change a tire.

Gannon was about to leave the hospital's door when he heard his name.

"Are you Agent Gannon?" asked an elderly woman in a gray uniform with a small gold pin near her left shoulder.

"I am."

"You just got a message that said you must go to Poughkeepsie and get Mr. Parker and proceed to Clinton Corners. More to come. That was all, sir."

"Thank you, madam." Gannon replied politely.

Now what? He quickly walked away to his car.

* * *

A late afternoon thunderstorm suddenly broke loose as Gannon and Parker darted from Gannon's car to the large oak doors at Radcliff Lindbergh's Clinton Corners estate house. The oppressive August humidity was about to disappear in the violence of a storm. Gannon banged on the doors' brass horseshoe knocker. Parker thought Gannon looked awful, and it was not due to the drenching rain that had caught them before they could make their dash across the courtyard.

Two hours earlier, Gannon had watched Otto Reinhardt die, but not before he incoherently revealed some awful things. And they became more terrifying on the ride from Poughkeepsie after Gannon had picked up Parker.

As Gannon raced through the back roads of Poughkeepsie and later onto New York State's winding Route 82, Parker read to him General Anderson's message about the Reischmans that Parker had received at Schroeder's house. Gannon mentally connected the dots as he dangerously maneuvered his coupe around a coal truck on the narrow two-lane road.

Parker told him the Reischmans once worked as servants on the estate of Radcliff Lindbergh III. It was Lindbergh who was instrumental in getting them hired as cooks at Vassar College. And it was Lindbergh who had taken back a mortgage from the Reischmans so they could acquire the house at 128 Church Street.

"It's you two again. Now what is it you want, may I ask?" the old man said as he opened the heavy door ever so little, still dressed in a silk bathrobe and slippers despite the time of day.

"We have some questions for you, Mr. Lindbergh. It appears you were not all that clean with us on our last visit." Gannon pushed in the door, almost knocking the unsteady man to the floor.

Stepping back to avoid falling and placing both of his hands on his cane, Lindbergh said, "Now listen here, young man. Do you know who I am? Are you aware that I have people in high places, only a telephone call away?"

Parker, now inside the house and standing alongside Gannon in the large, oval, marbled entry hall, said, "Look, old man, we really don't give a shit as to who you know. Why didn't you tell us about the Reis—"

Gannon interrupted as he saw Lindbergh becoming flustered. "Mr. Lindbergh, I'm not going to make any excuses for my associate here. I'm here for answers, and for your sake, they'd better be truthful and complete. Do you understand me, sir?"

"You are here about Warner and Thelma. The Reischmans, I suppose. May I sit down here, please?"

"Please do, and you're correct. Why didn't you tell me and Parker about them when we were here before?" Gannon demanded.

"You didn't ask, I suppose."

"That's pure rubbish, and you know it," Parker said angrily. He moved toward the elderly man in a threatening way.

"Enough, Corporal," Gannon cautioned. "Well, Mr. Lindbergh, what do you know about the Reischmans?"

Clutching his cane with both hands, his knuckles almost white, Lindbergh said, "The Reischmans did indeed work here ever since they came from Germany. I don't know exactly when. They were most outstanding in their work, and they were exceptionally loyal and dedicated. True Germans. However, they needed more money and better living quarters than just being on the second floor of the gatehouse."

Parker, taking in every word, said to himself, *What a cheapskate. With such an enormous house, at least a half dozen bedrooms, wasn't it so typical to put the help in the barn.*

Continuing, after Gannon brought him a glass of water, Lindbergh said, "Warner Reischman's mother's brother—in other words, his uncle—had a son, Warner's first cousin, whose name was Herbert Haupt. A boy in his early twenties who died last year. Do I have to give you the details, Agent Gannon, or will that suffice?"

"I know the details, sir. Again, why didn't you tell us this before? Why didn't you tell us that Haupt was Reischmans's cousin as well as his boyhood friend?" Gannon asked politely, ever so much annoying Corporal Parker, who preferred a more vigorous method of interrogation.

The old man had drunk most of the water. In doing so, he requested they move into the adjoining walnut-paneled library so he could obtain his heart medicine and take his pills with the remaining water.

Parker entered the room last and was immediately taken aback by its grandeur. The floor-to-ceiling bookshelves were impressive, and even more so was the fact that the upper shelves were accessed by climbing a ten-foot ladder that on its upper end locked into tracks to circle the room.

The room's deep red leather chairs and twin sofas accented the plush beige carpet. A model bi-wing plane took up the center of a partner's huge desk next to the room's bay window. A brass plaque screwed to the plane's stand read: *To Uncle Radcliff, your loving nephew, Charles, Pilot, The Spirit of St. Louis—1927.*

Lindbergh gestured with his cane to the two red-leather captain's chairs in front of his desk. Gannon and Parker obliged, and Lindbergh, sitting now on his side of the mammoth desk, said,

"Mr. Gannon, I may be a lot of things to you and the corporal here, but I am not a traitor to my country. Yes, I have disagreed with Mr. Roosevelt's policies and those of his Jewish backers, but so do many other Americans."

"Mr. Lindbergh—" Gannon began.

"Please, sir, let me finish, if you don't mind. I served this country for many years. I was with the president's cousin in San Juan and later served in Manila, in 1898."

"Sir, I don't mean to interrupt you, and we have not called you a traitor, nor do we think of you as one. But you must admit that you were hesitant, reluctant, if you will, in telling us about the Reischmans. Am I right?"

"Gentlemen, you need to hear me out. Exactly one year ago, this month, in Washington, D.C., Warner Reischman's cousin was electrocuted as a spy. He was only twenty-three years old." Lindbergh never raised his eyes from his glass-covered desk.

"What the hell is he talking about, Jim? And what does that have anything to do with us?" Parker asked Gannon.

"Tell him, Mr. Gannon, if you would."

"Haupt was born in Stettin, Germany, and came to the states with his mother when he was about six years old. His father was already here. They lived in or near Chicago. Haupt became a U.S. citizen at the same time his parents did. He left the states just before the war broke out in 1941 and floated around Mexico and Central America, and he had spent some time in Japan. And about a year later he was recruited, early last year—I don't know exactly when—to be part of a German sabotage team made up of former Americans then living in Germany."

"It sounds just like what we do, I suppose," Parker said, interrupting Gannon, who was not exceptionally pleased about Parker's loose comment.

Gannon continued as if he hadn't heard. "Haupt, along with seven others, divided into two teams of four who came into the U.S. in June at Long Island and Jacksonville, Florida, for one purpose: to meet up in New York City and Washington and blow things up. In other words, sabotage America's war industries."

"How were they found out?" Parker asked, thoroughly fascinated by Gannon's replay of what was secretly known as Operation Pastorius.

"Their leader, Dasch, once here in the states, called into the FBI. So he and his fellow spy, Berger, who were cooperative, were not executed. The rest were, in August of '42 in Washington, D.C. Is that about it, Mr. Lindbergh?"

"Yes, and the Reischmans were devastated, to be sure."

"Let's go back to Schroeder, sir, and her connection with them. What can you tell us? And hopefully this time we can have all of it," Gannon commanded.

Chapter Twenty-three

Mike Reilly was about to present to General Anderson his information on the missing OSS trainee, Kathe Schroeder, and the news of one dead New York City Water Department assistant chief engineer.

Reilly met Anderson at Springwood after the general had passed on instructions to Corporal Parker to have Gannon and Parker visit Radcliff Lindbergh. He wanted to meet privately with the general. Reilly had heard many good things about Anderson, not the least being the general's ability to take a series of apparently unrelated facts and piece them together logically and comprehensively. He was known as a good puzzle-solver, and Reilly believed he had one big, complex puzzle that needed to be solved quickly.

Only moments before, Reilly had heard from agent O'Neill that the president and his party were beginning to break up at Val-Kill. The picnic had run much later than anyone expected, in part because the president wanted his long-time trusted advisor, Steve Early, to be in on any of the planning with the prime minister. Also, FDR felt there was no reason why Early shouldn't be part of the celebration. Churchill was celebrating his thirty-fifth wedding anniversary, but his wife Clementine was not around. She was on a train due in from Montreal later in the evening.

Nestled in the back room of the U.S. Secret Service's quarters, on the second floor of the carriage barn at Springwood, Reilly was beginning to make notations on a small wooden easel that held a three-by-three-foot pad: "Let's see what it is that we know so far. Kathe Schroeder, a German-born immigrant, Vassar College graduate, and a trainee at the OSS camp, suddenly ups and leaves Camp Greentop. Question: why now?"

"And along with a bag full of high explosives, I might add, Mike," Anderson said as he sat at the oak desk watching Reilly write.

"Right. And then we got this guy Reinhardt, another foreigner, and an engineer with the water department. And we fish his car out of the river, but not before we find the car's decals at Schroeder's house. And when and how did Schroeder and Reinhardt connect? And above all, why?" Reilly asked as he wrote.

Now up from his chair and holding a cup of coffee, Anderson added, "And Reinhardt knows the servants up at Wilderstein, Miss Suckley's place. Based on the calls between them. What a coincidence."

"It's more than a coincidence. Jesus, and I was supposed to go there and meet with the Hildebrands. Let's get this done, and we'll go up there tonight."

"Getting back to your chart, Mike, now Reinhardt is dead, murdered. What do you make of it?"

Reilly moved away from the easel, leaned with both hands on the desk, looked up at his chart, and added, "Let's not forget there is a security guard found murdered at the chemical plant in Beacon."

"Do you believe that is connected in any way?" Anderson asked.

"That's just it. I don't know for sure, but the plant is only a couple of miles from where Reinhardt had his throat slashed. And the guard had his throat slashed as well. There're connected all right. And we know that a heap of bomb-making stuff plus some poisons were taken. And we know Schroeder had interned there while she was at Vassar."

"Mike, there are two things still puzzling to me."

"Just two. You're lucky, general," Reilly said half-sarcastically.

"Seriously, Mike."

"I'm sorry. It's just that I lost so much valuable time having to be at that goddamn party for that overbearing prime minister," Reilly said.

"Not a problem, but what about Miss Suckley's car showing up on Church Street and the fact that the Reischmans own the house and rented it to Schroeder?"

"This is no coincidence, John. There's at least a half-dozen people involved here, all, in one way or another, connected, and all German immigrants. The question or questions we should be asking: Are there more, and what are they up to?"

"It's coming together for me, Mike. They have explosives and chemicals. They are going to blow something up or poison and infect something, or both. I don't know the others, but I know Schroeder. She is brilliant, cunning, and deadly with explosives. Christ, we trained her, and her background is in chemistry," Anderson exclaimed.

"It's not your fault, John," Reilly said.

"And another thing. She's been taught to be elusive. But everything you've said and noted, Mike, makes me believe something is going to happen. Those people are all here, so it's going to happen in this area. Mike, just think for a minute. We know these people have been working between here or just north of here in Wilderstein and the pumphouses at Cold Spring. They got poisons and explosives. It's got to be sabotage of the water system and possible disruption of the summit between the president and the prime minister. Can there be anything else? But where and when? And all along, the Hildebrands had to be sending the president's timetable to them."

"Where the hell is Gannon? And do we know where the Reischmans are?" Reilly asked, wishing he had not heard what Anderson had just said.

* * *

Their eight-hour journey from Dennis Port on Cape Cod to Cold Spring on the Hudson was not going as planned for Thelma and Werner Reischman. They had wanted to be in Cold Spring by early evening, and they planned to stay at the Hudson Valley

Tourist Cabins for the night. At the tourist cabin, they would be passing the time before the next evening's rendezvous with Schroeder.

The Reischmans were not able to travel the Bourne Bridge across the Cape Cod Canal as quickly as they had thought. A vintage pick-up truck that had been loaded with vegetables and was on its way to the Boston market broke an axle and spilled its cargo onto the entrance to the four-lane bridge. It took the Reischmans and their fellow motorists almost two hours of waiting before they allowed the drivers to pass the now-spoiling vegetables strewn along the road.

And now they were in for another delay. The Reischmans were parked on the shoulder of U.S. Route 202. A military policeman on a motorcycle had signaled them to pull off to the side. Other civilians' cars and trucks also were on the road's shoulder, the drivers wondering how long a convoy it was going to be.

They had obeyed, and they waited. Darkness had fallen several hours previously. What seemed like an eternity to the German couple was less than fifteen minutes when the last of the military trucks hauling tanks, howitzers, and Jeeps passed. The last vehicle in the military convoy was the largest tow truck they had ever seen.

The Reischmans, along with their fellow travelers, got back on the highway as soon as the convoy had passed them by. And an hour later, they thought their journey would come to an abrupt stop. A police car's red light had commanded them to pull over again.

The burly, red-faced, uniformed state trooper took his time to approach Werner Reischman. He glanced at the Ford coupe's dirty windshield and asked, "May I see your license and the vehicle's registration, please?" in what sounded like a deep Irish brogue.

"Sir, we were not speeding I assure you," Reischman said, rather meekly.

"You're Germans, I see," the trooper said as Reischman handed over the car's papers and his license.

"Is that going to be a problem?" Reischman fired back.

"No, but what is a problem is the car has a C ration sticker, so what are you doing on the road with this car? Where are you going? That could be a problem and a violation of gas rationing regulations," the trooper said, never looking at Reischman as he read the information on the papers.

Werner and Thelma were aware of the laws on gasoline rationing as well as the rules that only certain professions had the freedom to use an automobile at any time. They were not in any one of the approved professions or occupations.

But what they did have was a letter from the pastor of St. John's Lutheran Church on 86th Street and First Avenue in New York City, noting that the Reischmans would be attending Thelma's Aunt Louise's funeral, an exception to the rules of restricted driving. The letter was a forgery. St. John's Lutheran Church on 86th Street in New York City did not exist. And the Reischmans were hoping their inquisitor had not lived in New York City.

The trooper read the letter for the second time and was still skeptical. "This here letter says you're going to New York City, and that you're from Cape Cod."

"That's correct, officer," said Thelma, the author of the forged letter.

"So why is it you didn't drive down U.S. 1 in Massachusetts and Rhode Island to get to New York? Why this way, and now here in Danbury?"

After what appeared to be an eternity of hesitation, Thelma finally said, "As you can see from my husband's license, sir, we reside and work most of the year in Poughkeepsie, New York. And we know the highways into New York better from that city."

"Well, if you ask me, you're going a roundabout way and wasting gasoline. I hope that you got plenty of coupons. You'll need them," the trooper said. He handed Werner back his papers.

Attempting, as best he could, to steady his shaking hands, Werner retrieved his documents.

"You can go. And by the way, I'm sorry for your troubles," the trooper apologized. He turned back to his car, its red light still swirling and lighting up the night. The trooper watched as the

Reischmans' car pulled back onto the highway. He made some notes on his pad.

* * *

Darkness had begun to fall on the thirty-two rolling acres at Wilderstein. It provided the uninvited guests with sufficient cover to move from the damp, poorly lit, and smelly root cellar to the estate's boathouse.

Colonel Krupp was relieved that the time to move from the house had finally arrived. He had been well aware of the living conditions of his colleagues for the last forty-eight hours—intolerable, even for these hardened German agents. Nothing they had experienced in prior covert operations had prepared them to inhabit a root cellar.

For Krupp, the physical conditions were far less a concern than having Kathe Schroeder and Ludwig Berger cooped up with the vegetables in the same twelve-by-twelve-foot space. He had known his fellow agents were beyond the breaking point. Their resentment and hatred of each other were intensifying by the hour. He felt it would be only a few more hours of confinement before one of them would kill the other.

Repeatedly, and ever since he became aware that Berger would be part of the mission, Krupp kept asking himself why the German High Command failed to recognize the animus that Berger held toward both Schroeder and himself. Krupp had believed that Berger's morbid suspiciousness and his neurotic temperament could not possibly have been overlooked by German security when they put together this mission. Once again, it had to have been Berger's rescue of Benito Mussolini that convinced his superiors he was the best to fill the mission's third position.

Miss Suckley's father's boathouse stood by itself two hundred yards beyond the main house and carriage barn. The ornate two-story structure had the capacity to store four to six boats when it wasn't holding ice harvested from the Hudson. The ice-harvesting practice had been discontinued years earlier. Krupp's second-floor vantage point on the building's east side gave him a sweeping view of the property back to the main house. From this perch, he had seen Hans Hildebrand limping behind an iron wheelbarrow as he made his way toward the boathouse.

"Herr Hildebrand, why are you limping? What has happened to you?" Krupp asked as he stood in the ramped entryway to the boathouse.

"It is nothing, sir. Please don't mind," Hans responded as he approached Krupp with his wheelbarrow loaded with blankets, food, and water jugs.

"Hans, I order you to tell me what happened to you. Did Berger have anything to do with this?"

"I was loading the wagon, sir. I was using the west veranda. It is closer, and Herr Berger felt I was moving too slowly. He shoved me down off the porch, and I just rolled down seven steps. That's all, sir. Please don't tell him I told you. It would not be good."

As Hans was telling Krupp what caused his limping, Schroeder was approaching the boathouse, carrying a wood box with *Dewars Whiskey Scotland* markings on its side. She was dressed in a khaki shirt and pants. The shirt collar bore her rank designation and unit. Krupp was mortified that she would brazenly display her SS uniform when secrecy had been their foremost concern.

Before he could say anything, the overly confident Schroeder said, "I've had this uniform at my house in Poughkeepsie for years and would only wear it when I knew I was alone." She placed her parcels on the boathouse wooden floor, ignoring Hans.

"Why now, Fraulein Schroeder, and why so openly?" Krupp asked.

"Herr Strandartenfuhrer, if I may be so formal, I have operated undercover for years. It has been most distasteful. I'm a Hauptsturmführer, in the Fatherland's SS, and my time as a spy, dressed in civilian clothes, is over as of right now."

Krupp felt it would amount to nothing had he continued to challenge Schroeder. It was more important that they complete their move from the main house to their new quarters, which in twenty-six hours, they would be vacating for good.

Not wanting Hildebrand to overhear his next question to Schroeder, Krupp ordered, "Herr Hildebrand, move these supplies up to the top floor."

Hildebrand pushed his wheelbarrow up the ramp between Krupp and Schroeder and moved into the building.

Krupp watched Hildebrand move to the westerly side of the building, where the staircase was located that led to the second floor. Krupp then asked, "Did you complete the placement of the charges?"

"I did. They are located in three rooms: in the library, on the third shelf of the bookcase, and on the opposite bookcase by the sofa. The other one has been placed in the dining room behind the logs in the fireplace. With this weather, I don't suppose they will be using it tomorrow night."

"And what about the third set?" Krupp asked as he closed the building's oversized sliding doors.

"That one is in the parlor. I placed it inside the piano, just behind the foot pedals," Schroeder said, wiping perspiration from her forehead.

"Well done. And where have you connected the detonator?"

"The wires all come down to the basement and out the window that faces that building," Schroeder noted, pointing to the carriage house.

"And the wires. How have you concealed them?" Krupp asked anxiously.

"That was not a problem, Strandartenfuhrer," Schroeder gloated. Krupp did not fail to notice.

"And why not?"

"I purposely did not splice the three wires from each of their placements into one wire at the window. In case one would be found, the other two would still work. From there, the wires are covered by the stones in the rear driveway and then by the vegetables in the garden," Schroeder continued. "There was one small problem. I did not have enough wire to go all the way into the carriage barn. So I ended it and placed it in the tool shed on the side of the barn. It's covered by paint cloths."

"Did you see Berger push Herr Hildebrand?" Krupp asked, satisfied with the accomplishments of his explosives expert.

"I did, and it was for no reason other than that pathological bastard's hatred of everyone."

"Where is he now?"

"I don't know, nor do I care. But what I do care about is if we fail and I am caught by the Americans, it will not be as a spy, but as an SS officer." Schroeder picked up her parcel and headed toward the staircase. "We have another problem to contend with. One that I've only discovered. When I looked out from the second-floor window, looking west down the river, I observed Navy patrol boats. They must be watching the river entrance to the president's house. That incompetent Reinhardt never told us about this, nor did the Hildebrands, Herr Krupp," Schroeder continued. "Do you think they will come up this far tomorrow evening?"

"Most certainly, with the two leaders here, yes. We will just have to deal with them. It's to our advantage that it will be dark when we leave."

* * *

Next to journaling in her diary and being with her companion, Margaret Suckley's other favorite pastime was playing the piano in the parlor at Wilderstein. As she sat at the instrument, the room's three oversized windows were opened from the bottom. The slight evening breeze was evident, even though damp. It floated the windows' white curtains and helped to neutralize the otherwise warm interior.

Arriving back from her all-day visit with the president and Mr. Churchill at Val-Kill, Daisy had changed into an all-white cotton dress. It was time to relax. While she was changing in her bedroom, she wondered why her Scottish terrier was not with her. Heather always was there to greet her, especially since she was gone most of the day. She made a mental note to ask Hans and Gert once again if they had found her. Also, she would ask the servants why there were some mud stains on the parlor and dining room floors. She had concluded that Mrs. Hildebrand must have been preoccupied in getting the house ready for to-morrow's dinner guests, and she just hadoverlooked it.

Before coming to the parlor, Daisy had added entries to her diary. The day's recordings took longer than usual. It had been a full day, a special day for both her and her dear friend, Franklin:

August 13, Thursday, a day full of new faces and names. Mr. P. wanted it so, and also wanted all to know it was W.C. and Mrs. Churchill's thirty-fifth wedding anniv. She was on her way from Montreal. The festivities were delayed until Steve Early had arrived.

Mr. Wallace does not like Mr. C. It was quite obvious. Some heated words were spoken.

W.C. was his usual self. He held court. Waxing ever so eloquently. That there should be one citizenship between America and the U.K. W.C. feels that together, we would rule the world. Mr. P. was upset, and so was Mr. Wallace.

No mention of E.R., now on her way to the Pacific.

Gave my book to Mary C.

Mr. P. whispered to me that he was looking forward to dinner at W. tomorrow.

Daisy's small, eloquent fingers found the keys on the piano. The soft notes echoed through the mansion's thirty-five rooms, most of which she had not seen in years. Her father, Robert Browne Suckley, might have been more conservative had he not replaced her grandfather's two-story Italianate mansion with his own design, a gaudy Queen Anne, which was so costly for her to maintain. She was able to afford only two servants, not the twenty he had employed.

"Oh, there you are, my dear Mrs. Hildebrand," Miss Suckley said as she heard Gertrude's footsteps enter the parlor.

"You rang for me, madam?" Gertie said politely.

Miss Suckley lifted her fingers off the keyboard and swung herself around on the piano stool. "What the devil do you think possessed Heather to have disappeared? She's never done anything like this. Never."

"I know. Hans is still outside looking for her. He went down to the boathouse, and he searched through the carriage barn, madam," Gertie said, her head bowed, staring at the room's red-and-blue Persian carpet.

"Mrs. Hildebrand, I would like for you and Mr. Hildebrand to do all you can to find her. If for no other reason, Mr. Roosevelt will be bringing Fala here tomorrow evening. And it would be very touching to see Fala's reaction when he meets his mother. Don't you agree?"

"Yes, madam, I do, and we will do all we can to find her. Is that all? May I get you something?"

"Thank you, Mrs. Hildebrand, yes, a small glass of sherry would be nice right now. It will help me to get to sleep. Tomorrow is a full and eventful day, and a long one at that," Daisy said, returning to the piano keys. Her selection was an old college tune she could play without any sheet music. She had picked up the melody nearly three decades ago while at Bryn Mawr College.

As her fingers located the black and white keys, Daisy had no concept of just how eventful tomorrow evening was going to be. It would be some time before the five floors of rooms at Wilderstein would hear the sound of the piano again, if ever.

"I'll get the glass of sherry," Gertie said, backing out of the room.

"One other thing I had failed to mention: Why are there mud stains on the floor?"

"Where, madam? I don't know."

"The parlor, right there, and in the dining room. Has that husband of yours been tracking in the mud? Or are you hiding someone else in the house and have not told me?" Daisy said with a smile.

Chapter Twenty-four

When Gannon and Parker drove into Springwood, returning from their visit with Radcliff Lindbergh, they sensed an added height in the estate's security detail. The entry road's gatehouse was being manned not only with Army military policeman, but also with Secret Service agents and a detective from Scotland Yard's Prime Minister's Protective Service division. Even the roving ground patrols, those walking and others in Jeeps, were in three-man groups—one soldier and two civilians.

Seeing his fellow agent, John O'Neill, standing outside the gatehouse, smoking his usual Chesterfield, Gannon brought the car to a stop and asked, "What's with all the security, John? What's going on?" He also wondered where his beloved Ellen was and what she was doing.

"The boss brought us up to Code Red an hour ago. He feels something might occur, and he wants to take no chances. As if it we weren't at that level already," O'Neill said, poking his head inside the driver's window, his breath reeking of tobacco.

"Where is he now?" Gannon asked.

"He's upstairs. He and Anderson just got back from Vanderbilt Annex, and was he ever in a hurry. Nearly drove right over the lot of us standing right here."

"Well, we'd better get back there, and I wonder what's happened, and if he's got more intelligence," Gannon said, moving the car forward.

"Oh, another thing. That fiancée of yours is waiting around back in the office. The general got talked into bringing her here. And I don't think the boss knows about it."

"Good God," Gannon exclaimed as the car rolled forward. "Not now, not here."

"Anything I can do?" Parker asked.

"Matter of fact, you can do something. I'll have you meet her and keep her busy until I get caught up with Mike and brief him on Lindbergh."

Gannon dropped Parker off at the front of the service garage, now converted to offices. He appreciated the young corporal's suggestion to meet with Ellen. And in doing so, he felt like a heel. But he had to see Mike Reilly and the general. His courtship with Ellen McCarthy would have to wait. When was she going back to Washington? Why is she still at Hyde Park? And why here, and at this time? He kept mulling it over as he got out of the car and headed for the second floor's wooden fire-escape stairs.

"I'm glad you're here, Jim, but why the back stairs?" Reilly asked. As Gannon entered the room he saw papers, photos, and maps spread out on the table and floor. Easel pad sheets covered two walls, with names, places, times, and arrows drawn on each, connecting all the names with places.

"Long story, boss, but I need to tell you about the Reischmans—information we got out of Lindbergh."

"Well, tell us what you've got, and we'll share some news that John also brought back about the Reischmans," Reilly said. He got up from the table and moved over toward the easel.

"Werner Reischman's first cousin was Herbert Haupt, the spy, one of the six who got the chair last August. And according to Lindbergh, the Reischmans hate the president—passionately, I should add. At one time, they worked for old man Lindbergh, and he paid for their house in Poughkeepsie. I suggest we pick them up and question them as to what they know about all of this," Gannon said, making his way to the coffee pot.

"Too late for that, I'm afraid, Jim," Anderson said.

"Why's that?" Gannon asked.

"Because, as I had just explained to Mike here, just before you came in, your Boston field office went out to Dennis Port to question them and their employer, a Mr. O'Malley, told your colleagues that the Reischmans just up and left. To go to an aunt's funeral in New York City, they were told."

"Can you believe that?" Gannon asked.

"I would have; they did leave a note saying just that."

"So?"

"Well, as it turns out, they don't have an aunt who died in New York, the Boston guys said. Never did have an aunt!"

"Where does that leave us now, Mike?" Gannon asked.

"I'll tell you where: in a critical and dangerous situation. The AIC in Boston had put out an all-points, and wouldn't you know, within the hour a Connecticut state trooper reported he had stopped the Reischmans on the other side of Danbury. They're not going to any goddamned funeral in New York City. They're coming here to Hyde Park to join up with Schroeder; I know they are. Why would they have lied to their employer and to the trooper? And why head west, when they should have been driving south to New York?" Mike Reilly's large Irish face became more flushed, turning a bright red.

"You can't be sure of that, boss. It could be a coincidence," Gannon said, wishing to calm things down.

Reilly exploded at his young protégé, "In a pig's ass, Jim. Tell him the rest, General. Tell him about Schroeder's past."

Gannon wished he had said nothing. He had never seen Reilly, whom he had admired so long and so deeply, become so enraged.

"It seems like Schroeder's father, a man named Siegfried Holtz, along with several others, blew up an ammunition ship docked at Black Tom Island in 1916. It was such an explosion, millions of pounds of ammunition went up, and so did the island and miles of shoreline in New Jersey. And I might add, dozens were killed in the blast. And by the way, Holtz was never caught."

"So how the hell does his daughter work her way into this country's secret spy agency?" Gannon asked Anderson.

"Someone, somebody at OSS in New York or Washington, clearly screwed up. That's all I can say. At least for now, and when I find out who, I'll personally shoot the bastard."

The room went quiet. For a time the three were at a loss. No one said anything for what seemed like an eternity, when Reilly said, "Jim, I'm sorry for having blasted off. You deserve better than that. Tomorrow the kitchen staff here at Springwood is going to Wilderstein. I want you to go with them and question the servants, the Hildebrands, and get from them anything that can be helpful."

"Just how far can I go with them?"

"If you must, put them under arrest, material witnesses for now, until we can sort all of this out. Assuming it's not too late."

"Mike, a pattern is beginning to develop here. The dots are connecting," Jim said. "Reinhardt's last words were, 'There's eight of us—they're going to destroy the—.'"

"So who are the other two, and where are they?" Reilly asked.

Anderson, now standing, recited names: "There's Otto Reinhardt, there's Kathe Schroeder, there's the two Reischmans and the two Hildebrands. That's six, so who are the other two?"

"And didn't the kids playing ball on Church Street tell us about a car and three guys in it? That couldn't have been the Reischmans. It was too soon," Gannon interjected.

"You're right, Jim. Assuming Schroeder was already in the house, I bet Reinhardt connected up with two of the bad guys in New York City. Left the city and brought them here because they didn't want to be exposed, and most likely they were unfamiliar with the route to Poughkeepsie," Reilly said.

"So why the visit to Church Street by Hans Hildebrand, the Packard, and the uniformed driver the kids told us about?" Gannon said.

"The only thing I can think of is, just like Reinhardt, the Hildebrands are 'sleepers', fifth columnists who are helping the other three professionals," Reilly responded.

"But helping to do *what* is the question, and with Schroeder's background in explosives it doesn't take much," Anderson said.

"John, I want you to alert the security office at the IBM factory," Reilly said.

"Mike, let me go down to Cold Spring. I want to see that pumphouse. We could learn something from Reinhardt—papers, maps, books, anything about who the other two are," Gannon asked.

"Not now. I just want you to go downstairs and take good care of that beautiful Irish lass who's been waiting hours to see you," Reilly said. He winked at Anderson.

"How did you know she was here?"

"Come now, Jim, it's my job to know. So get going, and I'll see you here in the morning, bright and early."

*   *   *

Franklin Roosevelt was not going to allow the evening to go by, just filling his stamp album or working on his coin collection. Especially when his houseguest was his dear friend, Winston Churchill. Churchill was hoping the president would take the advice of his doctor and just go to bed after experiencing such a long day of activities.

Grace Tully, along with Anna Roosevelt, seconded Dr. McIntire's advice and encouraged the president to retire for the night. The president thanked them and asked Agent O'Neill to see if the prime minister would join him for a nightcap and a cigar. A short while later, at around ten-thirty, the leader of the British Empire came into the president's library, dressed in a robe that covered his oversized night shirt. His leather slippers looked worn as the portly man, cigar in hand, was instructed to pour himself a glass of sherry and join his friend, who was now stretched out on the sofa.

"Franklin, where in God's name do you harvest the strength, the fortitude, and the courage to do what you do?" the prime minister asked as he lowered his body into the large upholstered chair next to the sofa.

"Winston, I must say that you're just patronizing this old and tired wreck of a human being."

"Indeed I'm not, sir. You are remarkable. Just where do you get it from?"

"And Winston, the same can be said of you. With all that you and your fellow countrymen have had to endure these past four years, you write and publish, and I hear you are working on what, a four- or five-volume history of the English-speaking people? You must now have a dozen books you have written," FDR said, holding his glass of spirits.

"There have been many, but you have not answered my question."

"Well, if you insist, my friend, I will tell you. And I haven't shared this with many, except of course with Babes, Daisy maybe, and Anna. It goes back to Warm Springs. Back some twenty years or so ago, Winston."

"The rehabilitation, the warm waters for your polio," Churchill added.

"Indeed, and while you and I had lost contact back then, I can assure you those years were the most difficult, the most despairing years of my life. I was about forty, and I was told by the best doctors we could find that I would never walk. Furthermore, the life I had and the life I wanted for Eleanor and the children was over."

"That's what the experts said. However, you proved them wrong."

"In the beginning, I agreed with them. But through the encouragement of Babes, Louie, and Basil O'Connor, and a few people who unfortunately you'll never get to meet, things changed. I changed when I witnessed the strength of so many of the stricken. They would not give up. And I won't either, then nor now. So enough of this. Would you pour this old man a patch?"

Churchill took the president's glass, moved to the bar, and prepared a drink for Roosevelt. For the next two hours, the two world leaders discussed, debated, and speculated over the war, the post war, new democracies, new economies, and how they would be remembered by history. Would historians treat them kindly or cruelly? Fairly or unjustly?

Churchill was game to keep on with the interchange of thoughts and ideas and speculation, when Arthur Prettyman came in and insisted he get the president to bed. Roosevelt was ready. He was extremely tired.

The president's valet lifted his charge and placed him in the wheelchair. Churchill was on his feet. He held the chair steady and asked Prettyman if he wouldn't mind if he could push the chair to the elevator. Prettyman nodded and watched the two tired, old men leave the room. A tear ran down on each of Churchill's cheeks. He was now pushing a wheelchair which held the man for whom he had the highest admiration; a man whose health he readily saw was deteriorating by the day; and a man whose decisions held the fate of most of the world's population. Churchill moved his arm and placed it on the president's shoulder. The gesture was not lost by the ever-watchful Arthur Prettyman as the elevator door opened.

Chapter Twenty-five

Hyman Ruckenstein and Hersh Morganstein had married two sisters, Natalie and Evy Goldman, in 1919, soon after the two World War I U.S. Army buddies were discharged. Months later, they opened a button-manufacturing business on Manhattan's Lower West Side. And after twenty years, the congestion of the teeming city as well as the competitiveness of the garment industry forced them to seek a less hectic life. At least these were the reasons they had given to their friends when they left the business. The real reason had been that Hy and Hersh no longer could get the material for their specialty button business because the sea lanes were basically closed. No longer could they acquire Mother of Pearl from Australia or Taturuga Corozo from Italy. Their top product line for years, rhinestones from Czechoslovakia, came to an end in 1939 when the Nazis invaded that country. Even their next highest seller, Taqua from Ecuador, no longer was safe to be shipped. And the two friends had little interest in manufacturing buttons for the military. The machinery was just too costly.

In 1940, the childless couples had moved some sixty miles northward, to Cold Spring, in Putnam County. There, the families bought a series of rundown tourist cabins on New York Route 9D. After six months of extensive painting, plumbing, carpentry, and landscaping, they opened the twenty-one newly furnished cabins for business and named their enterprise Hudson View Tourist Cabins.

Shortly after their grand opening, America was attacked at Pearl Harbor. And with the war came restrictions on travel for leisure purposes. The families initially had felt the war was going to take a financial toll, but it never materialized. Their location, halfway between the sprawling U.S. Military Academy at West Point and Stewart Field in Newburgh, brought a new type of business. Also, travelers who were in need of overnight lodging while on business at the sprawling International Business Machine plant in Poughkeepsie frequented their cabins. Since January of 1942, it was a rare night that the cabins had any vacancy. The former button manufacturers were delighted, even though they had to be open seven days a week.

Hy, the taller and less outgoing of the two partners, left it up to Hersh to be the greeter of their guests. Hersh made it his job to find out all he could from those who had signed their guest book. He was engaging and had the ability—at least he thought so—to address any subject. Their wives, Evy and Natalie, were present only on rare occasions at the front desk.

It was around nine-thirty at night when the office's squeaky door opened, tripping the bell hooked at the top. Hy Ruckenstein, who worked the night shift, looked up from his New York Daily Mirror, extinguished his Chesterfield, and greeted the couple.

"Welcome to Hudson View. Can I help you?" he asked in his heavy accent as he glanced at Thelma and Werner Reischman through his thick bifocals. Intuitively, Ruckenstein knew that the couple standing at the counter were Germans. Their look, mannerisms, and clothing gave them away; the wife had that typically stocky Prussian body. What he had not known was that every police agency in the North Atlantic region was on the lookout for his newly arrived lodgers.

"Yes, you can. We need a cabin for two or three nights. We may leave on Sunday or early Monday," Werner Reischman said, surveying the ten-by-twenty-foot office.

"Are you married?" Ruckenstein asked, looking down at his sign-in book.

"What kind of question is that supposed to be? Yes, we're married," Werner snapped, knowing full well that his host for the next three nights was a Jew. He had always boasted that he could spot a Jew a mile away.

"We're a decent family establishment, and no offense intended," Ruckenstein said, now on his feet, placing the register on the counter. "We have number fourteen, a hundred feet down the path to the left, Mr. and Mrs. Reischman. That will be twelve dollars for each night."

"That price is outrageous. There's a war on, or don't you know?" Thelma Reischman said.

"We've never raised our rates since Pearl Harbor, I want you to know. They're the same daily charges since we've opened. So do you want number fourteen or not?" Ruckenstein said matter-of-factly, attempting to mask his disgust for the Germans.

"We'll take it," Werner said, wishing his wife would not create any more of a scene or attract unnecessary attention.

Ruckenstein returned change to the couple, looked out the oversized office window at the Reischmans' Ford coupe, and said, "New York registration, but you're from Cape Cod, yes?"

"We've been loaned the car by a friend on the Cape. Are you always this inquisitive?" Werner asked.

"No, not always. But it does get lonely here, you know. Just trying to make small talk," Ruckenstein said, noticing how edgy his new guests were. They'd stick to themselves, inside their cabin, all day and night, he concluded. He watched the Reischmans go back to their car and observed Werner remove a tattered suitcase and hand it to his plump wife.

* * *

Jim Gannon was making his way north on Route 9D from the center of Cold Spring. He was alone, his mind revisiting all that had transpired within the past twelve hours. He was disappointed he did not go to the summit of Breakneck Ridge. It was too dark. What was most in his thoughts, however, was the meeting with Charles Lindbergh's uncle and the revelations that visit elicited. The Reischmans' connections to the Operation Pastorius spies were swirling inside his head. And the latest information, Agent Schroeder's connection to the Black Tom Island explosion in 1916, was somehow connected, he concluded as he drove past the wood-barricaded spot along the Hudson where, only the day before, Otto Reinhardt's submerged car had been discovered.

But Gannon wanted to dismiss it all except for one thing: his earlier meeting with his fiancée. He followed his boss's orders to take Ellen out, but not to Cold Spring. An hour ago, he had dropped Ellen off at a tourist cabin just a few minutes from where he now was. Ellen was not pleased with his leaving her at the Hudson River Tourist Cabins, but she understood that the love of her life needed to check out the harbor in Cold Spring.

As they drove into the tourist cabin parking lot, she asked, "Why have you come all the way down here, James? God, this place is dark. Aren't there any lights?"

"The office is just ahead," he said. "With the PM and the president at Springwood, there's not one empty room to be had but here."

"You've been here before, I see, and I hope not with any females," Ellen chided him as she pinched his ribs.

"Ouch, that hurts. Many times. This is where we put up extra personnel and no, there are no female agents, thank God!" Gannon said, pulling the car close to the walkway leading to the office.

"You've got to express my thanks to Mr. Reilly, James, for letting us spend some time together. I know you're terribly busy, and if I must say, somewhat preoccupied."

"He insisted, my dear, but here's what I would like for you to do. Check in with Mr. Ruckenstein. Call him Hy. We do it all the time. Nice guy, very New Yorkish, by the way. He'll put you in cabin fifteen. We got four cabins always in reserve. And if he asks if are we married, tell him almost. He knows you're coming." Gannon got out of the car and moved to Ellen's side to open her door.

Ellen picked up her overnight bag, gave her fiancé a kiss, and then moved toward the office and asked, "James, how does Mr. Ruckenstein know we were coming here? If it was only two hours ago—"

Interrupting, Gannon said, "Don't ask."

"James, we both know we shouldn't be going to a tourist cabin, not until we are married. What will we say when we go to Confession next Saturday?"

"Ellen, my dear, I've thought about that as well. But there's a war on, and the way things are going with my work, I might not see you for weeks. I can't wait until we are married. Will you be okay with that? I am, but I don't ever want to offend you."

"James, our time here will give me the chance to live out what I've been fantasizing for months."

* * *

If the Hudson View Tourist Cabins had appeared dark ninety minutes ago when Gannon dropped off Ellen, when he came back, the window in cabin fifteen was dark. The only light was a soft one inside the office, where Gannon was now heading.

"Well hello, Mr. Gannon. Welcome back. She's beautiful. Don't wait another day; get married tomorrow, before you lose her to a schmuck. Take my advice, young man," Hy Ruckenstein greeted a perplexed Gannon.

"I don't know if I haven't lost her already, Hy. She's not in cabin fifteen. Nothing's been touched. Could she have gone into another cabin by mistake?" He removed his hat and looked down at the guest register.

"I don't think so. Anyway, the other cabins are locked," Ruckenstein said.

"That's awfully strange. I wonder where she could have wandered off to?" Gannon stared out the office window.

"Now that I think of it, Mr. Gannon, she did meet the people staying in number fourteen. She seems to have been arguing with the Reischmans," said Ruckenstein, now joined by his wife, Evy.

"Did you say Reischman? Thelma and Werner Reischman, by any chance?" an anxious Gannon asked.

"Let me see." Hy looked at the register. "That's right. Germans they were. Came in a car with New York license plates, and not very nice, I'd have to say. Loners at that."

"Hy, I want you to call this number and tell them who you checked in to number fourteen. I'm going to fourteen right now. Tell them I'm here, and I need help. Go! Go!" Gannon ordered as he drew his .38 revolver and rushed out the door.

"Evy, I knew it the moment I set eyes upon those Germans. They are trouble, you wait and see. I'm right—I know it!"

"So what do you think it is, Hy?" Evy asked. She closed the office door, not wanting to be overheard.

"Evy, I don't know. But go wake up Hersh and your sister. We're going to need their help. I'm going to make the call Mr. Gannon wants. Quickly now. Did you see him run out of here with his gun? The Reischmans are bad people."

"I'll get Natalie and Hersh. I don't like this, Hy. I'm scared. This has never happened to us," a shaken Evy said. She left the office.

As she left, her husband said, "I just hope that no bad things have happened to Mr. Gannon's fiancée. I saw her and the Germans arguing—over what I don't know, and now she's disappeared." Ruckenstein paced back and forth in back of the counter, holding the telephone and waiting for an answer to his call.

* * *

"Mr. Reilly, I cannot locate them," Margaret Suckley said hysterically as she held the telephone receiver with both hands.

"Who is it you can't locate, Miss Suckley?" Mike Reilly responded. He looked at his watch and puzzled over receiving a call at eleven at night from the president's companion.

"They're nowhere to be found. I've been ringing for them and even went to their rooms. I just wished that I hadn't scolded her for the mud stains on the carpet. Where can they be?"

"Are you saying you can't locate the Hildebrands?"

"Yes, yes. That's who's not here. And hours ago, I heard an automobile in the driveway. I had thought Hans was putting the Packard in the garage. And Mr. Reilly, Heather has not been seen or heard from now for two days. What is happening?" Miss Suckley said. Her voice was quickly approaching hysteria.

"Margaret, I want you to sit down and stay calm. I'm sending two agents to you right now. You know one of them, John O'Neill. Okay?"

"Thank you."

"Now let me ask you something. Have the Hildebrands been acting strangely these past few weeks?" Reilly asked. He wondered if this was the proper time to put such a question to someone he knew was quite distraught.

"Now that you ask, Mr. Reilly, I did find Mrs. Hildebrand anxious, and I even asked her about it yesterday. She said it was all due to the work that needed to be accomplished for tomorrow's dinner. But it's not the first time I've seen her this way before a big event."

"But more so now, Miss Suckley. Is that right?" Reilly asked, sensing she was becoming more calm.

"Yes, and I also think it has to do with those calls that were being made by her to her cousin at the New York City Water Department. You remember; I spoke to you about them a few days ago," she said.

"Miss Suckley, a minute ago you mentioned that you heard an automobile in the driveway. By any chance, can you tell me if your Packard is still in the garage?" Reilly asked, knowing the answer.

* * *

Hans and Gertrude Hildebrand were driving in an excellent car, Miss Suckley's Packard. They had a nearly full tank of gasoline as well as three additional five-gallon containers in the trunk. The car also had the best automobile ration sticker, a "C," on its window, thanks in part to Margaret Suckley's friend, President Roosevelt. Hans had moved the old roadster back into the barn when he realized it had no gas-rationing sticker.

Nevertheless, it would take them four hours to drive from Wilderstein to Bennington, Vermont. They faced the danger of being stopped by a curious state trooper or county sheriff as they made their way across Dutchess County's Route 44 and on to U.S. Route 22 near the Connecticut border. The car might have had the proper sticker, but they did not have written permission from its owner. As the Hildebrands made their way north on U.S. Route 22 through the quaint towns of eastern Rensselaer County, they had no idea that an all-points bulletin was being broadcast for them and their stolen vehicle. They passed through the hamlet of Petersburg, and they still had some thirty miles of driving before reaching their destination in Vermont. Gert said, "Hans, how is your leg? You must be in terrible pain. May God condemn that Strandartenfuhrer Berger for pushing you down the stairs."

"It's the constant use of the clutch that aggravates it, Gertie, but we'll manage. I just hope the gasoline holds out. We've only got one jug left." Hans looked over at his wife. His hands gripped the large steering wheel, and he anxiously checked the Packard's fuel gauge.

"Hans, I'm so ashamed. We've done bad things. And worse things will happen tomorrow. And you and I still have the chance to see that it doesn't." Gert dabbed her handkerchief at her eyes.

"Gertie, you mustn't cry. It does no good. We had to do what we did. The children."

"But they're safe now. They're in Spain. And papa and momma are dead. I've had no chance to see them once more. I didn't know, but those terrible people and Herr Reinhardt can't use them to make us do things we shouldn't do. We must stop this madness and call someone," Gert mused.

Hans slowed the Packard as he approached a motorcycle with its lights flashing on the shoulder of the road. A gray-uniformed state trooper was writing in his pad with one foot on the rear bumper of a 1936 Chevy convertible that he must have pulled over for a traffic infraction.

"Gertie, when we get to his farm tonight, we will tell all to Uncle Ferdinand. He will guide us in doing what is right. He will also help us to get out of the country—to where, I don't know. But after what we have done, we can't stay any longer."

For the next thirty minutes, Gert and Hans went back and forth on how they would tell Uncle Ferdinand their story. They would not lie. He needed to hear all of it. They also knew that once he was told, he would be involved, and they would have put him at risk of being arrested. They felt they had no other choice.

They were now fifteen minutes from his apple-orchard farm as they drove east on Vermont Route 9.

A short distance before the sign that read *Welcome to Vermont—The Green Mountain State*, they saw flashing red lights ahead. Two police cars had the road blocked. They could not turn around. An oversized truck laden with logs was within twenty feet of the Packard's rear bumper.

"Oh my God, Hans, what are we to do?" Gert cried out upon seeing the road ahead blocked with red flares on each side.

Hans, with utter resignation in his voice, looked at his weeping wife and said, "How could we have come this far and so close to Uncle Ferdinand's farm and be arrested? Gert, we would be treated as spies. We're just like Schroeder, Berger, and Krupp."

* * *

Kathe Schroeder was not at all pleased that Colonel Krupp left her, hours before, alone in the boathouse with Ludwig Berger, that contemptible fellow Nazi. But she knew that if their escape route was ever going to materialize, Krupp had to make contact with the Reischmans.

Fortunately for Schroeder, Berger busied himself in a corner on the second floor of the icehouse by cleaning his Luger, sharpening his knife, and packing, unpacking, and repacking his haversack. Never once had he made eye contact or spoken to Schroeder or recognized her for providing his pack. At times, Schroeder could hear him mumbling over how he should have eliminated the Hildebrands. Little did he know that they were now a hundred miles away from Rhinebeck.

"Berger, you better hope that, for your sake, Krupp makes it back here safely," Schroeder said, breaking the eerie silence that had engulfed the darkened, spider-webbed room.

"Why just for my sake? You need him as much as I do to get away from this place, now don't you?" Berger said. He stuffed his sack for the second time.

"You forget, Herr Berger, I lived here. I went to a school here. I can blend in with these people. You would stand out like a fox in a hen house, and make no mistake about that," Schroeder observed, knowing every word she said would only provoke her comrade.

"You know, Schroeder, I don't know who I despise more, you or Herr Krupp. This mission can't come to an—"

Berger's voice went silent as he heard the door to the second floor open. Krupp appeared.

"Herr Krupp, where have you been? Why have you been gone so long?" Schroeder asked.

Krupp took off his suit jacket and placed it on the back of a chair. "You're wise to have kept the lights off, but unwise to be talking with no one on guard," he snapped.

"I stood my watch, Herr Krupp. Berger here was to busy to relieve me because no one is around here anyway."

"Still no reason to lower your guard, Schroeder. You know better, despite what Berger does," Krupp said disgustedly.

"Did you get to the Reischmans, Herr Colonel?" Schroeder asked.

"I did. I had to walk into the village. The telephone at the diner was not working."

"Are we all set?" Schroeder wanted to know.

"Yes but there was some trouble. A problem, but it is being taken care of."

"What kind of problem?" Berger got to his feet.

"Thelma Reischman said that a girl, a government person, was watching them at the tourist lodge. She was too nosey and asking too many questions, so they took her with them to the pumphouse."

"How stupid of them. They should have killed her right then," Berger shouted.

"Keep your voice down, Herr Berger. Do you want to give away our position?" Krupp said impatiently.

"Thelma said that was not an option. The area was too public, so they put her in their car. They did the right thing."

"We'll see if it is right soon enough, won't we?" Berger retorted.

Chapter Twenty-six

"Kramer, take your lamp with you. And just to be thorough, check out those buildings over there," agent John O'Neill said to the younger Secret Service agent, Don Kramer, as he pointed to the icehouse and garage.

"What about the boathouse?" Kramer responded.

"Yeah, go ahead. It's kinda dark, so don't twist an ankle getting down there," O'Neill cautioned. He was standing in the pea-stone driveway, not realizing his feet were directly over the detonation cords Schroeder had placed earlier in the day.

"John, on the porch," Kramer said to O'Neill. Standing on the back porch, arms folded over a light cotton white cardigan sweater, was Margaret Suckley.

It was a rare event. Miss Suckley infrequently ventured out to the back porch. Especially since, in order to do so, she would have to exit from the Wilderstein kitchen. It was a location in her house she was not predisposed to visit. Tonight, however, was one of those rare exceptions. Her servants had disappeared. And so had her dog and her Packard touring automobile.

"What can you tell me, Mr. O'Neill? Have you found them? They've been gone for hours. And what is so strange and disconcerting is that this has never occurred before," Miss Suckley added.

"Nothing yet, Miss Suckley. We've just got here. Agent Kramer is going to check out the other buildings. If you don't mind, I would like to see the servant's living quarters in the house."

"No, not at all. Please come in. The Hildebrands occupied all of the third floor. They always have," she said, returning to the kitchen.

"Kramer, need you here," shouted O'Neill. Kramer was pushing back the garage sliding door. Never once did he see what was under the tarp that covered the fifty-five gallon drums just to his right.

"What's up?" Kramer was almost out of breath as he jumped up the porch steps two at a time.

"Miss Suckley has given us the okay to check out the Hildebrands' apartment upstairs. So let's see what we can turn up on these two birds," O'Neill reported.

Agent Kramer was never aware that three sets of eyes and three weapons were pointed at him. The three unwanted boat-house guests were on their feet immediately once they heard agent O'Neill's car pull into the driveway.

* * *

Ellen McCarthy no longer had her white summer hat. She had lost it thirty minutes earlier when she was pushed into the Reischmans' coupe, back at the Hudson View Tourist Cabins. She was forced to lie down on the car's backseat floor. Thelma Reischman sat with her feet on Ellen's back. The Nazi sympathizer's Luger was not far from her distraught prisoner's head during the ten-minute ride to Breakneck Ridge.

Ellen's cotton cardigan sweater was in tatters. The thorny bushes along the rock-strewn path up Breakneck Ridge had seen to that. If it was any consolation to her—and it wasn't—Thelma Reischman's red blouse was torn as well.

Werner Reischman's wool jacket was bearing up to the bushes as he led the women up the 1,260-foot mountain. Thelma was behind Ellen. They still had another thirty minutes of climbing before they would reach the pumphouse. The thorns, bushes, and sharp stones and rocks were taking a toll on their bodies.

Scratches were now cuts, and blood was slowly streaking down Ellen's legs onto her white bobby-socks.

"Where are you taking me? What have I done? I don't know anything," Ellen screamed out as she clawed her way over a four-foot rock outcropping.

"Shut your mouth and keep climbing," Thelma Reischman commanded.

"Why me? What is this all about? Why have I been kid-napped? I don't have any money, nor do my parents," she pleaded, leaning on a birch tree.

"You foolish girl. Do you think we are kidnappers? Do you take us for gangsters? We are patriots for the Fatherland. And your watching us at the cabins has cost us precious time. You've interrupted our plan. You should—" Thelma shouted at Ellen, but she was interrupted by her husband, who had turned around and was coming back to them.

"Thelma! Good God, would you not speak to her? What are you saying, for Christ's sake? She was not to know, and we must keep it that way. Now look what's happened. Let's keep moving." Werner Reischman was clearly exasperated over his wife's out-burst. He now realized that Ellen McCarthy was going to have to be killed. She knew too much. It was unnecessary until Thelma revealed who they were.

"Get up," Thelma ordered Ellen.

"I don't take orders from Nazis. I'm not going anywhere with you. They'll be looking for me, and they'll soon find out what your plans are." A defiant Ellen McCarthy folded her arms across her chest, wondering if these were the people her fiancé was hunting.

Thelma responded. She backhanded her gun across Ellen's face. The impact caught the lower part of Ellen's right cheek and lower lip. Blood gushed from her mouth, and she slumped to her knees. Tears mixed with blood as Ellen brought her hands to her mouth.

"Why did you do that? Look at her. She's only going to slow us down. How senseless! Why don't you think for a change?" Werner berated his wife as he bent over, wrapped his arms around Ellen's thin waist, and lifted her to her feet.

"I'll do anything I want to do. And I won't let her speak to me with that tone," Thelma responded, attempting to ignore what Werner was doing.

"Miss, I'll hold you. You must keep walking. What is your name?" Werner asked, sending his wife a caustic stare.

* * *

"Sir, step out of the car and open the trunk," Corporal Baker of the New York State Police ordered Hans Hildebrand.

A minute earlier, the Hildebrands had entered the police road-block on the main entry road from New York toward south-western Vermont. Baker's partner, Cal Turner, was standing in front of the stopped Packard, just to the right of the car's head-lights. The trooper's hands clutched a sawed-off twelve-gauge shotgun.

Hans was visibly shaken. He had not expected to be asked to exit the car. He did not have the owner's permission, especially now, out-of-state and a hundred miles from where it should have been garaged. The gun-toting Turner added to his anxiety.

"Are you okay, sir?" asked Corporal Baker, who walked behind Hans to the rear of the car.

"Yes. I'm fine, officer, just fine," Hans replied, hoping that it was only he that the officer would be addressing, and not Gertrude.

"You look a bit distracted, sir. Have you been drinking? Where are you and the missus heading to?" Baker inquired. He looked into the Packard's oversized trunk and quickly noticed the gasoline containers and fumes.

"Oh no, officer. My wife and I are visiting our Uncle Ferdinand. He owns an apple farm just a few miles from here, that's all."

"Well, okay. I know the place. We're on the lookout for two escaped lunatics. They took off from New York's insane asylum in Wingdale and were reported headed to Vermont. Have you seen any hitchhikers?"

"No, officer, and we did drive by the big institution a few hours ago. We did not see any hitchhikers. May I shut the trunk?" Hans replied.

"Is this your automobile, sir? You shouldn't be storing gasoline in the trunk," Baker was saying when his partner shouted.

"Baker, watch it! A car's coming through!" Turner screamed as he ran out into the westbound lane of the two-lane road. Turner swung the flashlight back and forth with his left hand. His right hand held the shotgun.

The approaching car came to a complete stop in the westbound lane alongside the eastbound, backed-up cars. Its glassy-eyed driver rammed the car's transmission into reverse, grinding the gears. He backed the car up a hundred feet into a barbershop driveway and spun back out onto the road, headed west.

"The driver looks like our man. He had another guy up front with him," Trooper Turner shouted.

"Let's roll, Turner. You can go, Mr. Hildebrand, and get rid of that gasoline," Baker said, and he jumped into Turner's partially moving police car.

Chapter Twenty-seven

President Roosevelt always had surrounded himself with capable and loyal advisors and staff. Some were closer to his inner circle than others. After December 7, 1941, the inner circle had quadrupled in size. Nevertheless, and despite the buildup, Roosevelt still maintained a very tight group with whom he was comfortable in confiding. Near the top of that special list had always been Michael F. Reilly.

Reilly had but one goal: to serve out his years in the Secret Service by doing everything humanly possible to protect his charge, the president, from his enemies, his allies, and his friends. Franklin Roosevelt knew this, and as a result, he had the highest respect and even love for his bodyguard. Reilly was indeed one of his most trusted friends.

As far as the president was concerned, it was Reilly who got him safely back and forth from the White House, Hyde Park, Shangri-La, and Warm Springs. A year earlier, the president had thanked Reilly personally for making their Western trip safe and comfortable.

In early 1943, it was Reilly who had orchestrated the president's secret trip to the Mideast. Reilly, in January, had moved the president safely through Miami, Trinidad, Brazil, then to Gambia in West Africa, and from there to their final destination, Casablanca.

Always the historian, FDR knew the trip Reilly had laid out was precedent-setting—not only for its fourteen-thousand miles of travel, but because it was the first time a president had crossed the Atlantic in a plane; and more so because Mr. Roosevelt conferred with his allies and generals only a few short miles from the war's front lines.

"Mike, come in. Miss Tully tells me it's urgent. Mike, after all we've been through, what can be so urgent? Come, sit over here, and get yourself a cup of coffee," the president directed a very solemn Mike Reilly.

The president was seated in his armless oak wheelchair. Newspapers from Los Angeles, Chicago, Washington, and New York City were spread around the wheels. Fala raised his head when Reilly entered but just as quickly placed it back on top of the New York Times. The president had on his lap one of his dozen books on ornithology. It was months since he and Reilly had sneaked out of Springwood in the wee hours of the morning and gone bird-watching just off the shoreline near Red Hook, a few miles north of Rhinebeck.

"Mike, we just have to get out one of these mornings and see what new creatures have arrived and settled on the Hudson, don't you agree?" The president watched his friend retrieve a cup of coffee and sit on the plaid-covered sofa.

"Mr. President—" Reilly began to say, when Roosevelt interrupted.

"I know, you're not here to discuss bird-watching, are you? And can I offer you something better than coffee, Mike?"

"No, sir, this is fine. And yes, Mr. President, we've got a critically dangerous situation brewing." Reilly sipped his coffee.

Reilly was always deeply conscious of the burdens his boss carried. When he would have a private audience with his boss, he always would bring any issue to a head quickly and succinctly.

For the next five minutes, he summarized for the president all he knew of the latest threat upon his charge's life and that of his guest, the prime minister.

The president had heard these summaries on many other occasions. But this one was different. He knew it. Especially when Reilly told him about what agents John O'Neill and Don Kramer had uncovered in the third-floor apartment at Wilderstein. The revelation was visually upsetting to Mr. Roosevelt.

When he heard that spies were working at his friends' house, the president's demeanor changed immediately; these were spies he had met on numerous occasions when he visited Wilderstein.

Reilly outlined for the president the contents of a note written by Gertrude Hildebrand and left on the bed in her now-vacated apartment. She had written the letter to Margaret Suckley, apologizing for her and Hans's abrupt departure and the fact that they were taking the Packard and would not be coming back. Gertrude went on to write that she had hoped Miss Suckley would find it in her heart to forgive her and Hans, that what they were doing had to be done.

Reilly continued with his summary of events when he was interrupted once again by the president.

"Mike, I can't believe this. Daisy must be devastated, and I would like to speak to her. And Mike, before you even suggest it, the answer is no. I will not cancel tomorrow's dinner. It will go on, and it will be at Wilderstein," the president said, looking directly at the stunned Reilly.

"Mr. President, I must insist."

Roosevelt intervened: "Mike, I've made my decision, and it is final."

* * *

Jim Gannon had never appeared so dejected as he placed the telephone back into the receiver at the Hudson View Cabins' office. His deep reflection was interrupted by Hy Ruckenstein. "Mr. Gannon, are you okay? Can I get you something, some water or coffee, perhaps?"

"No, I'm fine," Gannon replied, turned his back, and faced the office front door.

"Well, to me you don't look fine, and I think you should just sit for a moment. Did you find out anything now about Miss McCarthy? What did Mr. Reilly have to say, if I can be so bold to ask?" Ruckenstein moved around the office counter with a cup of black coffee in hand.

"He wants me to stop the search and return to Springwood with the Secret Service team and Corporal Parker. That's what he said. Can you believe that? And Ellen is nowhere to be found, and for all we know, she could have been dumped in the woods or in the Hudson by the Reischmans."

"No, no, Mr. Gannon. Don't think like that. She'll be found, and she'll be just fine. You wait and see. Just drink the coffee." Ruckenstein tried to be as comforting as he could, still feeling his friend and customer was most likely right in his assumptions.

Gannon's phone call from Reilly had lasted ten minutes. Reilly informed Gannon about the letter agent O'Neill had found in the Hildebrands' apartment and that they had stolen Margaret Suckley's car. He restated all they knew about the plot without coming to a conclusion as to what was being plotted.

While Gannon was reluctantly taken Hy's advice by having a cup of coffee, Hersh walked in, ready to make an announcement. He was not able to do so. His wife, Natalie, and his sister-in-law, Evy, burst through the screen door even more excited than Hersh.

Hy told them to calm down and not to speak all at once. His suggestion was about to fall of deaf ears when Gannon got up from the sofa and demanded, "Hersh, what is it you've found? And girls, let Hersh go first."

"I called Mrs. Sands at the Fishkill telephone exchange. I asked her if she placed any long-distance calls from our pay phone. She said that early last evening she had placed a call from Rhinebeck to our phone. From a man who had a German accent. The call went on for close to twenty minutes, she told me." Hersh was noticeably proud he had some information to add.

"How would she know that?" Hy interjected.

"Because she had to keep asking the Rhinebeck caller to put more coins into the box," Hersh said.

"Good work, Hersh. Now, girls, what are you all so excited about?" Gannon asked as Corporal Parker entered the office, having no idea what was going on.

Evy decided to take charge and spoke first. "Mr. Gannon, we searched cabin number fourteen, and Natalie here found these crumpled-up notes in the bathroom next to the toilet. They have times on them and what looks like map descriptions. I just don't know, I'm not sure. Also, the writing is in German. Hy, maybe you can read it?" Evy started to hand the now-open sheets of paper to her husband.

"Evy, how many times have I told you I know Yiddish, not German?" Hy responded.

"I know German," Hersh said and reached for the papers.

Hersh took a couple of minutes to read and then reread the pages. The office was silent. All eyes were now on the five-foot-six, balding translator. Hersh looked up and said, "This is well written by someone who has been well educated, I think. It has five points, or better yet, commands:

> *Obtain petrol from tourist home—sufficient for trip east.*
> *Obtain food and water for five people.*
> *Must be at longitude 70.1323 degrees west and latitude 41.6452 degrees north by 0400 hours on 13 August.*
> *Have automobile standing next to mountain restaurant lot by 0600 hours on 12 August.*
> *Have U.S. clothing for two men and a woman.*

That's all it says." Hersh handed the note to Gannon.

Gannon looked at Parker, "Get Reilly back on the telephone. There are only three agents, plus the Reischmans. And does anyone have a map? I need to check out those coordinates."

"I can't say for dead certain, Jim, but it is close to Chatham on Cape Cod's southeast coast, east of Dennis Port," Parker said, dialing the telephone.

"How the hell do you know that, Parker?" Gannon asked.

"We use that area ourselves. To place agents on subs that will take them to Europe. But don't tell the general I told you so. He'd kill me."

"What's wrong, Mr. Gannon?" Hy asked.

"The note says five people. Where is Ellen?" Gannon ran his hands through his hair. "Parker, have you gotten through to Reilly?"

* * *

"Put your weapons away. He's not coming this way. He's turned back to the house, and it seems he did not see the wires under the stones," Colonel Krupp whispered to his fellow Nazis. He turned away from the second-floor window of the boathouse.

Krupp put the Luger into his belt and placed his Zeiss field glasses on the windowsill. "You see what I mean when I ordered you two to stay alert and on your post? What if he didn't stop and turn around, but came into the building? Where would you be? What would you have done then?"

"I'd kill him instantly with my dagger and think nothing of it, Herr Colonel," Ludwig Berger responded authoritatively.

"Strandartenfuhrer, you're such an arrogant ass. You've always have been, especially since you got the Iron Cross for rescuing that dog, Mussolini." Kathe Schroeder continued mixing a chemical compound.

"Shut up, you slut!" Berger yelled.

"Call me anything you wish, but you are the most arrogant, conceited, and vicious agent the Fatherland possibly could have sent on this mission. You completely missed the colonel's point. If we are discovered or have to expose ourselves, the mission is lost. It is as simple as that, you fool. Herr Colonel, you tell this swine, would you?"

"When will you two stop? No one is questioning your aggressiveness, Herr Berger. Nevertheless, Schroeder's right. We mustn't allow ourselves to be discovered. That will come soon enough, when the explosives go off—by my calculations, in less than twenty hours. So can you two control yourselves until then?"

"I surely can, Herr Colonel, but I am not sure if Strandartenfuhrer Berger here can," Schroeder retorted.
Krupp interrupted: "Enough! Let's review the plan once again. Berger, you stand by the window and pay close attention. Schroeder, at 1800 hours the guests will be arriving. At 1845 hours Berger will set the fuse…"

* * *

As the morning sun began to cross the Hudson Highlands, Ellen McCarthy did something she had never done before. She relieved herself in a wooded area, some fifty feet north of the pumphouse on top of Breakneck Ridge. Her moment of humiliation rapidly disappeared given her present circumstances. Her white cardigan sweater, in tatters from the previous night's climb up the mountain, was now completely soiled from blood and dirt. McCarthy had been given a corner in the pumphouse to sleep, but sleep never came. She lay awake all night and into the early morning. She wondered if her fiancé had begun a search for her and whether she would be found before Thelma Reischman had her way. She found Werner more compassionate, but she had no illusions; he would kill her just as soon as his wife would. The question she kept asking herself was, why had they not done so by now? What good was she to them?

One factor Ellen did not know was the conversation the Reischmans had in their car while driving from Cape Cod to Cold Spring. Although the couple were in complete sympathy with the cause of Nazi intruders Krupp, Schroeder, and Berger, if discovered, they did not want to be implicated in the mission and electrocuted as spies. Their feelings for the Fatherland did not run that deep. They were in Cold Spring only to provide transportation for the mission, a mission whose nature they did not know.

Nevertheless, Ellen was alert enough during her captivity, pretending to be asleep, that she had overheard the Reischmans' conversation speculating on the purpose of the mission—the assassination of Roosevelt and Churchill and the poisoning of the water supply to New York City.

Ellen felt she had to escape. She had to get word to Gannon. She kept wondering how she could overcome the eagle eye of Thelma Reischman. Then it came to her. There was a way, and it could be at noon when Thelma was to prepare lunch. Earlier she had heard them talking about their next meal. It might be the only time that the Luger would not be in Thelma's hand. Adjusting her skirt and sweater, Ellen walked back to the pumphouse to the ever-watchful glare of Thelma Reischman.

* * *

Ferdinand Metz's two-hundred-acre apple orchard that gently rolled up the north face of Bennington's Mount Anthony was the subject of many tourist photographs. Hundreds of trees were heavily laden with ripening McIntosh, Delicious, and New York Red apples. They were within three weeks of being harvested, if Metz could get the apple pickers to his orchard. That was difficult last year because those who had picked in past years were working in Bennington's factories, producing war goods. Other residents were off fighting in the Pacific or in Italy.

The orchard had been named Vermont Apple Orchards by his father. The older Metz had immigrated in 1913 to America with his family from Bavaria and had grown grapes and apples near the foothills of the German Alps, close to the border with Austria. The senior Metz had not liked what was in store for Germany under the reign of Kaiser Wilhelm, so he moved to America with his wife and only child, Ferdinand.

Ferdinand, like his father, was keen on the history of his adopted country, and also like his father, he was true to his new country's government and freedoms. To Ferdinand there was no better friend to farmers and growers than the man who now occupied the Oval Office.

Just before Ferdinand had taken over the management of the family orchard in 1938, he listened to the words of his dying father. Hitler was going to do to Germany what the Kaiser had done before him, bring the country to war, and untold suffering was to befall the German people.

The thousands of apples hanging from scores of trees at the Metz orchard were ripening daily. Ferdinand Metz knew this, and so did the army of worms that soon would invade the fruit. The crop was a few weeks short of needing to be harvested. What it needed more immediately, on this pleasant pre-fall Saturday morning, was to be sprayed.

Before sunrise, not wanting to disturb his late-night arrivals, his niece and her husband, Metz had come out to the mixing shed and filled two fifty-five-gallon drums with a watered-down concoction of insect repellent. His apples, if they were to survive this year's invasion of parasites, had to be inundated with his home-made solution, especially today. The temperature, wind, and sunshine made for perfect conditions to drag the drums by his tractor through the trees.

Yet the orchard man abruptly stopped what he was doing. The apples could wait. What couldn't wait, he told himself, was the survival of his country and its leader. He would go back to the house, meet with Gertrude and Hans, and insist that she tell the authorities the Nazis' dastardly plan.

Ferdinand sat at his kitchen table, stoked his pipe, and watched his guests finish their strudel. He poured another cup of coffee for them and himself and said, "Earlier this morning, I came to a conclusion: Gertie, you must call the authorities."

"Uncle, I can't do this. It's too late, and we must still think of the children, Kurt and Erich. The Nazis can still reach them. I'm sure of it. They've reached us. Here in America. And next to the president's house," Gert appealed to her uncle.

"You have no idea how ruthless, how vicious these killers are, Uncle Ferdinand," Hans broke in. "They are dedicated to Hitler and all that he stands for. I've seen and felt their brutality. Just yesterday I was beaten by this killer, Ludwig Berger. His stare at you is so frightful." Hans got up and moved over to Gert to place his hands on her shoulders.

"I know how you must feel, children, but we mustn't allow for these people to carry out their deed. And Erich and Kurt are in Madrid, with Carl. They're safe," Metz went on, losing his patience.

"You can't possibly know what it is that we feel," Gert tried to explain. "You live on this beautiful farm surrounded by apple trees and hills. Live with three hardened Nazi murderers in your cellar for three days, giving them food and water, and listening and watching them plot their mission. I saw them beat up my husband and kill Miss Suckley's dog. No, Uncle Ferdinand, you can't feel how we do. Never."

"No, child, you're right, I can't ever know what it was that you two must have lived through. But if you are to stop these people, bring their mission to failure, you must act now, I tell you!" Metz insisted. "You never should have run away. What you know and what is being planned by those Nazis will bring tragedy to our adopted country. My dear Hans and Gertie, no matter how great the threats to you were, no matter how intimidating those swines were to you and your loved ones, your duty was to let the authorities know what you've been asked to do. This is a free country. We can toil in the fields and factories and shop in peace. We can go to whatever church we want, and so can the Jews. You're not doing anything will bring disgrace to our name and family. So this is what we will do after you finish breakfast."

Tears flowed down Gertrude Hildebrand's cheeks as she and Hans listened to Metz. Hans held his wife's hand. They both knew what her uncle had said was the truth, and their conduct was cowardly. Gert finally responded, "Uncle Ferdinand, Momma and Poppa are dead. The Nazis said they died in the bombing of Stuttgart. Hans and I are ready to do what you think we should. We no longer can be held hostage by these people."

Chapter Twenty-eight

Margaret Suckley was not in a good mood. Strangers from Springwood were in her kitchen and dining room. A half-dozen Secret Service agents followed and observed each and every movement of the cooks and waitstaff. She wished she never had made the suggestion to host a dinner for her dear friend and his guests. She did, however, find solace in one area. Gertrude Hildebrand had set the dining room table magnificently for the fourteen guests who would be arriving at Wilderstein in seven hours.

Miss Suckley never had played much of a role in preparing Wilderstein for social events. She always had depended on her Gertrude; and the recently arrived staff knew it all too well. Their questions for her regarding the location of appliances, kitchen tools, wine and liquor, linens, and a myriad of other food and beverage preparation essentials were met with a blank stare. Miss Suckley was a lost soul in her own house. She retreated to her study and picked up her trusted friend, her diary. She sat at her desk, inked up her pen and began to write:

Aug, 12th, Saturday
It is pure chaos here. There is at least a dozen strangers in the house, getting dinner ready. Why did Gertrude leave? What are she and Hans up to? Did they have anything to do with Heather's disappear-

ance? Fala will not have his playmate tonight. How dreadful. Why can't the strangers be quieter? I've never heard such noise, commotion, coming from the kitchen.

The knock on her door was quiet: three gentle knocks. "Yes, who is it? I did not want to be disturbed," she said, the pen still clutched in her fingers.

"Miss Suckley, it's me and agent Kramer. We're sorry to have to bother you, but can we see you for a minute?" agent John O'Neill announced as he and Kramer stood in the hallway outside of her study.

"Mr. O'Neill, can it wait? I am in the middle of something," she responded with a tone of disgust. The two agents looked at each other on the hallway side of the walnut door.

"We don't believe so, ma'am. It will only take but a minute. We need to ask you a few questions," Kramer said.

"Well then, come in if you must. And please try to keep it brief. I have fourteen guests arriving in a few hours, and my kitchen and dining room are in a state of pandemonium. My servants have left me. My Heather is gone, and so is my automobile. Can you blame me for being short with you? This has been a most trying morning," Miss Suckley told the two agents, who proceeded to enter her study.

The burly O'Neill had no intention to keep his questioning of the president's friend brief. He wanted answers. He and Kramer had completed a survey of the house only minutes before. As far as O'Neill was concerned, Miss Suckley's present state of mind was secondary to O'Neill's passion to protect Mr. Roosevelt. At this moment, he had little patience and even a certain level of contempt for the mistress of Wilderstein.

"Miss Suckley, who has been living in your root cellar, and were you aware of this?"

* * *

Kathe Schroeder, alias Kathe Holtz, was, on this warm Saturday afternoon, in her element. She was sitting on a wooden crate on the second floor of the Wilderstein boathouse. Spread out before her were a dozen bottles of chemicals, some large, while others were one quart in size.

Her hands were encased in large black rubber gloves as she poured one mixture after another into and out of a five-gallon glass bottle. And while doing so, she recalled her chemistry training from when she was a student at Vassar Collage, a few miles south of where her present improvised lab was now located.

Schroeder's seven weeks of training at Camp Greentop had augmented her work today. Just one of her prime motivating factors was the opportunity to get back at those Americans who dishonored her family name. The German-American Claims Commission would wish they had never come to judge her father, Siegfried Holtz, as the perpetrator of the 1916 Black Tom ammunition explosion. For Schroeder it was a dream come true. Her admission to Vassar College as a chemistry major, and then her recruitment into the SS, provided her with the tools to seek out the revenge that dominated her very being. Her assignment to Colonel Krupp was all she required.

"How are you able to determine the right mixture if you don't have a scale or proper measuring vessels?" Colonel Krupp asked, watching her pour chemicals from one bottle to the next.

"I don't, but it will do the job in any event. Just one quart of the compound of arsenic and cyanide when mixed will, when poured into a controlled water environment, completely contaminate for a week the city's water. Now just imagine what damage and havoc six of these will accomplish? Not to worry, Herr Colonel. Just the knowledge that their precious water has been poisoned will create so much fear," she speculated. "Finally, these Americans will come to realize that Germany has brought the war to their soil."

"Herr Colonel, if I were you, I would worry," Berger interjected. "She never has done this before, so what makes her so goddamn sure this will work?" Berger continued his sentry duty, looking out of the second-floor window.

"The SS Strandartenfuhrer makes a good point, Fraulein Schroeder. Why are you so certain it will work? We have only one chance at this. There won't be a second chance," Krupp said.

"I'll answer you, Herr Colonel, but not that swine. It will work because I had done this on a smaller scale as a secret research product when I interned at the Hudson River Chemical Company. The security guard, the late Mr. Kelly, wanted the carp out of his fishing pond, so he let me test my concoction at his house."

"And with what results?" Krupp asked.

"The fish died within twenty minutes. All of them. Mr. Kelly told me, very quietly, last week. He also said that nothing now grows or lives in his pond." Schroeder stood up proudly from her box seat and squeezed corks into the six bottles.

"A pond is not a reservoir, especially five of them, and the sizes that they are, Herr Colonel. This is a bad plan, and I'll have no part in its failure," Berger persisted.

"Your problem, Strandartenfuhrer, is that it can't be achieved unless a knife or gun is involved. Well, I got news for you, you arrogant and conceited ass. This will work, and we don't need you and your ignorance to see to it that it happens," Schroeder snarled.

"Berger, get back on your post, and stay there. Never mind what is taking place here," Krupp ordered.

"I'm putting my life on the line for what, I ask?" Berger responded.

Krupp wasted no time: "We are all putting our lives on the line. Schroeder, pack up the bottles. The guests will be here in a few hours. Also, try and get some sleep."

* * *

Corporal Parker had made it very clear to his friend, Agent Gannon. He would stay in Cold Spring and not return to Springwood, as ordered, along with the rest of the Secret Service search team. He would do this even if it meant disobeying an order from General Anderson and a possible court-martial. Parker was convinced the Reischmans were holding Ellen McCarthy at a place close to the Hudson River Tourist Cabins, and that it was only going to be a matter of hours before they would be discovered and Ellen rescued.

But Gannon did not want the young corporal to risk his army career. He coaxed him back to Springwood. They were now in the office above the converted garage along with a very determined General Anderson and an equally resolute Mike Reilly, who had called the meeting.

"Gentlemen, in three hours we leave with Mr. Churchill and the president for Wilderstein. The boss, in so many words, made it perfectly clear that the dinner would go on as scheduled." Reilly said. He paced back and forth in front of his plain oak desk.

"But I thought you had the final say, Mike, when it came to presidential security. If I'm not mistaken, you even have federal law that gives you the final say. So why have you abdicated your authority?" Anderson asked.

"Get real, John. When the boss gets into the mood I just witnessed, you don't pull rank or cite laws. As far as he's concerned, he's been in a lot worse security situations than this one. The goddamn problem is he doesn't have the same understanding or comprehension of it that we have."

"I'd say so," Gannon interjected.

Reilly, ignoring Gannon's remark, continued, "We have three possible assassins or saboteurs on the lam, along with two collaborators, the Reischmans, who we know are up to doing some evil thing. If I had my way, we'd be back at the White House or Shangri-La, and the hell with this dinner and Miss Suckley's feelings about it."

"Mike," Anderson asked, "do you believe that what we've got here is a second round of Operation Pastorius? You know, another attempt by the Nazis to infiltrate and blow up things? The first pass was a disaster for them. And from our intelligence, it appears this group is made up of professionals."

"Possibly, and I've thought of that, John. But what's the connection to Wilderstein and the late Mr. Reinhardt?" Reilly responded. "And one other thing. Saboteurs don't hit and run and go back to Germany. The note you found at the cabin clearly dictates that their operation will be big, and they are to get out of the country. And Parker, you were right that their rendezvous is off Cape Cod, and we've notified the Navy and Coast Guard."

"Sir, if I might add," Parker broke in. "For two reasons, sir. First, they need safe houses. That's what we train our people to do."

"He's right, Mike," Anderson said, impressed with his corporal's interjection. "And what's your second point, Parker?" Gannon asked, breaking his silence of the last fifteen minutes, wondering why he was in this meeting and not searching for Ellen.

"The second point should be pretty clear to all of us," Parker went on. "Reischman's cousin, Herbert Haupt, got tried last year for being a saboteur. Lindbergh also told us that. And Schroeder's father was involved in blowing up the ammunition dump in New York City or around there someplace, twenty-five years ago."

"Parker, your points are good, but what I don't get is why these people have come here to set up shop. Why in Poughkeepsie and Rhinebeck? This area has the highest concentration of security in the country, and they know it." Reilly said.

General Anderson responded, "Your point, Mike, is that if they were out to destroy defense facilities and war-manufacturing plants, why come here in the first place? To my knowledge, there are only two located here, the IBM factory and the chemical factory where Mr. Kelly was murdered. We've have no airplane, ship-building, or tank-manufacturing facilities within a hundred miles. It's the president and Mr. Churchill, isn't it Mike?"

"That's my conclusion, general, but when and where, I don't know," Reilly said.

"Or how they plan on doing it, and why take Ellen?" Gannon said. "That's a part of this puzzle that doesn't make any sense, Jim," Reilly added.

"Would it be that the Reischmans are pumping her for information? Do you think they've made a connection between her and you, Jim?" Parker asked.

"I can't imagine—" Gannon began when Reilly broke in.

"Sorry to interrupt, Jim, but I'm of the opinion that Ellen just got in the way. You've said that the innkeeper, what's his name, Rubinstein or something—"

"Ruckenstein, Mr. Reilly," Parker corrected.

"Yes, that's it. He said Ellen had just arrived, and it was in the parking lot and that she ran into the Reischmans. And he saw them having some words."

Reilly was out of his chair, running hands through his thick, black hair when the door to the office opened. Standing there was the president's personal secretary and Reilly's dear friend, Grace Tully.

"Come in, Grace, and to what do we owe this visit, do tell me? Is it because the boss has changed his mind and come to his senses?" Reilly said with a smirk.

Before the slim, immaculately dressed secretary could respond, Parker, Gannon, and Anderson were on their feet. And not solely because a lady had entered the room, but also because she was the president's trusted assistant.

"Thank you, gentlemen, but please be as you were," Miss Tully acknowledged.

"Parker, would you give Miss Tully your chair? Please sit here, Grace, if you will," Reilly said.

"Thank you, Mike. I'll stand. I'll not be long, and the answer is no. Mr. Roosevelt and his guests are still planning to go to Wilderstein in about two hours."

"I wish that were not the case, Grace. I'm against this dinner, and I tried to persuade the boss to cancel it, you know," Reilly said.

"I know, Mike. The president told me all about your meeting. Matter of fact, he was upset with himself and felt he was too harsh with you. But you must realize, Mike, Mr. Roosevelt does not in any way want to disappoint Miss Suckley. She has been planning this event for some time, and the disappearance of the Hildebrands has only added to her stress—significantly, I might add," Miss Tully said. She changed her mind about standing and took Parker's chair.

"Miss Tully, can you bring any influence at all to this—" agent Gannon began to ask.

"Forgive me for interrupting you, Mr. Gannon, and also, I was deeply saddened to have heard from Mr. Roosevelt about Ellen. I hope and pray she will be found safe."

"Thank you, ma'am," Gannon responded, wondering how the president knew about Ellen.

"But Mike, the switchboard over at the house only moments ago received two calls. The first was from the New York State Police. It was from a Corporal Baker. He was calling in response to your bulletin on Miss Suckley's Packard."

"Why didn't the call come in here, Grace?" Reilly said explosively.

"Just a moment, Michael, and please calm down. There is more, if I can just continue."

"Please do, Grace, and I'm sorry. Please go ahead," Reilly said. He began once again to pace behind his desk.

"Trooper Baker told the switchboard that last night he and his partner stopped the Hildebrands a few miles west of Bennington, Vermont. He said the occupants were on their way to see a relative who owned a farm nearby, but he couldn't recall the farm or relative's name."

"Jesus, Mary, and Joseph. Do you have any idea what this means, Grace? We need those two. They're the possible link, the key to these others we've been looking for," Reilly said.

"Michael, you must stay calm. We have a new girl on the board, and she's not fully trained. You know as well as I do, it is so difficult to get people. All she did was take the messages, and she didn't want to interrupt your meeting. That is why she came and told me."

"I'm calm, Grace, I assure you. I'm calm. You said there's more. What's more?"

"The second call, Mike. The operator said it was from Vermont. A collect call, person-to-person for you or Mr. Gannon here. The caller spoke with a deep German accent. The caller was a woman, and she sounded distressed. Nevertheless, she requested to speak to only you or Mr. Gannon, and she said both of you would know her."

"So why wasn't she put through to us, Miss Tully?" Gannon asked.

"You know the policy, Mr. Gannon. Our White House operators have been instructed never to accept collect calls, or for that matter, person-to-person calls," she responded.

"Good Christ, Grace! I don't believe what I'm hearing," Reilly said, his hand covering his face.

"The caller said she would call back in two hours. In other words, around five, Mike, and in the meantime, Trooper Baker said they will locate the farm and be back to us about the same time your five o'clock call is due to come in," Miss Tully added.

Chapter Twenty-nine

The silence in the Metz kitchen went on for several minutes and was broken by Hans. "Uncle Ferdinand is right, Gertie. We must do something. Our running away does nothing but help Berger's cause," Hans acknowledged, his hands tightly gripping his wife's shoulders.

"I just don't know what is the right thing to do. I'm so confused, so torn," Gert said, her eyes looking down at an empty plate.

Metz tried again: "Gert, let me see if I can help both of you. You love this country. Hans loves it, and so do I. By running, you will have betrayed your adopted country and Miss Suckley. You'd be helping the Bergers, the Schroeders, and Krupps of this world, not Mr. Roosevelt and Mr. Churchill. You must not continue to run. You must call the authorities and alert them." Metz went back to the stove to retrieve the coffee pot.

The three German immigrants debated making the telephone call. Tears were uncontrollable from Hans and especially Gertrude. Her tears were not so much for her possible betrayal of the country or its leader, but for the mistress of the house where she had worked for the last twelve years.

Gert left the kitchen. A few minutes passed, but to Hans it felt like an eternity.

Hans and Metz looked up from the table as Gert came back into the kitchen from the parlor. Her normally red-flushed cheeks were ashen. She slowly entered. Hans got up and went to her. Metz asked, "Did you tell them?"

"The operator at Springwood did not accept my call. They don't take collect calls, she said. And they don't accept person-to-person calls."

"Was that all?" Metz asked.

"No, I told her I'll call back in two hours, and that I have to speak to Mr. Reilly or Mr. Gannon."

* * *

To many residents of the Rocky Mountain states, Breakneck Ridge in Cold Spring, New York, would be better described as a small hill. At nearly thirteen hundred feet above sea level at its highest point, where the pumphouse is located, it is no match for the grandeur of the Rockies or the Cascades. Nevertheless, the vertical drop on the mountain's south face is hundreds of feet. The bottom of the cliff is a mere fifty yards from the Hudson River.

Ellen McCarthy was aware of the dropoff just to the right of the pumphouse. Also, from what she could ascertain during her visit to the outdoor necessary, she realized there was no possible escape to the north or east. The north was too dense, and a run to the east provided no coverage from her captors; clearing for the pipeline had taken care of that as an escape route. Her only route to safety was back the way she came, the mountain's west face. But this time, it would not be a slow climb through bushes and over rocks and boulders. It would be a terrifying run with no sure way to stop until she reached the state road, assuming she could make it that far.

Despite their present circumstances and environment, Thelma Reischman proved ever the dutiful German housewife. And at noon on this cloudless Saturday afternoon, she began preparing lunch for her husband.

"Werner, why are we even here? Why aren't we back at the cabin? It's a lot better to sleep in a bed than in this god-forsaken place that has no water, no toilets, nothing. I hate it. And what are we to do with that bitch?" Thelma drew a stale sandwich from her brown paper bag and placed it alongside a vacuum bottle.

"Do you think that for one moment we had a choice with her?" Werner yelled. "I didn't, so we had to come here. And let's hope no one is looking for her. We can't be sure of that, can we? And as long as she is here and under guard, we have nothing to fear. So shut up. I need to think. And she is not a bitch." Werner watched his wife lay out her two sandwiches.

"Don't tell me to shut up. I resent that. But what are we going to do with her? We have to get back to the cabin. We're to meet Oberst Krupp and Fraulein Schroeder early tomorrow morning," Thelma barked.

"And don't forget Strandartenfuhrer Berger. When Krupp called, he told me Berger has been a serious problem; he's placed the mission in jeopardy a number of times. But it's not at the cabins we are to meet them with the car. We'll go back to the cabins for petrol and food."

While the Reischmans began to have their sandwiches, Ellen pushed her legs out from under her. The corner she had been placed in was excruciatingly uncomfortable, and Thelma knew it. Ellen had no appetite for a stale liverwurst sandwich, which she could smell from thirty feet away. Instead she was intent on hearing every word the Reischmans spoke.

"So what is the mission? Did Herr Krupp tell you anything? Don't you think we should know, after all we've done?" Thelma asked.

"Do we have anything for Miss McCarthy to eat, Thelma?" Werner wondered.

"No, we don't. Let her starve. I didn't plan on her being with us too much longer anyway. And don't you get too cozy and teary-eyed over that bitch. In a few hours, she'll be out of our lives forever," Thelma declared.

"I don't know where or when you've become so hard and cruel, Thelma. And it certainly has changed you. That pretty young girl has not done anything to us, and you know it," Werner said.

"I don't want to hear your sentimental tripe. Just tell me about Herr Krupp's mission before I take my nap. When I wake up, you should take one as well. It's going to be a long night. We won't be back on the Cape until late tomorrow morning," Thelma said, removing a speck of mustard from her lips.

"If you insist, I'll tell you. There are two parts. The first part is in Rhinebeck, and the next part is…"

* * *

A thousand feet below and five miles south of where the Reischmans were holding their hostage, New York State Troopers Sergeant Ryan and Trooper Fanelli were sitting in their police car. Like the Reischmans, they were each having a sandwich. The spot they had selected for lunch was off New York State Route 9D at a scenic Hudson River pulloff. Because of the war and the rationing of gasoline, they did not expect to see much automobile traffic. Their patrols since the beginning of the war were mostly uneventful.

Ryan and Fanelli's troop commander, upon instructions from the Secret Service, had ordered the two troopers to keep their patrol on the state highway limited to the area just south of Cold Spring to a few miles north of Beacon. Their earlier discovery of the bloody body of Reinhardt, the finding of the sunken water department automobile, and now the kidnapping of Ellen McCarthy all placed a high priority on patrolling their assigned route.

"What a day, wouldn't you agree, Sarge?" Trooper Fanelli ventured.

"Yeah, it sure is. A great day to be on that river catching some sturgeon or a big bass. And here I am, sitting with you, driving up and down this road. Our late lunchtime is over, Fanelli. Get us back on the road and, just to breakup the monotony, point us north to Beacon," Ryan said. He wiped his hands with his handkerchief and placed his vacuum bottle back into its holder in a metal lunch box.

The two troopers had closed the distance from where they lunched and were within several hundred feet of the Route 9D road and railroad tunnel when Ryan shouted, "Holy good Christ, look at that! Stop the damned car, Fanelli. Look up there, at two o'clock. Someone is running down the goddamn hill. He's crazy. He'll go right over the cliff."

Fanelli pulled the police car onto the gravel shoulder and picked up the image his sergeant was screaming about. "Sarge, it's not a guy. It's a girl, and she looks to be injured."

"You're right. It's a girl, and she going to be a lot more injured if she doesn't slow the hell down," Ryan exclaimed.

"Sarge, are you thinking what I'm thinking?"

"You bet I am. Pull the car up to the other end of the tunnel. She'll come out on top of the tunnel. God, I hope to Christ she doesn't go over the side onto the road or the tracks."

"She's not going to be able to stop! She's going too fast," Fanelli exclaimed.

"It's too late. Oh God, stop the car now!" Ryan shouted as he watched Ellen's body come into sight as it fell from the roof of the tunnel on to the Route 9D concrete roadway.

Thelma Reischman was staring at the Luger she was holding. She was shaking her head as she stood by the pumphouse door. Until today she had never had to fire a gun before. Her first shot was lucky for her. She clipped her escaping charge in the right shoulder. Thelma wished her aim had been just a bit more to the left. Then she and her husband would not be in the dilemma they were in now.

"You missed her. She's still running, you fool!" Werner yelled at his startled wife as she looked down the hill.

"Fool? You're the fool for falling asleep. You said you wouldn't nap, that you were okay and would guard her. Now look what's happened."

Werner Reischman did not want his prisoner to be shot. Neither did he want her to escape. He had known, ever since Ellen was shoved into their car, that Thelma was going to have her killed. For Werner, the cause was not great enough for him to be a partner in the murder of an innocent, young, and beautiful girl. He had to act while Thelma was napping if he were to prevent the killing of Ellen. And he did. At least he thought he had prevented her death when he had told her earlier, "Miss McCarthy, you must get out of here right away. My wife's been sleeping now for forty-five minutes. She never naps for more than an hour. You must get out of here before she wakes up." Werner untied the rope on Ellen's feet.

"Why are you helping me?" she had asked, her eyes still swollen from lack of sleep and constant tearing.

"I have no time to explain. I just want you out of here. As soon as I get your hands free, you must get down the hill as fast as you can run. Do you understand?"

"I do, but still don't know why. Are you going to shoot me in the back?"

Still whispering so as not to wake his wife, Werner had said, "We are involved in something that is too important, and you have nothing to do with it. You're an innocent bystander. And now you are going to be a victim, if you don't stop talking. You must leave." Werner's breath, his body odor, and his grisly face were repulsive to Ellen. But at that moment, she did not care. All she wanted was to get away from the Reischmans and let her fiancé know she had been held captive by the two Germans he and Reilly were hunting.

Earlier, the Reischmans had no idea their prisoner had not been asleep when they discussed Colonel Krupp's plans for Roosevelt and Churchill. Ellen wanted to keep it that way. She had to make her escape. She had to act on Werner's order and leave.

Ellen's fear for her own safety quickly vanished. She had to get word to Gannon, but how?

Her opportunity was at hand.

As Werner undid the last cord on Ellen's arms, his wife had started to wake up. Her yawning could barely be heard over the constant humming of the water pumps that brought water up the mountain.

Ellen had gotten to her feet and staggered out through the pumphouse door. Her legs felt like rubber. She had been tied up too long. The brilliant sunlight blinded her momentarily as she rubbed her eyes to adjust from the almost pitch-black pumphouse interior into daylight. Once out the door, she knew she had to turn left. Her bearing was Storm King Mountain, the solid granite hulk on the opposite side of the Hudson. She had started to run west, but her legs did not respond. Bending forward, she vigorously rubbed her calves and knees and at the same time did all she could to get to the edge of the hill and down the mountain.

Seconds later, an eternity for Ellen, she was on the edge of the mountain. She never looked back, and suddenly she felt an excruciating pain in her right shoulder. Werner had lied to her. He had shot her in the shoulder as she was making her escape. He had said he wouldn't do such a thing. Ellen fell forward. Her fall was broken by a half-dozen four-foot-high balsam fir trees. Had they not been there to break her fall, she would have crushed her skull on the jagged rock outcroppings.

The pain in her shoulder became more severe as she pushed her way out of a small grove of trees and resumed her race down the mountain. Her legs were now responding, and she was aware she was losing blood. She couldn't see it, but she felt dampness on her lower back and side. It didn't matter. What mattered was she had to get back to Jim.

"I'm not a fool, and I wasn't napping. I just wanted—" Werner stammered.

"She's got to be stopped. She knows too much. I'm going after her," Thelma insisted as she re-gripped the Luger and pointed the barrel toward the spot where Ellen was shot.

"Thelma, just let her go. She knows nothing, I tell you. The shot will have been heard all around the mountain. We must leave this place," Werner pleaded.

"I'm not leaving until I get that bitch. I'm going after her." Thelma moved her stocky legs as fast as they would take her toward Ellen.

Werner grabbed his wife's shoulder to prevent her from moving, even though she weighed close to one hundred pounds more than he did.

With the Luger in her right hand, Thelma swung around and struck her husband squarely on the left side of his face and mouth. Werner never saw the arm coming at him. Blood gushed from his nose and mouth. A large gash appeared just below his eye, and he fell to the ground.

Ellen's pain was now excruciating. The scratches on her arms, face, and legs were of small consequence as she raced down the hill. Her youth and stamina allowed her to distance herself from her pursuer. Thelma barely could keep her balance as she raced after Ellen. The portly Fräulein never looked back at her husband. Twice she fell, and the second fall stripped the Luger from her clutch. It fell to the path and discharged. The sound echoed throughout the valley, and the bullet ricocheted off a boulder and came back to Thelma, barely missing her forehead. Thelma picked herself up and retrieved the Luger. She continued her pursuit.

"Sarge, did you hear that?" Trooper Fanelli asked as they got out of their patrol car to come to Ellen's assistance.

"I sure did. It came from up there, I think."

"Hunters, you think, Sarge?" Fanelli asked.

"In August, no way. What the hell is that? Look, another person coming down the hill. Fanelli, get down. She's got a goddamn gun. She looks crazy as hell!" Thelma, with the Luger in hand, started to close the distance on her captive. She did not see that Ellen was already at the bottom of the hill. Her run had come to its end on the pavement of Route 9D.

"Drop the gun, lady!" Fanelli shouted as he and Ryan drew their Colt .38 revolvers. And in the same movement, they instinctively took cover behind the left front fender of their car, which was now shielding an unconscious and bleeding Ellen McCarthy.

Thelma Reischman did not heed the order from Trooper Fanelli. She kept advancing, raised her Luger, and aimed it at the troopers. She let go two rounds that went into the door of the patrol car. Fanelli and Ryan unhesitatingly fired off three shots each. Four bullets hit the target. Thelma's forward momentum had been so forceful, the entry wounds from four direct hits to her abdomen and chest did not slow her down. She clutched her stomach, bent over, and rolled the last thirty feet down the mountain. Her lifeless body came to a rest on the shoulder of the highway, less than twenty feet from the woman she wanted to kill. Her husband, attending to himself and in great pain, stood at the edge of the mountain, wondering if Ellen was safe. He could not see what had happened. But he could distinguish the shots fired from his wife's Luger and then a fusillade of shots fired from different weapons—and then silence. His wife would not be coming back up the mountain. He had to leave.

Chapter Thirty

The driveway that led into Margaret Suckley's Wilderstein estate was less than spectacular, especially when compared to those tree-lined drives of the dozen or so mansions of her neighbors. And the same held for Miss Suckley's Queen Anne-Italianate Villa, which when compared with the others was nondescript. Frankly, Wilderstein was in the middle phase of being run down, even decrepit.

Miss Suckley's grandfather's dream was deteriorating daily, and she knew it. It bothered her deeply, especially when Hans Hildebrand drove her home and up the driveway. The last time the house had been painted was before World War I, around 1910. And it showed. The awnings no longer had their dark green luster. Where the fabric had not been ripped by the weather, a faded green hue had taken over.

Margaret knew it didn't have to be this way. If only her brother had wisely invested the inheritance from their father. Instead, the over-confident and self-centered sibling lost untold amounts by speculating in foreign currencies. He did so against the advice of wiser minds who had foreseen the economic turbulence of the last decade, as well as the unrest in Europe and the war. Arthur Suckley did not believe it, so his stubbornness cost the family most of its fortune.

Margaret long ago had resigned herself to the fact that she would do all she could to maintain the house with her monthly trust allowance. It did not matter what her grandfather, Robert Browne Suckley, would say had he been alive to see the estate that he and the world-renowned architects, Calvert Vaux and Arnout Cannon Jr., had designed. Her goal this evening was to please her guests and especially her companion the president— not her ancestors.

* * *

"Herr Oberst, they're arriving. I can see the automobiles. Now there's one just leaving. How will we know when Churchill and Roosevelt have arrived? The trees are blocking my vision," Schroeder said, lowering her Zeiss binoculars. She looked over at Krupp, who was placing the last two jars of chemicals and poisons into the haversack.

"Are the automobiles that brought the guests leaving once they've dropped them off?" Krupp asked.

"*Herr vol*," responded Schroeder. "It is getting darker, too. We should have taken up a position in the carriage barn. We would see better."

"Too risky. The gazebo is in between the house and the barn. Is there a guard in the gazebo? And where the hell is Berger?" Krupp asked Schroeder.

"There is a man standing in the gazebo. And there's Berger. He's behind the barn, down between the oil drums."

"He doesn't listen. I did not want him to leave until it was completely dark. If they send out a patrol, he'll be discovered, and we'll have failed," Krupp said desperately.

"The automobiles, Oberst. How will we know?"

"I have already gone over this with Berger. All the guests' cars will go around the circle drive, and their chauffeurs will drive them to the road that leads out the back way. Only Mr. Roosevelt's car will remain at the house with his backup car. Schroeder, as soon as he has arrived, let me know. It will be time to move, and it must be done quickly. Did you get the boat ready?"

It was difficult for Berger, with his six-foot-two frame, to conceal himself within the circle of oil drums, but he had managed to do so. Earlier, when Schroeder had laid the explosives and drew the detonator wire back to the carriage house and barn, he had built himself a hideout. The roof of his shelter was a wooden delivery pallet with a black tarpaulin covering it and the drums. The drums were touching one another, except for a four-inch space that allowed him to use his spyglass to observe the driveway.

The cool evening air on this August night had no effect on the perspiring Berger. It did not help that he was in his wool, full-collared SS uniform. For Berger the clock was his worst enemy. Even the swarm of mosquitoes and fireflies had little effect on him.

As he squatted in the circle of oil drums, Berger was thinking that in one hour he would be the hero of the Third Reich. He alone would be given credit for bringing to an end the reign of two of the world's most powerful leaders. It would be SS Strandartenfuhrer Ludwig Berger of the village of Halle, Prussian Saxony, who will be given a medal by the Fuhrer himself. It would be a new medal, the Berger Cross. It will be more significant than the Iron Cross. It would just be a matter of time now. Using his sleeve to wipe his forehead, Berger mumbled, "Where is that crippled, Jew-loving old man?"

* * *

Werner Reischman, noticeably anxious, was driving his car into the Hudson River Tourist Cabins driveway. His hands, when not on the steering wheel, were shaking as he attempted to control the sporadic blood still flowing from his nose. Did his wife's blow break his nose, he wondered? His shirt and pants were laden with dirt and blood. His wool jacket was torn in several places. He needed to get back to cabin fourteen, bathe, and put on fresh clothes. After that he would drive to the railroad station and take the train to New York City. He had to disappear. He no longer had any interest in assisting the Nazis. There would be no car to take them to Cape Cod. That conclusion came to him only moments before, when he slowly drove by the scene of carnage at Cold Spring. Fire department personnel and policemen were warning motorists to keep moving slowly as other police and ambulance workers were attending to the two women being placed on stretchers.

Panic gripped Reischman as he watched through his car's dirty windshield the chaos in front of him. He knew Ellen McCarthy was still alive. The army medics were giving her a transfusion as well as oxygen. How did they get here so quickly, he wondered? It took only forty-five minutes for him to gather his belongings at the pumphouse and work his way down the mountain to his car. If he felt he did one thing correctly, it was how he concealed his car. He had driven it onto the grounds of an abandoned estate just south of the railroad tunnel. The grounds were strewn with empty soda and beer bottles. Weeds, brush, and leaves had taken over the stone patio of what must have been a beautiful country home.

His curiosity came to an abrupt halt when he saw the other roadside casualty. The victim's arms lifelessly hung over the side of the gurney. She was not covered with a sheet. Her dress was reddish brown, and her rotund face had been badly bruised. It was unmistakable. Thelma Reischman was dead. And for Werner Reischman, so was the mission.

* * *

"Hersh, get the shotgun quickly. He's back!" Hy Ruckenstein shouted to his partner..

"Who's back, and why the shotgun, Hy?" Hersh got up from behind the office counter and looked out the window. He saw the car entering the grounds.

"Reischman, I think. And it looks like he's by himself, and he's going to his cabin. Get the goddamn gun, and make sure it has shells in it."

"Hy, let's call the police. This is not our business. We can't go after Mr. Reischman, and not with a gun. You're crazy. I'm not doing nothing. I'm calling the police."

"Well, call the police. But first give me the gun, and if you don't, I'll get it myself and just might use it on you. Reischman kidnapped Mr. Gannon's fiancée at our place. I'm going to personally have that Nazi son of a bitch tell me what he and his Nazi wife did with Miss McCarthy," Hy said. He turned toward his partner with a look of terror in his eyes.

Reischman pulled his car in front of cabin fourteen. A half-dozen other automobiles were also in front of other cabins. Music could be heard coming through the screen doors and windows. Little girls were playing jump rope on the concrete walkways. Boys were playing catch.

Reischman waited a few minutes in his car before he reached into his torn pants pocket and removed the cabin's oversized key. He slowly walked to the cabin door, pulled open its screen door and placed the key into the lock.

"Just keep moving inside, you Nazi creep, or I'll blow you to hell," Ruckenstein ordered. He jammed the shotgun into the small of Reischman's back.

"I'll do what you say. Just don't shoot," a trembling Reischman responded.

"Just keep moving and put your hands on top of your head, you Jew-hater. And get on your knees."

"Kill me if you wish. I'm a dead man," the distraught Reischman moaned.

"Not yet. Where is Miss McCarthy? If you or that other Nazi, your wife, harmed that girl in any way, I'll blow your head off right here in this cabin."

Werner Reischman was on his knees, his hands were atop his bald head, now covered with scratches. His mouth and nose were terribly damaged. He needed medical attention, which was not to be forthcoming from the man standing in front of him, holding a shotgun two feet from his chest. Werner said, "Mr. Ruckenstein, the girl was not harmed by me. I untied her, and I helped her escape. It was my wife's idea to take her from here. I didn't want to do it. I swear to you. I did not want any harm to come to her."

"Look at you, begging for your life, on your knees. You're not so big and powerful now, are you, you Nazi bastard? Now that the gun is not in your hand, but in mine—a Jew?" Ruckenstein relished the contempt he summoned up for his terrified and wounded prisoner whose head was touching the cabin's nearly threadbare carpet.

"I must tell you what these people are going to do. In just a few hours. And you must listen to me," Reischman pleaded.

"Once again, I'll ask you: Where is Miss McCarthy?"

"She's on her way to the hospi—" were Reischman's last words before a resounding noise was heard by the children playing outside cabin fourteen. Hersh could be seen coming down the path, shouting, "Hy, I've called the police. They'll be right here."

* * *

"Jim, don't disappear on me. I've got something to tell you," Reilly told Gannon as he and agent O'Neill carried the president up the back porch steps and into the kitchen at Wilderstein.

Mr. Roosevelt did not want the guests to see him carried into the house. He had Mr. Churchill and Lady Churchill dropped off at the front entrance. Mrs. Churchill had arrived only hours before from Montreal. Mr. Roosevelt's affliction provided the prime minister an excuse to make his own grand entrance into the house and be greeted by Miss Suckley's guests. Roosevelt knew this would be quite pleasing to the prime minister.

Once Reilly had seen that FDR was comfortably seated in his armless wheelchair and led into the parlor by Daisy Suckley, Reilly retreated to the back porch and found Gannon and Parker. Reilly had instructed O'Neill stay in the house.

"Jim, I don't want to be out here too long. I'll want to get back inside. Too many people, and the space is so goddamn confining. But I did want to give you the news about Ellen," Reilly said. He lit up a cigarette.

"You've found her. She's okay, isn't she? Where is she?" Gannon insisted.

"Yes, we've found her, but she's been badly injured. She took a slug to her shoulder. Lost a lot of blood, and she's got a severe concussion and maybe a slight head fracture. They don't know yet for sure," Reilly said. He looked at Gannon and Parker.

"How'd you find her, Mr. Reilly?" Parker asked.

Reilly ignored Parker's question. "The information is still sketchy, Jim. We picked it up on our radio coming up from Springwood, just twenty minutes ago."

"Where is she, Mike? Will she make it?" Gannon's hands were tightly clasped behind his head.

"Remember those Army guys we heard about who were climbing the mountain when they found Reinhardt? Well, they were still below in Cold Spring and were called up. They had a medical team and a doctor with them and got Ellen stabilized. They took her right to Poughkeepsie, to St. Frances Hospital. They've got a first-class emergency and operating room there. You know that already anyway. And from what we know, she'll pull through," Reilly assured him.

"Mike, do you need me here? Can I go and see here? Just for an hour. They'll be all inside and—"

"Sorry, Jim." Reilly interrupted his protégé. "Ellen was found on 9D by the same two troopers who found Reinhardt. Ellen had escaped from the Reischmans. They had her held up on Breakneck, and it appears that somehow, we don't know how for sure, she got away. But in doing so, she took a bullet."

"From who, the Reischmans, Mr. Reilly?" Parker asked.

"The troopers think so. Matter of fact, they're sure it was Thelma Reischman who shot her," Reilly said.

"Why the woman and not Werner Reischman?" Gannon inquired.

"Because Thelma Reischman also shot at the troopers when they stopped to help Ellen. Unfortunately, they returned fire and dropped her."

"That's not unfortunate. That's good news, Mr. Reilly. One less Nazi. How good is that?" Parker said, not witnessing the same excitement from Gannon or Reilly.

"Not really, Parker. We wanted her alive. She could have told us about Schroeder and the others. Mike, did they get Werner?" Gannon asked.

"They didn't, but your friend Ruckenstein did. Reischman eluded the police in Cold Spring and went back to the tourist cabins. Ruckenstein confronted him to find out what he had done with Ellen. When he heard she was injured, Ruckenstein blew his head off with a twelve-gauge. The cops are holding him for now as a material witness." Reilly crushed his cigarette on the porch deck with his shoe.

"That's too bad, but can you blame him?" Gannon wondered.

"Not really. He'll be okay. One other thing. Before she fell unconscious at St. Frances, Ellen told the troopers she had overheard the Reischmans mention that a Colonel Krupp—he must be their leader—told Werner Reischman there were two events planned. That was all they could get from Ellen before she went under anesthesia. I've got to get back inside. You two keep a close eye on things out here," Reilly said. He pulled open the kitchen screen door.

* * *

"Daisy, you have done a wonderful job. Everything is so beautiful, and your dress and shawl are just brilliant. They bring out all that makes you so stunning," Roosevelt told his friend and hostess.

"Thank you, Franklin, but you are such with the words. I only want to make certain the prime minister and Lady Churchill have a good time. I understand they'll be leaving us tomorrow." Miss Suckley pushed the president's wheelchair from the parlor out into the hallway and then on to the library.

The president had whispered to Daisy moments before that he wasn't interested in hearing Winston pontificate about his vision for a new world order. Margaret and her dear friend were well aware that after a fourth scotch, the prime minister was all her guests required for entertainment for the evening.

Churchill was seated in an armchair in the white-and-blue room, which had all the trappings of a parlor. He was surrounded by Vice-President Wallace, Secretary Morgenthau, and Dr. McIntire, the president's physician, who was also a vice admiral in the Navy. Secretary of War Stimson sat himself on the piano bench next to Anna Roosevelt and Lady Mary.

Churchill raised a glass of scotch with his right hand, holding the cigar with his other, and announced, "I would like to make a toast to that grand lady who is not with us tonight but is somewhere off in the Pacific with our boys. May she come back safe and with God's speed."

"To the First Lady, Mrs. Roosevelt," was the response.

Churchill went on, "Now, let me advance to my summary on how we and our American cousins will bring this war…"

Chapter Thirty-one

The president's secretary, Grace Tully, along with his press secretary, Steve Early, were doing all they could to stay out of the way of the kitchen's staff. Wilderstein's kitchen never was designed to have a crew of eight prepare and serve a meal. It was even more confining with agent John O'Neill and his two associates watching over every step of the food and beverage preparation. Chief Petty Officer Orlando had been detached from his Springwood duties to oversee his fellow Filipino staff. He was accustomed to having O'Neill look over his shoulder, but never in such tight quarters. The tension in Miss Suckley's kitchen was close to the breaking point. It was Orlando's job to bring steadiness and calm to his crew.

The evening's hostess, Margaret Suckley, was enjoying a quiet moment in the library with the president. She became oblivious to the chaos taking place in her kitchen. The Filipino chefs, cooks, and waitstaff were shouting orders at each other—mostly in broken English, even though they were all members of the U.S. Navy.

Pots, dishes, cutlery, towels, and many other kitchen tools could not be readily found, and it was evident to the Secret Service bystanders that frustration was building by the minute. The agents wondered if the dinner was ever going to be cooked, let alone served and enjoyed.

"Why the hell don't they speak English?" Steve Early asked Miss Tully.

"Because we took over their country forty-five years ago. Just give them—" Miss Tully responded when the telephone next to her rang.

She leaned over, placed the receiver next to her ear, and used her right hand to cover the other ear. Her complexion went ashen. The whites of her eyes grew larger. Her hand tightened its grip on the receiver.

"Quiet, everyone!" she shouted as loud as she could.

"What is it?" Early asked.

"Quiet, everyone! John, get Mr. Reilly in here right away. Please hurry. And not a sound from anyone!" Tully's hand covered the telephones mouthpiece.

"Who is on the phone, Grace?" Early insisted.

"Gertrude Hildebrand. And she wants to speak with Mr. Reilly and no one else."

* * *

"Herr Oberst, the boat is ready. Everything is in its place, and I also placed the charts of the river up front. I repacked the chemicals. The way you had them stored in the haversack, we would not have gotten beyond the dock," Schroeder said to her colonel.

"What's he waiting for? Berger knows all the guests have arrived. Roosevelt himself was carried in the back entrance thirty minutes ago," Krupp said angrily.

"Berger, that pompous ass, wants to let us know that he's in charge, that this is his show. And he wants to take his time. He even told me when you were out that he'll be the hero of the Fatherland for what he'll have accomplished."

"That arrogant bastard, and right to the end. Doesn't he realize that his pushing that detonator plunger is only the beginning? We've got to make our escape and get to the pumphouse," Krupp said. He placed his field glasses on top of a box in the boathouse.

"You picked the wrong man, Herr Oberst. He does not work for the good of the cause. He works for what is good for Herr

Donald B. Keelan

Berger," Schroeder said. She leaned over Krupp's shoulder to obtain her own view of the house and barn.

"Blow it! Blow it, you fool. Now!" Krupp shouted out, doing all he could to muffle his voice.

* * *

"Can you all shut the hell up? I can't hear the goddamn telephone," Reilly said angrily.

Moments before, Grace Tully had told him who was on the telephone, and he raced back from the library. "Mrs. Hildebrand, are you telling me that all this time you knew about these three Nazis? That they lived in the damn house for three days, and you said nothing and told nobody?" Reilly shouted into the telephone.

Reilly waited for a response. There was no immediate answer from Gertrude to his questions. And then he got her response. His red face turned white when she told him what the Nazis had placed in the house. The phone was left hanging.

* * *

"Jim, look here, in the gravel. A bunch of wires," Parker shouted to Gannon, who was standing at the top step of the back porch. Gannon was pondering whether he should just leave and get to St. Frances Hospital to see Ellen. He was trying to convince himself he was not needed here, that Ellen needed him a lot more than Mike Reilly.

"What is it, Parker? What wires?" Gannon responded.

"Jim, the house has been booby trapped! These are explosive wires, and they're leading right there, through the goddamn windows. They go off in that direction, that way, to the barn." Parker slowly moved across the gravel driveway, picking up the wire as he crossed and headed toward their source.

Gannon leaped off the porch and onto the gravel drive. He took up the wires in his hands and said to Parker, "Go inside and tell Mike to evacuate the house. Go, go! I'll track this way."

232

Instantly, Parker acted on Gannon's order. He bounded up the porch stairs two at a time and headed toward the kitchen door.

Reilly did not get to finish his telephone conversation with Gertrude Hildebrand. The moment she told him she and Hans had seen the Nazis place wires and small packages in the parlor, library, and dining room, Reilly dropped the telephone receiver and raced back to the library. Parker was now in the parlor and was about to tell Reilly about the wires when Reilly issued an order: "Miss Suckley, you and Parker here get all of the guests and staff out of the house. It is rigged to explode." Reilly reached down to the president's wheelchair. As he had practiced countless times before, he lifted Mr. Roosevelt up and placed the crippled man over his shoulder.

Parker followed Miss Suckley out of the library and into the parlor. The prime minister's aide-de-camp, Lieutenant Colonel Montgomery, stood in the corporal's way and said, "Here here, young man, what is this interruption? What is your business, may I ask?"

"My business, sir, is that this house is set to blow up, and if you don't get the hell out of my way and start getting everyone out of here, we're all going to be blown to kingdom come."

Agent John O'Neill was even less diplomatic. He pushed the colonel aside and shouted, "Not the doors. Get to the windows, and get through them. Hurry. Let me help you, prime minister."

Reilly got his charge out of the side door and onto the south porch. From there he carried FDR to the president's automobile, which had been moved from the back of the house. FDR had not said a word after Reilly yanked him from his wheelchair. He didn't have to. When he and Reilly were clear of the porch steps, FDR knew full well why he was being moved. Reilly stumbled, but never fell. The force of the blast pushed him forward. Agent Kramer was now with both men. The car door was opened, and FDR was pushed onto the back seat. Reilly lay on top of them.

The white-and-blue room's three oversized three-over-four mullion windows were flung open by Secretary Morgenthau. Once opened, the area of the raised window was almost the size of an opened door—for which it had been designed. The ladies were first to exit. It was a slow and difficult task not made easy with high heels and ankle-length dresses.

* * *

Ludwig Berger was unaware that agent Gannon was slowly making his way toward the oil drums. The Nazi was too engrossed in making sure his first plunger was set to discharge its electrical circuit. He pushed down hard on it. Instantly there was a loud explosion as the front room on the north side of Wilderstein blew out onto the estate's grounds.

Gannon dove to the ground. The concussion was overbearing. His immediate thought was, *How could anyone inside have survived?* When he looked back toward the house, he realized the explosion had taken out only one room. That must be the reason for the three wires. There were to be more explosions.

Meanwhile, Berger threw off the tarp-covered roof of his hiding place. He stood to see his accomplishment as he placed the second plunger on top of an oil drum. He shouted, "Death to the Jew-lover," as he placed his hand over the plunger.

Berger's rage toward FDR prevented him from seeing Gannon, who was now only thirty feet from the crazed assassin. Berger kept shouting out his words of hatred, not caring if he was to be seen or, for that matter, heard.

They were to be his last words. Gannon's first shot caught the Nazi between the eyes. The would-be hero of the Fatherland fell back, but not before a resounding second blast rocked the house. Margaret Suckley's dining room was instantly turned into an inferno. There had to be casualties, Gannon slowly realized, as he approached the Nazi, his .38 revolver still aimed at the mortally wounded Berger.

Gannon went over to Berger. He pushed the empty oil drums aside, then shoved the wooden pallet to the side, still holding his .38. He placed two fingers under the neck of Berger's uniform. There was no pulse.

Gannon stood up and turned toward the house. He had to get back. He had an awful feeling about what he was going to find. *Are the president and Mr. Churchill safe?* he kept asking himself. He ran down the dirt road from the barn to the back of the house. His fears grew worse with each step as he saw black smoke and flames coming from the windows that only moments before had shattered the mansion's dining room and library. *Who has been killed?* He bounded up the back porch steps. It was on the porch that he saw the kitchen staff, their faces blackened. Some had cuts and bruises, and all were coughing. Smoke was billowing out the screen door. Orlando Lopez, navy chief petty officer, and head chef, was attending to his people.

"Chief," Gannon said, "Get your men off the porch. Get them over to the gazebo, and give me a count. Where's Mr. Reilly?"

"Señor Mike is okay. He got Mr. Roosevelt out. And Mr. Churchill, I think. Mr. Gannon, what's happening?" Lopez said, placing a towel around the leg wound of one of his sailors.

Orlando no sooner finished speaking when Gannon heard the screeching of tires. He quickly went to the end of the porch, his revolver still in his hand, and got a glimpse of agent Don Kramer at the wheel of the president's roadster. The towering John O'Neill was standing on the running board. O'Neill was cradling a Thompson submachine gun.

"Jim, is the president safe?" a weakened voice asked Gannon.

Gannon turned from the driveway and the car that was speeding away to see Grace Tully on the porch holding a seriously injured Steve Early. The president's press secretary had been on his way to the dining room through the butler's pantry when the room exploded. He was thrown back, clear into the kitchen. Chief Lopez had assisted him onto the porch and into the care of Miss Tully.

"I don't know, Miss Tully, I just don't know. I need to find Mike. Have you seen him? Are you okay? Can I leave you here for a minute?" Gannon responded. He looked down at the helpless and disheveled woman and the unconscious Steve Early.

"He was right, Mr. Gannon. Mike was right. He did not want the president to come here. But it is too late now," Miss Tully said, her voice becoming weaker.

"Let's not worry about that now, Miss Tully. I need to find Mr.—"

Grace Tully interrupted him. "Jim, find out if Daisy is safe. Please, would you do that for me?"

As was the custom with Churchill's Scotland Yard security detail, they stayed away from any gathering between the president and their prime minister. At Miss Suckley's dinner party, it was no different. The two-man British detail relied on Reilly's men to provide the security protection. The British team stayed outside next to their cars. That was the case until the library windows came crashing toward them.

As the two six-foot-four agents ran toward the house, they saw their leader being carried out over the shoulder of an army corporal. Corporal Parker had wasted no time when he had entered the library and told off Mr. Churchill's military aide. Parker warned everyone to get out, then leaned over and placed the nearly inebriated prime minister over his back.

Seconds later, Parker placed the British leader into the waiting arms of the Scotland Yard detail, but not before he had fallen through the porch door from the blast of the explosion. He and the prime minister were on the porch deck. Parker got up, picked up the heavy-set man, and handed him over. Parker turned back and re-entered the burning and smoke-filled room.

There were others to bring out.

* * *

"Herr Oberst, I have heard only two explosions. There should have been three. And that gunshot noise—it did not come from a Luger. Do you think they may have discovered Herr Berger?" Kathe Schroeder wondered. She held her binoculars up, trying to observe what was taking place at the house and the carriage barn. The darkness and billowing smoke made it impossible to see the chaos.

"Berger was to set the charges off instantly, one right after the other. Didn't you notice the delay between his first charge and the second one? What the hell was the delay for?" Krupp was asking as he moved their gear to the boathouse's second-floor staircase.

"I'll tell you what he was doing. He was admiring his work. That's so typical Berger. And that's all that was needed to draw attention to his hiding place," Schroeder said sarcastically.

"Schroeder, you're probably right. And we now must leave. It's been ten minutes since the first explosion. They'll be all over this place in minutes, just as soon as they recover the guests from the house. The worst is we can't tell for sure if Roosevelt and Churchill were killed," Krupp lamented.

"We don't want to wait for Herr Berger?" Schroeder asked.

"I'm not certain if we were successful in killing Roosevelt and Churchill. But I am certain Berger is not coming back here. He's dead, and we have to leave now."

"Herr Krupp, if that is true, and Berger's been killed, that pleases me even more than knowing if we got the president and the prime minister," Schroeder said as she and Krupp ran to Margaret Suckley's boat. Krupp had no response. He wanted to get far away from Wilderstein, and quickly.

Chapter Thirty-two

Wilderstein was inundated with ambulances and fire trucks from Rhinebeck, Hyde Park, Wappingers Falls, and Poughkeepsie. Thirty minutes earlier, an all-hands call had been sounded. Firemen were rolling up their hoses, throwing burned chairs and other damaged items out the windows, while others were venting smoke from the house. A company of one hundred and ten fully armed soldiers from Hyde Park cordoned off the entire estate and surroundings. Dozens of soldiers, an arm's length from one another, could be seen slowly walking toward the river. Their orders were to locate anything or anybody.

St. Francis Hospital trauma teams joined with U.S. Army medics to attend the seriously injured guests and staff. The president's physician, Dr. McIntire, also was in attendance at the hospital emergency room. Once he had seen to it that the president was safely back at Springwood, he asked if he could assist with the injured. The president gave his immediate permission.

At Wilderstein, miraculously, none of Miss Suckley's guests was killed. The three who had been killed from the explosions were laid out on the driveway next to the back porch. Chief Lopez had brought out tablecloths from the Wilderstein linen closet to cover them.

Mike Reilly, along with Jim Gannon, had set up a temporary office in the carriage barn, the only structure with an operating telephone. Three uniformed New York state troopers were standing guard around the corpse and former hideout of Ludwig Berger. A uniformed Army soldier and a civilian were snapping photographs of the dead Nazi.

Reilly could be heard talking on the telephone to General Anderson, who had not come to the dinner party. He had wanted to stay at Springwood to gather more information on the Nazis.

"John, I'm awfully sorry to have to tell you that your young corporal, Parker, is dead," Reilly said into the telephone, then paused. "He was killed when the second blast went off. Shortly, ever so shortly, after he had evacuated the prime minister, I'm told. Just after that, Gannon saw him pick up an injured Filipino waiter. He threw the guy over his shoulder and was headed to the kitchen, through the dining room, when the room went up." Reilly paused once again. He looked over at Gannon, who was trying to hold back his emotions, but to no avail.

"John, did he have a family? Will you take care of that?" Reilly asked, then continued, "John, again, I'm so sorry. He was a good kid and a good soldier. And when we're through with this, I personally will ask the boss to bestow our country's highest decoration on him. Parker saved a lot of lives tonight. Jim told me it was Parker who discovered the detonator wires."

For the next five minutes, Reilly did not say a word. He just listened to General Anderson and then said, "John that is most helpful, and we will get on it right away. But no FBI guys, agree? We'll finish this ourselves and tonight, so help me Christ."

Reilly placed the receiver back on the phone box on the wall, turned to Gannon, and said, "I know you liked the kid, Jim. He was a big help to us. I'm going to miss him too. Anderson just told me that one wish he had always heard from Parker was that he wanted to get into the war as a real soldier. He did not want to serve his time as the general's aide. Well, tonight his wish came true."

"Mike, you know I once asked him if he would consider joining the service when he finished his Army tour. He told me—"

Reilly interrupted. "I know, Jim, there's much to do right now, and we've lost precious time. I've got a lot to tell you, and I'll do it as we drive."

"What did you mean no FBI, that it's our thing?" Gannon asked.

Reilly did not answer. He guided his assistant out through the barn's sliding doors. For the next thirty minutes while they drove back to Springwood, Reilly filled Gannon in on his telephone conversation with Gertrude Hildebrand. He mentioned how the housekeeper had given him the message that Wilderstein was set to be blown up with explosives by the three Nazis. She also said they had had a large batch of chemicals and poisons and had plans to use them, not at Wilderstein, but somewhere else.

Gannon had two questions but waited until Reilly finished speaking as the car roared south at sixty miles per hour down U.S. Route 9. He wanted to know what had happened to Schroeder and Krupp.

"It was just after the second explosion that the other two escaped," Reilly said in response.

Gert Hildebrand had told Reilly their names, and how Berger and Krupp gained entry into the country. Just before she told Reilly about the explosives, she related how Otto Reinhardt was involved, and that he had told them something awful was going to happen to the water supply to New York City. It was that part of the mission that had brought Schroeder in as well as Reinhardt, and Reinhardt wanted out. When he became aware of their plans for the water system, he defected.

"Mike, I still don't understand how Schroeder and Krupp got away. Where the hell are they now?" Gannon asked. Their car pulled up to the gate sentry house at Springwood.

"The boat, Miss Suckley's boat. It's gone, and so are Krupp and Schroeder. Anderson was explaining it all to me when I was on the phone with him. Just think about it. A chemical factory break-in, a dead guard, Schroeder's a chemist, and all the action that has taken place down at Cold Spring." Reilly moved the car forward from the gatehouse and observed another perimeter around the president's mansion, manned by soldiers from Stewart Field, toting M-1 rifles.

"Are you saying it was not just the president and Churchill they were here for, but they also intend to poison the water supply to New York City?" Gannon asked. Agent John O'Neill approached their car opposite the back entrance to Springwood.

"That's right. And you know what is situated at the top of Breakneck Ridge?"

"I think I do."

"Well, let me refresh your memory for sure. One-thousand horsepower pumps that send drinking water into pipes that are six feet or more in diameter," Reilly said.

"So what are we going to do? And don't we need to get there, pronto?" Gannon responded.

"All in good time. Anderson told me the Coast Guard said it would take Krupp's boat, at full speed, an hour or more to reach Cold Spring, even a bit longer because of the movement of the current and tide. I couldn't believe the tidal change can affect the river, but it does all the way up to Beacon. But no matter. Krupp and Schroeder are on their way to destroy the water supply, and we've got to stop them, not the FBI."

"Mike, what happened here tonight was in part an FBI matter, and we never alerted them—and all hell is going to break loose."

"I know that, and so does General Anderson. We and the OSS and had no business going after saboteurs. But we knew the bastards were after our boss, and he was not harmed. Nor was Mr. Churchill. Now we got to get the other two before they harm the water system, and while we still have our jobs."

Chapter Thirty-three

According to a long line of river captains who for the past three centuries had navigated the Hudson River, dating back to Henry Hudson, it's a difficult encounter, the Hudson River. It was the same for Schroeder. She was unfamiliar with the river and its current and tides. To make matters worse, it was dark. And she was still not familiar with the charts she had obtained.

Several thousand feet south of Wildenstein and two hundred feet from the east bank of the Hudson, Margaret Suckley's riverboat was knifing its way south on the waveless river. The night air had grown silent as complete blackness took over. Only the sound of a railroad steam engine dragging a hundred or more box cars and tankers broke the night silence. The freight train was heading south on the west side of the Hudson. Kathe Schroeder took her eyes off the direction she was steering the boat when suddenly, a passenger train to her left startled her with its whistle blast as it entered a railroad crossing not far from Hyde Park.

"Herr Krupp, the petrol gauge, why is it so low? Wasn't Berger to check it out? Again, the fool failed to do what he was told," Schroeder said. She tapped the glass on the boat's fuel gauge.

Colonel Krupp had been standing next to his colleague ever since they left the dock at Wilderstein. His hands tightly gripped the boat's windshield as the spray from the dirty brown river poured over them. The threat of possibly running out of fuel was now joined by the threat of the boat filling with water. Schroeder's pushing the boat to maximum speed was causing too much water to pour over the gunnels. There was also an additional problem: the boat's motor was over heating. It never was designed to be pushed so hard. Schroeder had to reduce her speed. She was fast approaching Poughkeepsie's Selkirk railroad bridge.

"Schroeder, you must reduce our speed. The boat will not be able to sustain this pounding, nor will the packed chemicals. Also, it will conserve our fuel." Krupp shouted into Schroeder's left ear and looked up river to see if they were being followed.

Krupp continued, "The noise we're making and the turbulence will attract the patrol boats. We've been fortunate they did not see us leave the boat dock. They had to have heard the explosives. And even if they didn't, they must have been radioed that there has been an assassination of their president."

Schroeder yelled back, "I saw the patrol boat. It was well out in the middle of the river and near Red Hook. I'm certain they didn't see us, and we don't have lights on, either."

"Right now I'm more concerned about the fuel. You also will need the fuel to counter the southern current we'll run into shortly," Krupp added.

"What do you mean? We are moving with the current," Schroeder shouted back to Krupp.

"Reinhardt told Berger and me that from where we are at this point, we will run into the current from the ocean that comes up this way. Also, there's an island ahead on your left, approximately four hundred meters from the shore. We must go by it slowly, and above all, in quiet."

"Will there be anyone on the island?"

"There could be, but I'm not sure. It is shown here on the map, Bannerman Island. It has a different name than what Reinhardt had told me, Pollope Island. He said it is just used to store old military hardware," Krupp said, using a pail to bail out the rear of the boat.

"Colonel, for nearly an hour now, you've never said anything about Berger. Do you think he has survived? If he has, he will be furious that we left without him." Schroeder glided the boat quietly to the west of Bannerman Island and began the turn eastward toward the shore at Cold Spring. She received no answer from Krupp.

It was there that the Reischmans were to be waiting for them with means to get their supplies and themselves to the base of Breakneck Ridge. The Reischmans' automobile was also the escape vehicle that would have taken the five of them to Cape Cod. There they were to rendezvous with U-214 and return to the Fatherland, their mission accomplished.

"Herr Oberst, how did you know about this trail?" Kathe Schroeder asked as she struggled, carrying fifty pounds of chemicals up a narrow timeworn path toward the summit of Breakneck Ridge.

She and Krupp had waited for fifteen minutes at the river inlet for the Reischmans. Colonel Krupp would wait no longer. He felt something had happened to them, and he and Schroeder needed to move.

"Herr Reinhardt took us down this path when we came here last week," Krupp said. "He said it was an easier route for him, but longer. And with all of these supplies, I'm thankful now that we are on it. The other way would have been nearly impossible." Krupp also was having a difficult time carrying the heavier portion of their supplies.

"Herr Oberst, we still don't know if our mission at Wilderstein was successful. Do you think the two explosives were sufficient to have accomplished it?" Schroeder persisted. She stopped for a moment and rested her pack and herself against a huge boulder alongside the winding path.

"We won't know for some time. Maybe you were right; we should have stayed and found out for ourselves. On the other hand, we would have stood a good chance of being discovered. And this part of the mission never would have been accomplished. We must keep going." Krupp adjusted the straps on his pack and started to head up to the steepest part of the trail. But it was not before he had responded to a question from Schroeder, an important question also he had kept asking himself ever since they left the inlet:

"Herr Oberst, how do you plan for us to get back to the Cape and meet U-214?"

His response was not what she had expected. It sent cold shivers through her perspiring body. It made her nauseous, especially when he said, "We're splitting up. We are not going to Cape Cod. There will be no meeting with the submarine. We will be on our own. You should be able to blend in better than me, but I'll try."

Some thirty minutes had elapsed since Schroeder and Krupp's last rest stop on the Breakneck Ridge trail. They now stopped walking. They were at the summit, and they pulled their packs from their backs. Their bodies were drenched with sweat. They were exhausted.

The clearing was pitch black. They could barely see the outline of the pumphouse. They were guided to it mainly from the humming sound of the massive pumps that broke the nighttime stillness.

They would have preferred to drag their packs to the door of the pumphouse, but the rubbing of the glass vessels against the rocky ground cover would have broken them open. Instead they clutched them, held them close to their chests, and walked toward the steel door.

The two Germans gently placed their loads on the concrete apron that surrounded the door. As they stood up, the pumphouse door swung open. A dozen flashlights beamed at them. A strong light came from inside the pumphouse and splashed upon the faces of the startled Nazis. They heard a stern voice say, "I'm Michael Reilly of the United States Secret Service, and you two are under arrest for attempting to kill my boss."

Schroeder and Krupp froze. What did he mean by *attempt?* They both instantly realized that Berger had failed.

Jim Gannon, his .38 revolver in hand, slowly worked his way around his boss's left side so he could be outside the building and stand next to Krupp. The dozen other field agents came up closer from the woods line, each carrying a flash-torch and gripping a Thompson submachine gun.

Reilly continued, "The president and prime minister are safe. They were not even scratched by what you Nazi bastards tried to accomplish. And your partner, Ludwig Berger: He's dead. He was shot and killed, which is what's going to happen to you two."

Krupp regained his composure as well as his authority and announced, "That is not acceptable. We are German soldiers. Yes, we have been captured while attempting to carry out a military mission. We are in uniform, and we are German officers of the Wehrmacht. And under the Geneva Convention—"

Reilly did all he could to restrain his Irish temper. He placed himself within inches of the colonel's sweating face. "You're not soldiers. You're a bunch of killers. And we're going to treat you as such. You're the second act of what happened here last summer—what did you call it, Operation Pastorius? And you're going to fry just like your cousins did."

"I object and—"

Once again Reilly interrupted the obstinate Krupp. "Object, you say? You son of a bitch! You killed a guard at the chemical plant. You slit the throat of one of your own conspirators, Otto Reinhardt, and—"

Now Reilly was interrupted by an angry Jim Gannon. "And you kidnapped and shot in the back an innocent girl who had nothing to do with your scheme." The seething Gannon shouted into Krupp's ear. "And you killed with your bombs three military personnel who were just doing their jobs."

"It was Berger who did all of that," a trembling Krupp exclaimed. "Not us, I assure you. You can't blame us for his cruelty. He was insane. From the beginning, he was that way. It was not us. It was not me. I don't know about a girl being shot. It was not us. It must have been the Reischmans."

Schroeder, standing motionless on Krupp's left, couldn't believe what she was hearing. She felt the man she had respected was about to turn on her. Just like he was doing with Berger and the Reischmans. The colonel, she thought, was pleading to save his life and could care less about anyone else. She needed to think. How was she going to get away? She was now all alone, and if held by the Americans, she would be executed.

"No, Colonel, it was all you," Reilly shouted. "You were in charge. You allowed for all of this to happen. You did not stop Berger from beating up Hans Hildebrand. And by the way, his wife, Gert, provided us with the details. But you know what really stinks here, Colonel? You killed Miss Suckley's dog, Heather."

Suddenly Krupp screamed, "Run, Schroeder, run!"

Instantly, Krupp pushed his arm up and knocked the revolver from Gannon's hand. In the same motion, he shoved Gannon against the brick wall of the pumphouse. The approaching agents were helpless to open their guns on Krupp. He stood between Gannon and Reilly.

The instant Krupp made his move, Schroeder ran to her left and around the pumphouse. She ran as fast as her weakened legs could carry her to the mountain's south face.

Krupp was now in a full dash, taking the same direction Ellen McCarthy had taken only a few hours before.

"Jim, get Schroeder. Don't let her escape. We'll get that bastard, Krupp," Reilly ordered. Immediately he heard a barrage of Thompson .45 caliber submachine guns go off. They were pointing in the direction Krupp had taken. The flashlights had illuminated the scene. Krupp, who three years earlier had failed in his mission to capture the Duke of Windsor in an aborted raid in Portugal, now lay dead at the edge of the westerly side of Breakneck Ridge. He had failed for the final time.

Schroeder, unlike her leader, was not familiar with the top of Breakneck Ridge. Otherwise she would not have been in the predicament in which she now found herself. Her dash to freedom came to an abrupt halt. She was at the top of the three-hundred-foot cliff on the south side of the mountain and had no place to run. Agent Gannon cornered her and said, "There are no more places to turn, Schroeder. Give it up, and step away from the edge."

Schroeder looked down the sheer cliff, her back to Gannon. She paused for a moment and contemplated Gannon's order. She was not going to be his prisoner. She swung her body around. In the same motion, she unhooked the button on her holster and with her right hand drew out her Luger. Gannon's first shot went into her left shoulder. It didn't stop her. She drew up the Luger and aimed it at Gannon, who was now standing within twenty feet of her. Gannon's second shot ripped into the center of her chest. She dropped the Luger and fell backward, over the cliff.

Gannon ran forward and looked down. The lack of moonlight concealed Schroeder's body at the base of the cliff. Gannon looked back at an approaching Mike Reilly and said, "Boss, it's over. Thank God. And can I now get to Ellen, and I pray she is awake so I can tell her too."

Chapter Thirty-four

The Present

In the White House's Oval Office, Professor Michael Ferguson arose from the sofa and walked over to the fireplace. He wondered whether, after he told his story, the president's offer for lunch would still stand. He looked at his watch. Three hours had passed since President Smyth had asked him to describe what occurred at Hyde Park in 1943.

Earlier, the president had removed his suit jacket and suggested that his guest, who was describing an unbelievable story, do likewise. Ferguson moved from the fireplace to one of the twin sofas. He sat down again. The president had taken a seat on the other twin sofa.

"Mr. President, you are the first to know the full story of what occurred during those three weeks in August of 1943. I haven't told a soul," Ferguson said, reaching for another cup of coffee. He already had consumed two since he had arrived in the Oval Office.

"Mike, this event, this incident, is so dramatic and historic, it must be told. Just as we have done with Nikita Khrushchev's Camp David attempted assassination story."

"I would agree, sir. It's time now that someone makes every aspect of it known. More than seventy years have gone by, and everyone who was involved has passed on, Mr. President."

"Mike, I have a lot of questions. And I do agree it must be told, but first, in your opinion, why was it kept secret up to now? Why bury the details in boxes and store them or hide them at Camp David? It was Shangri-La back then, of course. Was it because the information would be out of reach there?"

"I've spent considerable time pondering that very question, Mr. President. I keep coming back to the rationale that Mr. Roosevelt did not want the American people to have any additional fear or distress than they already were enduring from the war."

"I'm not sure I understand." the president said.

"Sir, this was the second time in fourteen months that the Nazis had landed saboteurs and killers on American soil. And with the second group, their purpose was to kill the president and Mr. Churchill. Also, I might add, whose mission it was to poison the New York City water system. Mr. Roosevelt felt this information was just too much for the American people to handle. Could Americans ever feel safe at home if this was made known to them? Also, how demoralizing it would be to our forces who were overseas, worrying about their families back home."

For the next thirty minutes, the president asked questions. He specifically wanted to know what had happened to all of the people who were involved.

Ferguson was able to accommodate him. He had known this was a question the president would ask. Also, he wanted the answers himself. He recorded his research on index cards and read each one to the president:

"The Hildebrands were arrested at Metz's apple orchard and were detained for the duration of the war. In 1946 they were sent back to Germany over the objections of Margaret Suckley. With her friend, the president, dead more than a year, she had no one. The Truman Administration didn't want to be involved in a simple deportation hearing when many others also were taking place. In August of 1943, she, along with everyone else, was sworn not to reveal what had happened.

"Margaret Suckley, along with Grace Tully, was at the president's side when he died in 1945 at Warm Springs, Georgia. She continued to live at Wilderstein until her death in June of 1991. She was one hundred years old. Her letters and diaries were discovered in a suitcase under her bed. In 1995 her writings were published by Geoffrey Ward. He titled his work *Closest Companion*, but there was no mention, in any publication for that matter, of what had occurred on that Saturday night in August 1943 at Wilderstein."

Professor Ferguson was moving to his next index card when the president asked, "How was it, Mike, that with the fire, rescue, and others at the estate soon after the explosions, no details reached the news media?"

"The official report was there was a gas explosion. The stove in the kitchen, something like that. I can tell you at the time, not many bought into that version of what had happened, but because of the Secrets Act and all that, it was hushed up and, in time, forgotten."

Ferguson went on to note that President Roosevelt secretly had sent money to his friend to have her house repaired. Today it is open to the public for tours, weddings, and other events. The Wilderstein Preservation Organization maintains it, as they have done since 1983 when Miss Suckley turned it over to them.

"Michael Reilly stayed with Mr. Roosevelt until the president's death. He then left the service and created a private investigation agency in Washington. True to his word, he was able to secure for Corporal Parker's family the nation's second-highest award, the Distinguished Service Cross, for their son. Unfortunately it had to be done secretly. The president bestowed it to the family in a private ceremony in the White House in 1944. President Roosevelt had to intervene when the head of the FBI, J. Edgar Hoover, wanted Reilly and Anderson charged with obstruction of justice. Hoover dropped his case only after the president told him the public would be made aware of the fact that it was not his FBI who captured the first group of saboteurs. Needless to say, Hoover was upset and upstaged by FDR," Ferguson said.

"Mike, this is so fascinating. What a job you've done. Please continue," President Smyth said.

"The owners of the tourist cabins also were honored in a private ceremony held at Hyde Park later that year. They sold the cabins and moved to Montreal, where they opened businesses that produced buttons and material for children's clothes. Like everyone else involved, they never revealed what had occurred in August 1943 at their tourist cabins. Today there is a two-hundred-room hotel on the property.

"I should also note, Mr. President, that to maintain security, Mike Reilly had all of the Germans' remains buried in a small plot at Springwood. He knew he could keep the press at bay by doing this. In 1947, all six bodies were exhumed and sent back to Germany. They were on the same plane as George Dasch. He was the German infiltrator who, in July 1942, ratted on his comrades in Operation Pastorius.

"The incident came pretty close to being made public late in 1944. Questions were being asked from two separate quarters. The people in Beacon and Mr. Kelly's family wanted to know who had murdered him. At about the same time, the officials at the NYC water department were asking questions concerning the disappearance of the engineer. You will recall, sir, Reinhardt was second in charge."

"So how was it all hushed up?" the president asked.

"Government agents got to visit those who were asking questions. They were told both men were killed by an escaped patient from the Matawan State Mental Hospital, which is located nearby in Beacon. And that ended any more questions.

"I believe that about sums it up, sir," Ferguson said. He placed his index cards in his shirt pocket.

"Mike, I have a question," the president said. "How was it that Reilly, Gannon, and the other agents were able to get to the pumphouse at Cold Spring before Krupp and Schroeder?"

"You will recall, Mr. President, that General Anderson did not go to Wilderstein the evening of the dinner. Instead he stayed back at Springwood. He had believed, and correctly as it turned out, that there was to be another event—at Breakneck. On his own, he sent the dozen agents there ahead of Gannon and Reilly. They, by the way, were put on top of the mountain by a Sikorski helicopter from Stewart Field the first time it was used outside of a test run."

"Jim Gannon and his fiancée, Ellen—What ever happened to them?" the president asked excitedly, as if he did not want the story to end.

"Oh yes, Jim Gannon and Ellen McCarthy, forgive me. It took Ellen close to three months to recover, not so much from the bullet, but from the head injury sustained when she fell from the roof of the railroad tunnel. In July of 1944, she and Jim were married in St. Peter's Roman Catholic Church in Poughkeepsie. President Roosevelt and his secretary of treasury were there, as were Grace Tully and Margaret Suckley. Jim stayed with the Secret Service and took over Mike's head of detail post. Soon after the near-attempt on President Truman in 1951, he left the service and joined one of the large aircraft companies, Boeing, I believe, to head up its security. He retired to Vermont in 1977, not far from the Metz farm in Bennington. And he passed away in 1984. Metz, by the way, was never charged with anything."

"Any children?" The president inquired.

"Oh, yes indeed. Just like me, sir, he had five. Matter of fact, Mr. President, the Secret Service agent outside your office is James Gannon, III—Jim's grandson."

"Oh my God, what a coincidence! The treacherous conspiracy the Nazis had created to poison the region's water system, as well as to bring untold harm on the president and prime minister—what a story, professor! And it's a story that needs to be told, each and every aspect of it, from Cold Spring up to Reinbeck. It has been a secret for too long. And if I may be so bold as to suggest its title: *Conspiracy on the Hudson.*"

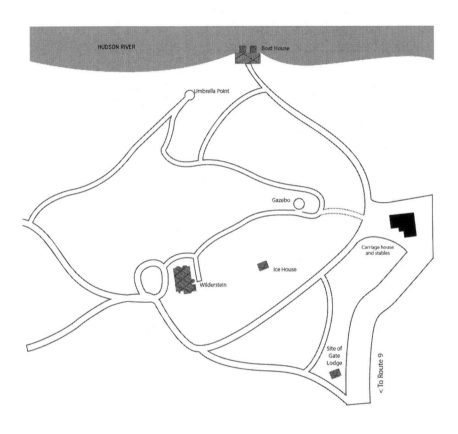